The yellowbacks... classics of popular fiction

The yellowjackets or yellowbacks were a great series of bestselling adventure and crime thrillers that had its origins in the mid to late 19th century following on from the 'penny dreadfuls'. They virtually began the mass market revolution of the early 20th century with a clear standard format and imprint/series livery (what would today be called branding). Hodder & Stoughton published the yellowjackets in two main series with series run dates of: 1923-1939 and later 1949-1957.

As the tagline ('where thrillers really began') on the back cover implies, the imprint and series focused on thrillers that were the bestsellers of their time. This current reissue or retro revival if you will, brings back many of these masterpieces, now classics in their own way and extends it further by including key titles from that period that were either great crime or thriller or even general commercial fiction (including sub-genres of noir, horror, gothic, romance, westerns, etc.) influences of their time. There are some perennial favourites and many rarities either lost or not easily available being revived in the current series. Writers and characters ranged from adventure heroes like Bulldog Drummond, Allan Quatermain, Richard Hannay or the Saint through thriller grandmasters Edgar Wallace and E. Phillips Oppenheim, crime and mystery maestros like Patricia Wentworth, GK Chesterton, Agatha Christie and the Detection club, to western and swashbucklers like Zane Grey, Max Brand, Captain Blood and even romance or general fiction classics like Hermina Black, Denise Robins, Marie Corelli or Stella Morton. These were books that had storytelling at their heart and always entertained.

The yellowbacks had both hardback (with varying design elements) and paperback (which built the series look) versions with the latter still carrying the imprint 'yellowjacket'. The current reissues pay tribute to both and use an amalgam of elements from both editions while retaining the complete yellow (or 'mustard-plaster') livery with the author's name in blue beveled type with a 'simulated emboss' effect and a white outer 'outline', and the book title in black. These reissues retain the distinctive size of the original mass market paperback and follow the three main category variations—the thrillers (crime, westerns, mystery, adventure) had blue lettering for the author's name, while Romance and softer general fiction had red; and other categories like humour had green.

For more detail and a full list of titles visit https://www.hachetteindia.com/home/yellowbacks

THE LONE WOLF

THE LONE WOLF

Louis Joseph Vance was an American novelist, screenwriter and film producer. Best known for the popular character Michael Lanyard, a criminal-turned-detective known as *The Lone Wolf* who featured in eight books and 24 films between 1914 and 1949 and also appeared in radio and television series.

He wrote short stories, verse and many popular novels.

Vance moved to Los Angeles to work with Universal Pictures on films based on his work, including *The Trey o' Hearts* (1914) and a serial and film series (1914–1916) based on his Terence O'Rourke stories. In 1915, he founded Fiction Pictures, Inc., a motion picture production company whose films were distributed by Paramount Pictures. The studio was sold to Famous Players in June, when Fiction Pictures went out of business.

Vance died alone in his New York City apartment on December 16, 1933, in a fire that resulted from his falling asleep with a lighted cigarette.

THE LONE WOLF

Louis Joseph Vance

hachette

The Lone Wolf
First published by A.L. Burt. New Yorkin 1914.

The first of the series, *The Four Just Men*, was published in 1905 by Tallis Press in the United Kingdom. This was followed by *The Council of Justice*, published in 1908 by Ward Lock & Co. in the United Kingdom. Then came *The Just Men of Cordova* in 1917 by Hodder & Stoughton in the United Kingdom, *The Law of Four Just Men* in 1921 by Hodder & Stoughton in the United Kingdom

1

The texts in these editions in most cases have been reprinted as is, with minimal editorial changes and by and large no bowdlerizing for political correctness; though in some editions, a few words and phrases considered archaic, or those considered offensive now, along with archaic punctuation may have been modified in places to make the text more accessible to today's readers. The narratives, language, beliefs, social mores and/or cultural depictions, in these volumes are a reflection of their times and must be viewed as such. They may also contain certain cultural, racial and gender prejudices and stereotypes that may be outdated or clearly wrong then and wrong today; but their removal would be tantamount to claiming these prejudices never existed. The Publisher does not endorse or support those depictions or stereotypes; and these books have been made available for a discerning audience that will read it for entertainment value and a chronicle/record of popular fiction of past times.

Cover design by Priya Singh adapted from the original classic yellowjacket by Hodder & Stoughton.

Cover illustration by Ishan Trivedi.

Series note: Some of the books in the series (unless otherwise credited) may have cover or inside illustrations from the original yellowbacks or early editions, and while full restoration has been attempted, some images may be grainy or faded due to the condition of the original material. The end notes or bonus material or blurb details may have been sourced from the public domain or free use publications such as Wikipedia and attribution is hereby made also allowing similar free use reproduction from here. Sources requiring further specific attribution may write in and further detailing and/or corrections shall be made in subsequent printings/editions.

Reprint specifications may be subject to change including but not limited to finishes, paper, colour sections.

ISBN: 978-93-5731-056-7

Hachette Book Publishing India Pvt. Ltd.
4th & 5th Floors, Corporate Centre,
Plot No. 94, Sector 44, Gurugram - 122 003, India

Typeset in Electra LT STD 10/12.5 pt by Manipal Technologies Limited, Manipal

Printed and bound in India by Manipal Technologies Limited, Manipal

MIX
Paper from responsible sources
FSC™ C043100

CONTENTS

I

TROYON'S

It must have been Bourke who first said that even if you knew your way about Paris you had to lose it in order to find it to Troyon's. But then Bourke was proud to be Irish.

Troyon's occupied a corner in a jungle of side-streets, well withdrawn from the bustle of the adjacent boulevards of St. Germain and St. Michel, and in its day was a restaurant famous with a fame jealously guarded by a select circle of patrons. Its cooking was the best in Paris, its cellar second to none, its rates ridiculously reasonable; yet Baedeker knew it not. And in the wisdom of the cognoscenti this was well: it had been a pity to loose upon so excellent an establishment the swarms of tourists that profaned every temple of gastronomy on the Rive Droit.

The building was of three storeys, painted a dingy drab and trimmed with dull green shutters. The restaurant occupied almost all of the street front of the ground floor, a blank, non-committal double doorway at one extreme of its plate-glass windows was seldom open and even more seldom noticed.

This doorway was squat and broad and closed the mouth of a wide, stone-walled passageway. In one of its two substantial wings of oak a smaller door had been cut for the convenience of Troyon's guests, who by this route gained the courtyard, a semi-roofed and shadowy place, cool on the hottest day. From the court a staircase, with an air of leading nowhere in particular, climbed lazily to the second storey and thereby justified its modest pretensions; for the two upper floors of Troyon's might have been plotted by a nightmare-ridden architect after witnessing one of the first of the Palais Royal farces.

Above stairs, a mediaeval maze of corridors long and short, complicated by many unexpected steps and staircases and turns and enigmatic doors, ran every-which-way and as a rule landed one in the wrong room, linking together, in all, some two-score bedchambers. There were no salons or reception-rooms, there was never a bathroom, there wasn't even running water aside from two hallway taps, one to each storey. The honoured guest and the exacting went to bed by lamplight: others put up with candlesticks: gas burned only in the corridors and the restaurant—asthmatic jets that, spluttering blue within globes obese, semi-opaque, and yellowish, went well with furnishings and decorations of the Second Empire to which years had lent a mellow and somehow rakish dinginess; since nothing was ever refurbished.

With such accommodations the guests of Troyon's were well content. They were not many, to begin with, and they were almost all middle-aged bourgeois, a caste that resents innovations. They took Troyon's as they found it: the rooms suited them admirably, and the tariff was modest. Why do anything to disturb the perennial peace of so discreet and confidential an establishment? One did much as one pleased there, providing one's bill was paid with tolerable regularity and the hand kept supple that operated the cordon in the small hours of the night. Papa Troyon came from a tribe of inn-keepers and was liberal-minded; while as for Madame his wife, she cared for nothing but pieces of gold...

To Troyon's on a wet winter night in the year 1893 came the child who as a man was to call himself Michael Lanyard.

He must have been four or five years old at that time: an age at which consciousness is just beginning to recognize its individuality and memory registers with capricious irregularity. He arrived at the hotel in a state of excitement involving an almost abnormal sensitiveness to impressions; but that was soon drowned deep in dreamless slumbers of healthy exhaustion; and when he came to look back through a haze of days, of which each had made its separate and imperative demand upon his budding emotions, he found his store of memories strangely dulled and disarticulate.

The earliest definite picture was that of himself, a small but vastly important figure, nursing a heavy heart in a dark corner of a fiacre. Beside him sat a man who swore fretfully into his moustache whenever the whimpering of the boy threatened to develop into honest bawls: a strange creature, with pockets full of candy and a way with little boys in public surly and domineering, in private timid and propitiatory. It was raining monotonously, with that melancholy persistence which is the genius of Parisian winters; and the paving of the interminable strange streets was as black glass shot with coloured lights. Some of the streets roared like famished beasts, others again were silent, if with a silence no less sinister. The rain made incessant crepitation on the roof of the fiacre, and the windows wept without respite. Within the cab a smell of mustiness contended feebly with the sickening reek of a cigar which the man was forever relighting and which as often turned cold between his teeth. Outside, unwearying hoofs were beating their deadly rhythm, *cloppetty-clop*...

Back of all this lurked something formlessly alluring, something sad and sweet and momentous, which belonged very personally to the child but which he could never realize. Memory crept blindly toward it over a sword-wide bridge that had no end. There had been (or the boy had dreamed it) a long, weariful journey by railroad, the sequel to one by boat more brief but wholly loathsome. Beyond this point memory failed though sick with yearning. And the child gave over his instinctive but rather inconsecutive efforts to retrace his history: his daily life at Troyon's furnished compelling and obliterating interests.

Madame saw to that.

It was Madame who took charge of him when the strange man dragged him crying from the cab, through a cold, damp place gloomy with shadows, and upstairs to a warm bright bedroom: a formidable body, this Madame, with cold eyes and many hairy moles, who made odd noises in her throat while she undressed the little boy with the man standing by, noises meant to sound compassionate and maternal but, to the child at least, hopelessly otherwise.

Then drowsiness stealing upon one over a pillow wet with tears... oblivion...

And Madame it was who ruled with iron hand the strange new world to which the boy awakened.

The man was gone by morning, and the child never saw him again; but inasmuch as those about him understood no English and he no French, it was some time before he could grasp the false assurances of Madame that his father had gone on a journey but would presently return. The child knew positively that the man was not his father, but when he was able to make this correction the matter had faded into insignificance: life had become too painful to leave time or inclination for the adjustment of such minor and incidental questions as one's parentage.

The little boy soon learned to know himself as Marcel, which wasn't his name, and before long was unaware he had ever had another. As he grew older he passed as Marcel Troyon; but by then he had forgotten how to speak English.

A few days after his arrival the warm, bright bedchamber was exchanged for a cold dark closet opening off Madame's boudoir, a cupboard furnished with a rickety cot and a broken chair, lacking any provision for heat or light, and ventilated solely by a transom over the door; and inasmuch as Madame shared the French horror of draughts and so kept her boudoir hermetically sealed nine months of the year, the transom didn't mend matters much. But that closet formed the boy's sole refuge, if a precarious one, through several years; there alone was he ever safe from kicks and cuffs and scoldings for faults beyond his comprehension; but he was never permitted a candle, and the darkness and loneliness made the place one of haunted terror to the sensitive and imaginative nature of a growing child.

He was, however, never insufficiently fed; and the luxury of forgetting misery in sleep could not well be denied him.

By day, until of age to go to school, he played apprehensively in the hallways with makeshift toys, a miserable, dejected little body with his heart in his mouth at every sudden footfall, very much in the way of femmes-de-chambre who had nothing in common with the warm-hearted, impulsive, pitiful serving women of fiction. They complained of him to Madame, and Madame came promptly to cuff him. He soon learned an almost uncanny cunning in the art of effacing himself, when she was imminent, to be as still as death and to move with the silence of a wraith. Not infrequently his huddled immobility in a shadowy corner escaped her notice as she passed. But it always exasperated her beyond measure to look up, when she fancied herself alone, and become aware of the wide-eyed, terrified stare of the transfixed boy...

That he was privileged to attend school at all was wholly due to a great fear that obsessed Madame of doing anything to invite the interest of the authorities. She was an honest woman, according to her lights, an honest wife, and kept an honest house; but she feared the gendarmerie more than the Wrath of God. And by ukase of Government a certain amount of education was compulsory. So Marcel learned among other things to read, and thereby took his first blind step toward salvation.

Reading being the one pastime which could be practiced without making a noise of any sort to attract undesirable attentions, the boy took to it in self-defence. But before long it had become his passion. He read, by stealth, everything that fell into his hands, a weird mélange of newspapers, illustrated Parisian weeklies, magazines, novels: cullings from the débris of guest-chambers.

Before Marcel was eleven he had read "Les Misérables" with intense appreciation.

His reading, however, was not long confined to works in the French language. Now and again some departing guest would leave an English novel in his room, and these Marcel treasured beyond all other books; they seemed to him, in a way, part of his birthright. Secretly he called himself English in those days, because he knew he wasn't French: that much, at least, he remembered. And he spent long hours poring over the strange words until; at length, they came to seem less strange in his eyes. And then some accident threw his way a small English-French dictionary.

He was able to read English before he could speak it.

Out of school hours a drudge and scullion, the associate of scullions and their immediate betters, drawn from that caste of loose tongues and looser morals which breeds servants for small hotels, Marcel at eleven (as nearly as his age can be computed) possessed a comprehension of life at once exact, exhaustive and appalling.

Perhaps it was fortunate that he lived without friendship. His concept of womanhood was incarnate in Madame Troyon; so he gave all the hotel women a wide berth.

The men-servants he suffered in silence when they would permit it; but his nature was so thoroughly disassociated from anything within their experience that they resented him: a circumstance which exposed him to a certain amount of baiting not unlike that which the village idiot receives at the hands of rustic boors—until Marcel learned to defend himself with a tongue which could distil vitriol from the vernacular, and with fists and feet as well. Thereafter he was left severely to himself and glad of it, since it furnished him with just so much more time for reading and dreaming over what he read.

By fifteen he had developed into a long, lank, loutish youth, with a face of extraordinary pallor, a sullen mouth, hot black eyes, and dark hair like a mane, so seldom was it trimmed. He looked considerably older than he was and the slightness of his body was deceptive, disguising a power of sinewy strength. More than this, he could care very handily for himself in a scrimmage: la savate had no secrets from him, and he had picked up tricks from the Apaches quite as effectual as any in the manual of jiu-jitsu. Paris he knew as you and I know the palms of our hands, and he could converse with the precision of the native-born in any one of the city's several odd argots.

To these accomplishments he added that of a thoroughly practised petty thief.

His duties were by day those of valet-de-chambre on the third floor; by night he acted as omnibus in the restaurant. For these services he received no pay and less consideration from his employers (who would have been horrified by the suggestion that they countenanced slavery) only his board and a bed in a room scarcely larger, if somewhat better ventilated, than the boudoir-closet from which he had long since been ousted. This room was on the ground floor, at the back of the house, and boasted a small window overlooking a narrow alley.

He was routed out before daylight, and his working day ended as a rule at ten in the evening—though when there were performances on at the Odéon, the restaurant remained open until an indeterminate hour for the accommodation of the supper trade.

Once back in his kennel, its door closed and bolted, Marcel was free to squirm out of the window and roam and range Paris at will. And it was thus that he came by most of his knowledge of the city.

But for the most part Marcel preferred to lie abed and read himself half-blind by the light of purloined candle-ends. Books he borrowed as of old from the rooms of guests or else pilfered from quai-side stalls and later sold to dealers in more distant quarters of the city. Now and again, when he needed some work not to be acquired save through outright purchase, the guests would pay further if unconscious tribute through the sly abstraction of small coins. Your true Parisian, however, keeps track of his money to the ultimate sou, an idiosyncrasy which obliged the boy to practise most of his peculations on the fugitive guest of foreign extraction.

In the number of these, perhaps the one best known to Troyon's was Bourke.

He was a quick, compact, dangerous little Irishman who had fallen into the habit of "resting" at Troyon's whenever a vacation from London seemed a prescription apt to prove wholesome for a gentleman of his kidney; which was rather frequently, arguing that Bourke's professional activities were fairly onerous.

Having received most of his education in Dublin University, Bourke spoke the purest English known, or could when so minded, while his facile Irish tongue had caught the trick of an accent which passed unchallenged on the Boulevardes. He had an alert eye for pretty women, a heart as big as all outdoors, no scruples worth mentioning, a secret sorrow, and a pet superstition.

The colour of his hair, a clamorous red, was the spring of his secret sorrow. By that token he was a marked man. At irregular intervals he made frantic attempts to disguise it; but the only dye that would serve at all was a jet-black and looked like the devil in contrast with his high colouring. Moreover, before a week passed, the red would crop up again wherever the hair grew thin, lending him the appearance of a badly-singed pup.

His pet superstition was that, as long as he refrained from practising his profession in Paris, Paris would remain his impregnable Tower of Refuge. The world owed Bourke a living, or he so considered; and it must be allowed that he made collections on account with tolerable regularity and success; but Paris was tax-exempt as long as Paris offered him immunity from molestation.

Not only did Paris suit his tastes excellently, but there was no place, in Bourke's esteem, comparable with Troyon's for peace and quiet. Hence, the continuity of his patronage was never broken by trials of rival hostelries; and Troyon's was always expecting Bourke for the simple reason that he invariably arrived unexpectedly, with neither warning nor ostentation, to stop as long as he liked, whether a day or a week or a month, and depart in the same manner.

His daily routine, as Troyon's came to know it, varied but slightly: he breakfasted abed, about half after ten, lounged in his room or the café all day if the weather were bad, or strolled peacefully in the gardens of the Luxembourg if it were good, dined early and well but always alone, and shortly afterward departed by cab for some well-known bar on the Rive Droit; whence, it is to be presumed, he moved on to other resorts, for he never was home when the house was officially closed for the night, the hours of his return remaining a secret between himself and the concierge.

On retiring, Bourke would empty his pockets upon the dressing-table, where the boy Marcel, bringing up Bourke's petit déjeuner the next morning, would see displayed a tempting confusion of gold and silver and copper, with a wad of bank-notes, and the customary assortment of personal hardware.

Now in as much as Bourke was never wide-awake at that hour, and always after acknowledging Marcel's "bon jour" rolled over and snored for Glory and the Saints, it was against human nature to resist the allure of that dressing-table. Marcel seldom departed without a coin or two.

He had yet to learn that Bourke's habits were those of an Englishman, who never goes to bed without leaving all his pocket-money in plain sight and—carefully catalogued in his memory...

One morning in the spring of 1904 Marcel served Bourke his last breakfast at Troyon's.

The Irishman had been on the prowl the previous night, and his rasping snore was audible even through the closed door when Marcel knocked and, receiving no answer, used the pass-key and entered.

At this the snore was briefly interrupted; Bourke, visible at first only as a flaming shock of hair protruding from the bedclothes, squirmed an eye above his artificial horizon, opened it, mumbled inarticulate acknowledgment of Marcel's salutation, and passed blatantly into further slumbers.

Marcel deposited his tray on a table beside the bed, moved quietly to the windows, closed them, and drew the lace curtains together. The dressing-table between the windows displayed, amid the silver and copper, more gold coins than it commonly did—some eighteen or twenty louis altogether. Adroitly abstracting en passant a piece of ten francs, Marcel went on his way rejoicing, touched a match to the fire all ready-laid in the grate, and was nearing the door when, casting one casual parting glance at the bed, he became aware of a notable phenomenon: the snoring was going on lustily, but Bourke was watching him with both eyes wide and filled with interest.

Startled and, to tell the truth, a bit indignant, the boy stopped as though at word of command. But after the first flash of astonishment his young face hardened to immobility. Only his eyes remained constant to Bourke's.

The Irishman, sitting up in bed, demanded and received the piece of ten francs, and went on to indict the boy for the embezzlement of several sums running into a number of louis.

Marcel, reflecting that Bourke's reckoning was still some louis shy, made no bones about pleading guilty. Interrogated, the culprit deposed that he had taken the money because he needed it to buy books. No, he wasn't sorry. Yes, it was probable that, granted further opportunity, he would do it again. Advised that he was apparently a case-hardened young criminal, he replied that youth was not his fault; with years and experience he would certainly improve.

Puzzled by the boy's attitude, Bourke agitated his hair and wondered aloud how Marcel would like it if his employers were informed of his peculations.

Marcel looked pained and pointed out that such a course on the part of Bourke would be obviously unfair; the only real difference between them, he explained, was that where he filched a louis Bourke filched thousands; and if Bourke insisted on turning him over to the mercy of Madame and Papa Troyon, who would certainly summon a sergent de ville, he, Marcel, would be quite justified in retaliating by telling the Préfecture de Police all he knew about Bourke.

This was no chance shot, and took the Irishman between wind and water; and when, dismayed, he blustered, demanding to know what the boy meant by his damned impudence, Marcel quietly advised him that one knew what one knew: if one read the English newspaper in the café, as Marcel did, one could hardly fail to remark that monsieur always came to Paris after some notable burglary had been committed in London; and if one troubled to follow monsieur by night, as Marcel had, it became evident that monsieur's first calls in Paris were invariably made at the establishment of a famous fence in the rue des Trois Frères; and, finally, one drew one's own conclusions when strangers dining in the restaurant—as on the night before, by way of illustration—strangers who wore all the hallmarks of police detectives from England—catechised one about a person whose description was the portrait of Bourke, and promised a hundred-franc note for information concerning the habits and whereabouts of that person, if seen.

Marcel added, while Bourke gasped for breath, that the gentleman in question had spoken to him alone, in the absence of other waiters, and had been fobbed off with a lie.

But why—Bourke wanted to know—had Marcel lied to save him, when the truth would have earned him a hundred francs?

"Because," Marcel explained coolly, "I, too, am a thief. Monsieur will perceive it was a matter of professional honour."

Now the Irish have their faults, but ingratitude is not of their number.

Bourke, packing hastily to leave Paris, France and Europe by the fastest feasible route, still found time to question Marcel briefly; and what he learned from the boy about his antecedents so worked with gratitude upon the sentimental nature of the Celt, that when on the third day following the Cunarder Carpathia left Naples for New York, she carried not only a gentleman whose brilliant black hair and glowing pink complexion rendered him a bit too conspicuous among her first-cabin passengers for his own comfort, but also in the second cabin his valet—a boy of sixteen who looked eighteen.

The gentleman's name on the passenger-list didn't, of course, in the least resemble Bourke. His valet's was given as Michael Lanyard.

The origin of this name is obscure; Michael being easily corrupted into good Irish Mickey may safely be attributed to Bourke; Lanyard has a tang of the sea which suggests a reminiscence of some sea-tale prized by the pseudo Marcel Troyon.

In New York began the second stage in the education of a professional criminal. The boy must have searched far for a preceptor of more sound attainments than Bourke. It is, however, only fair to say that Bourke must have looked as far for an apter pupil. Under his tutelage, Michael Lanyard learned many things; he became a mathematician of considerable promise, an expert mechanician, a connoisseur of armour-plate and explosives in their more pacific applications, and he learned to grade precious stones with a glance. Also, because Bourke was born of gentlefolk, he learned to speak English, what clothes to wear and when to wear them, and the civilized practice with knife and fork at table. And because Bourke was a diplomatist of sorts, Marcel acquired the knack of being at ease in every grade of society: he came to know that a self-made millionaire, taken the right way, is as approachable as one whose millions date back even unto the third generation; he could order a dinner at Sherry's as readily as drinks at Sharkey's. Most valuable accomplishment of all, he learned to laugh. In the way of by-products he picked up a working acquaintance with American, English and German slang—French slang he already knew as a mother-tongue—considerable geographical knowledge of the capitals of Europe, America and Illinois, a taste that discriminated between tobacco and the stuff sold as such in France, and a genuine passion for good paintings.

Finally Bourke drilled into his apprentice the three cardinal principles of successful cracksmanship: to know his ground thoroughly before venturing upon it; to strike and retreat with the swift precision of a hawk; to be friendless.

And the last of these was the greatest.

"You're a promising lad," he said—so often that Lanyard would almost wince from that formula of introduction—"a promising lad, though it's sad I should be to say it, instead of proud as I am. For I've made you: but for me you'd long since have matriculated at La Tour Pointue and graduated with the canaille of the Santé. And in time you may become a first-chop operator, which I'm not and never will be; but if you do, 'twill be through fighting shy of two things. The first of them's Woman, and the second is Man. To make a friend of a man you must lower your guard. Ordinarily 'tis fatal. As for Woman, remember this, m'lad: to let love into your life you must open a door no mortal hand can close. And God only knows what'll follow in. If ever you find you've fallen in love and can't fall out, cut the game on the instant, or you'll end wearing stripes or broad arrows—the same as myself would, if this cursed cough wasn't going to be the death of me... No, m'lad: take a fool's advice (you'll never get better) and when you're shut of me, which will be soon, I'm thinking, take the Lonesome Road and stick to the middle of it. 'He travels the fastest that travels alone' is a true saying, but 'tis only half the truth: he travels the farthest into the bargain... Yet the Lonesome Road has its drawbacks, lad—it's *damned* lonely!"

Bourke died in Switzerland, of consumption, in the winter of 1910—Lanyard at his side till the end.

Then the boy set his face against the world: alone, lonely, and remembering.

II

RETURN

His return to Troyon's, whereas an enterprise which Lanyard had been contemplating for several years—in fact, ever since the death of Bourke—came to pass at length almost purely as an affair of impulse.

He had come through from London by the afternoon service—via Boulogne—travelling light, with nothing but a brace of handbags and his life in his hands. Two coups to his credit since the previous midnight had made the shift advisable, though only one of them, the later, rendered it urgent.

Scotland Yard would, he reckoned, require at least twenty-four hours to unlimber for action on the Omber affair; but the other, the theft of the Huysman plans, though not consummated before noon, must have set the Chancelleries of at least three Powers by the ears before Lanyard was fairly entrained at Charing Cross.

Now his opinion of Scotland Yard was low; its emissaries must operate gingerly to keep within the laws they serve. But the agents of the various Continental secret services have a way of making their own laws as they go along: and for these Lanyard entertained a respect little short of profound.

He would not have been surprised had he ran foul of trouble on the pier at Folkestone. Boulogne, as well, figured in his imagination as a crucial point: its harbour lights, heaving up over the grim grey waste, peered through the deepening violet dusk to find him on the packet's deck, responding to their curious stare with one no less insistently inquiring... But it wasn't until in the gauntlet of the Gare du Nord itself that he found anything to shy at.

Dropping from train to platform, he surrendered his luggage to a ready facteur, and followed the man through the crush, elbowed and shouldered, offended by the pervasive reek of chilled steam and coal-gas, and dazzled by the brilliant glare of the overhanging electric arcs.

Almost the first face he saw turned his way was that of Roddy.

The man from Scotland Yard was stationed at one side of the platform gates. Opposite him stood another known by sight to Lanyard—a highly decorative official from the Préfecture de Police. Both were scanning narrowly every face in the tide that churned between them.

Wondering if through some fatal freak of fortuity these were acting under late telegraphic advice from London, Lanyard held himself well in hand: the first sign of intent to hinder him would prove the signal for a spectacular demonstration of the ungentle art of not getting caught with the goods on. And for twenty seconds, while the crowd milled slowly through the narrow exit, he was as near to betraying himself as he had ever been—nearer, for he had marked down the point on Roddy's jaw where his first blow would fall, and just where to plant a coup-de-savate most surely to incapacitate the minion of the Préfecture; and all the while was looking the two over with a manner of the most calm and impersonal curiosity.

But beyond an almost imperceptible narrowing of Roddy's eyes when they met his own, as if the Englishman were struggling with a faulty memory, neither police agent betrayed the least recognition.

And then Lanyard was outside the station, his facteur introducing him to a ramshackle taxicab.

No need to speculate whether or not Roddy were gazing after him; in the ragged animal who held the door while Lanyard fumbled for his facteur's tip, he recognized a runner for the Préfecture; and beyond question there were many such about. If any lingering doubt should trouble Roddy's mind he need only ask, "Such-and-such an one took what cab and for what destination?" to be instantly and accurately informed.

In such case to go directly to his apartment, that handy little rez-de-chaussée near the Trocadéro, was obviously inadvisable. Without apparent hesitation Lanyard directed the driver to the Hotel Lutetia, tossed the ragged spy a sou, and was off to the tune of a slammed door and a motor that sorely needed overhauling...

The rain, which had welcomed the train a few miles from Paris, was in the city torrential. Few wayfarers braved the swimming sidewalks, and the little clusters of chairs and tables beneath permanent café awnings were one and all neglected. But in the roadways an amazing concourse of vehicles, mostly motor-driven, skimmed, skidded, and shot over burnished asphalting all, of course, at top-speed—else this were not Paris. Lanyard thought of insects on the surface of some dark forest pool...

The roof of the cab rang like a drumhead; the driver blinked through the back-splatter from his rubber apron; now and again the tyres lost grip on the treacherous going and provided instants of lively suspense. Lanyard lowered a window to release the musty odour peculiar to French taxis, got well peppered with moisture, and promptly put it up again. Then insensibly he relaxed, in the toils of memories roused by the reflection that this night fairly duplicated that which had welcomed him to Paris, twenty years ago.

It was then that, for the first time in several months, he thought definitely of Troyon's.

And it was then that Chance ordained that his taxicab should skid. On the point of leaving the Ile de la Cité by way of the Pont St. Michel, it suddenly (one might pardonably have believed) went mad, darting crabwise from the middle of the road to the right-hand footway with evident design to climb the rail and make an end to everything in the Seine. The driver regained control barely in time to avert a tragedy, and had no more than accomplished this much when a bit of broken glass gutted one of the rear tyres, which promptly gave up the ghost with a roar like that of a lusty young cannon.

At this the driver (apparently a person of religious bias) said something heartfelt about the sacred name of his pipe and, crawling from under the apron, turned aft to assess damages.

On his own part Lanyard swore in sound Saxon, opened the door, and delivered himself to the pelting shower.

"Well?" he enquired after watching the driver muzzle the eviscerated tyre for some eloquent moments.

Turning up a distorted face, the other gesticulated with profane abandon, by way of good measure interpolating a few disconnected words and phrases. Lanyard gathered that this was the second accident of the same nature since noon that the cab consequently lacked a spare tyre, and that short of a trip to the garage the accident was irremediable. So he said (intelligently) it couldn't be helped, paid the man and over-tipped precisely as though their journey had been successfully consummated, and standing over his luggage watched the maimed vehicle limp miserably off through the teeming mists.

Now in normal course his plight should have been relieved within two minutes. But it wasn't. For some time all such taxis as did pass displayed scornfully inverted flags. Also, their drivers jeered in their pleasing Parisian way at the lonely outlander occupying a position of such uncommon distinction in the heart of the storm and the precise middle of the Pont St. Michel.

Over to the left, on the Quai de Marché Neuf, the façade of the Préfecture frowned portentously—"La Tour Pointue," as the Parisian loves to term it. Lanyard forgot his annoyance long enough to salute that grim pile with a mocking bow, thinking of the men therein who would give half their possessions to lay hands on him who was only a few hundred yards distant, marooned in the rain!...

In its own good time a night-prowling fiacre ambled up and veered over to his hail. He viewed this stroke of good fortune with intense disgust: the shambling, weather-beaten animal between the shafts promised a long, damp crawl to the Lutetia.

And on this reflection he yielded to impulse.

Heaving in his luggage—"Troyon's!" he told the cocher...

The fiacre lumbered off into that dark maze of streets, narrow and tortuous, which backs up from the Seine to the Luxembourg, while its fare reflected that Fate had not served him so hardly after all: if Roddy had really been watching for him at the Gare du Nord, with a mind to follow and wait for his prey to make some incriminating move, this chance-contrived change of vehicles and destination would throw the detective off the scent and gain the adventurer, at worst, several hours' leeway.

When at length his conveyance drew up at the historic corner, Lanyard alighting could have rubbed his eyes to see the windows of Troyon's all bright with electric light.

Somehow, and most unreasonably, he had always believed the place would go to the hands of the house-wrecker unchanged.

A smart portier ducked out, seized his luggage, and offered an umbrella. Lanyard composed his features to immobility as he entered the hotel, of no mind to let the least flicker of recognition be detected in his eyes when they should re-encounter familiar faces.

And this was quite as well: for—again—the first he saw was Roddy.

III

A POINT OF INTERROGATION

The man from Scotland Yard had just surrendered hat, coat, and umbrella to the vestiaire and was turning through swinging doors to the dining-room. Again, embracing Lanyard, his glance seemed devoid of any sort of intelligible expression; and if its object needed all his self-possession in that moment, it was to dissemble relief rather than dismay. An accent of the fortuitous distinguished this second encounter too persuasively to excuse further misgivings. What the adventurer himself hadn't known till within the last ten minutes, that he was coming to Troyon's, Roddy couldn't possibly have anticipated; ergo, whatever the detective's business, it had nothing to do with Lanyard.

Furthermore, before quitting the lobby, Roddy paused long enough to instruct the vestiaire to have a fire laid in his room.

So he was stopping at Troyon's—and didn't care who knew it!

His doubts altogether dissipated by this incident, Lanyard followed his natural enemy into the dining-room with an air as devil-may-care as one could wish and so impressive that the maitre-d'hotel abandoned the detective to the mercies of one of his captains and himself hastened to seat Lanyard and take his order.

This last disposed of; Lanyard surrendered himself to new impressions—of which the first proved a bit disheartening.

However impulsively, he hadn't resought Troyon's without definite intent, to wit, to gain some clue, however slender, to the mystery of that wretched child, Marcel. But now it appeared he had procrastinated fatally: Time and Change had left little other than the shell of the Troyon's he remembered. Papa Troyon was gone; Madame no longer occupied the desk of the caisse; enquiries, so discreetly worded as to be uncompromising, elicited from the maitre-d'hôtel the information that the house had been under new management these eighteen months; the old proprietor was dead, and his widow had sold out lock, stock and barrel, and retired to the country—it was not known exactly where. And with the new administration had come fresh decorations and furnishings as well as a complete change of personnel: not even one of the old waiters remained.

"'All, all are gone, the old familiar faces,'" Lanyard quoted in vindictive melancholy—"damn 'em!"

Happily, it was soon demonstrated that the cuisine was being maintained on its erstwhile plane of excellence: one still had that comfort...

Other impressions, less ultimate, proved puzzling, disconcerting, and paradoxically reassuring.

Lanyard commanded a fair view of Roddy across the waist of the room. The detective had ordered a meal that matched his aspect well—both of true British simplicity. He was a square-set man with a square jaw, cold blue eyes, a fat nose, a thin-lipped trap of a mouth, a face as red as rare beefsteak. His dinner comprised a cut from the joint, boiled potatoes, brussels sprouts, a bit of cheese, a bottle of Bass. He ate slowly, chewing with the doggedness of a strong character hampered by a weak digestion, and all the while kept eyes fixed to an issue of the Paris edition of the London Daily Mail, with an effect of concentration quite too convincing.

Now one doesn't read the Paris edition of the London Daily Mail with tense excitement. Humanly speaking, it can't be done.

Where, then, was the object of this so sedulously dissembled interest?

Lanyard wasn't slow to read this riddle to his satisfaction—in as far, that is, as it was satisfactory to feel still more certain that Roddy's quarry was another than himself.

Despite the lateness of the hour, which had by now turned ten o'clock, the restaurant had a dozen tables or so in the service of guests pleasantly engaged in lengthening out an agreeable evening with dessert, coffee, liqueurs and cigarettes. The majority of these were in couples, but at a table one removed from Roddy's sat a party of three; and Lanyard noticed, or fancied, that the man from Scotland Yard turned his newspaper only during lulls in the conversation in this quarter.

Of the three, one might pass for an American of position and wealth: a man of something more than sixty years, with an execrable accent, a racking cough, and a thin, patrician cast of features clouded darkly by the expression of a soul in torment, furrowed, seamed, twisted—a mask of mortal anguish. And once, when this one looked up and casually encountered Lanyard's gaze, the adventurer was shocked to find himself staring into eyes like those of a dead man: eyes of a grey so light that at a little distance the colour of the irises blended indistinguishably with their whites, leaving visible only the round black points of pupils abnormally distended and staring, blank, fixed, passionless, beneath lashless lids.

For the instant they seemed to explore Lanyard's very soul with a look of remote and impersonal curiosity; then they fell away; and when next the adventurer looked, the man had turned to attend to some observation of one of his companions.

On his right sat a girl who might be his daughter; for not only was she, too, hallmarked American, but she was far too young to be the other's wife. A demure, old-fashioned type; well-poised but unassuming; fetchingly gowned and with sufficient individuality of taste but not conspicuously; a girl with soft brown hair and soft brown eyes; pretty, not extravagantly so when her face was in repose, but with a slow smile that rendered her little less than beautiful: in all (Lanyard thought) the kind of woman that is predestined to comfort mankind, whose strongest instinct is the maternal.

She took little part in the conversation, seldom interrupting what was practically a duologue between her putative father and the third of their party.

This last was one, whom Lanyard was sure he knew, though he could see no more than the back of Monsieur le Comte Remy de Morbihan.

And he wondered with a thrill of amusement if it were possible that Roddy was on the trail of that tremendous buck. If so, it would be a chase worth following—a diversion rendered the more exquisite to Lanyard by the spice of novelty, since for once he would figure as a dispassionate bystander.

The name of Comte Remy de Morbihan, although unrecorded in the Almanach de Gotha, was one to conjure with in the Paris of his day and generation. He claimed the distinction of being at once the homeliest, one of the wealthiest, and the most-liked man in France.

As to his looks, good or bad, they were said to prove infallibly fatal with women, while not a few men, perhaps for that reason, did their possessor the honour to imitate them. The revues burlesqued him; Sem caricatured him; Forain counterfeited him extensively in that inimitable series of Monday morning cartoons for Le Figaro: one said "De Morbihan" instinctively at sight of that stocky figure, short and broad, topped by a chubby, moon-like mask with waxed moustaches, womanish eyes, and never-failing grin.

A creature of proverbial good nature and exhaustless vitality, his extraordinary popularity was due to the equally extraordinary extravagance with which he supported that latest Gallic fad, "le Sport." The Parisian Rugby team was his pampered protégé, he was an active member of the Tennis Club, maintained not only a flock of automobiles but a famous racing stable, rode to hounds, was a good field gun, patronized aviation and motor-boat racing, risked as many maximums during the Monte Carlo season as the Grand Duke Michael himself, and was always ready to whet rapiers or burn a little harmless powder of an early morning in the Parc aux Princes.

But there were ugly whispers current with respect to the sources of his fabulous wealth. Lanyard, for one, wouldn't have thought him the properest company or the best Parisian cicerone for an ailing American gentleman blessed with independent means and an attractive daughter.

Paris, on the other hand—Paris who forgives everything to him who contributes to her amusement—adored Comte Remy de Morbihan...

But perhaps Lanyard was prejudiced by his partiality for Americans, a sentiment the outgrowth of the years spent in New York with Bourke. He even fancied that between his spirit and theirs existed some subtle bond of sympathy. For all he knew he might himself be American...

For some time Lanyard strained to catch something of the conversation that seemed to hold so much of interest for Roddy, but without success because of the hum of voices that filled the room. In time, however, the gathering began to thin out, until at length there remained only this party of three, Lanyard enjoying a most delectable salad, and Roddy puffing a cigar (with such a show of enjoyment that Lanyard suspected him of the sin of smuggling) and slowly gulping down a second bottle of Bass.

Under these conditions the talk between De Morbihan and the Americans became public property.

The first remark overheard by Lanyard came from the elderly American, following a pause and a consultation of his watch.

"Quarter to eleven," he announced.

"Plenty of time," said De Morbihan cheerfully. "That is," he amended, "if mademoiselle isn't bored..."

The girl's reply, accompanied by a pretty inclination of her head toward the Frenchman, was lost in the accents of the first speaker—a strong and sonorous voice, in strange contrast with his ravaged appearance and distressing cough.

"Don't let that worry you," he advised cheerfully. "Lucia's accustomed to keeping late hours with me; and whoever heard of a young and pretty woman being bored on the third day of her first visit to Paris?"

He pronounced the name with the hard C of the Italian tongue, as though it were spelled Luchia.

"To be sure," laughed the Frenchman; "one suspects it will be long before mademoiselle loses interest in the rue de la Paix."

"You may well, when such beautiful things come from it," said the girl.

"See what we found there today."

She slipped a ring from her hand and passed it to De Morbihan.

There followed silence for an instant, then an exclamation from the Frenchman:

"But it is superb! Accept, mademoiselle, my compliments. It is worthy even of you."

She flushed prettily as she nodded smiling acknowledgement.

"Ah, you Americans!" De Morbihan sighed. "You fill us with envy: you have the souls of poets and the wealth of princes!"

"But we must come to Paris to find beautiful things for our womenfolk!"

"Take care, though, lest you go too far, Monsieur Bannon."

"How so—too far?"

"You might attract the attention of the Lone Wolf. They say he's on the prowl once more."

The American laughed a trace contemptuously. Lanyard's fingers tightened on his knife and fork; otherwise he made no sign. A sidelong glance into a mirror at his elbow showed Roddy still absorbed in the Daily Mail.

The girl bent forward with a look of eager interest.

"The Lone Wolf? Who is that?"

"You don't know him in America, mademoiselle?"

"No..."

"The Lone Wolf, my dear Lucia," the valetudinarian explained in a dryly humourous tone, "is the sobriquet fastened by some imaginative French reporter upon a celebrated criminal who seems to have made himself something of a pest over here, these last few years. Nobody knows anything definite about him, apparently, but he operates in a most individual way and keeps the police busy trying to guess where he'll strike next."

The girl breathed an incredulous exclamation.

"But I assure you!" De Morbihan protested. "The rogue has had a wonderfully successful career, thanks to his dispensing with confederates and confining his depredations to jewels and similar valuables, portable and easy to convert into cash. Yet," he added, nodding sagely, "one isn't afraid to predict his race is almost run." "You don't tell me!" the older man exclaimed. "Have they picked up the scent—at last?"

"The man is known," De Morbihan affirmed.

By now the conversation had caught the interest of several loitering waiters, who were listening open-mouthed. Even Roddy seemed a bit startled, and for once forgot to make business with his newspaper; but his wondering stare was exclusively for De Morbihan.

Lanyard put down knife and fork, swallowed a final mouthful of Haut Brion, and lighted a cigarette with the hand of a man who knew not the meaning of nerves.

"Garçon!" he called quietly; and ordered coffee and cigars, with a liqueur to follow...

"Known!" the American exclaimed. "They've caught him, eh?"

"I didn't say that," De Morbihan laughed; "but the mystery is no more—in certain quarters."

"Who is he, then?"

"That—monsieur will pardon me—I'm not yet free to state. Indeed, I may be indiscreet in saying as much as I do. Yet, among friends..."

His shrug implied that, as far as *he* was concerned, waiters were unhuman and the other guests of the establishment non-existent.

"But," the American persisted, "perhaps you can tell us how they got on his track?"

"It wasn't difficult," said De Morbihan: "indeed, quite simple. This tone of depreciation is becoming, for it was my part to suggest the solution to my friend, the Chief of the Sûreté. He had been annoyed and distressed, had even spoken of handing in his resignation because of his inability to cope with this gentleman, the Lone Wolf. And since he is my friend, I too was distressed on his behalf, and badgered my poor wits until they chanced upon an idea which led us to the light."

"You won't tell us?" the girl protested, with a little moue of disappointment, as the Frenchman paused provokingly.

"Perhaps I shouldn't. And yet—why not? As I say, it was elementary reasoning—a mere matter of logical deduction and elimination. One made up one's mind the Lone Wolf must be a certain sort of man; the rest was simply sifting France for the man to fit the theory, and then watching him until he gave himself away."

"You don't imagine we're going to let you stop there?" The American demanded in an aggrieved tone.

"No? I must continue? Very well: I confess to some little pride. It was a feat. He is cunning, that one!"

De Morbihan paused and shifted sideways in his chair, grinning like a mischievous child.

By this manoeuvre, thanks to the arrangement of mirrors lining the walls, he commanded an indirect view of Lanyard; a fact of which the latter was not unaware, though his expression remained unchanged as he sat—with a corner of his eye reserved for Roddy—speculating whether De Morbihan were telling the truth or only boasting for his own glorification.

"Do go on—please!" the girl begged prettily.

"I can deny you nothing, mademoiselle... Well, then! From what little was known of this mysterious creature, one readily inferred he must be a bachelor, with no close friends. That is clear, I trust?"

"Too deep for me, my friend," the elderly man confessed.

"Impenetrable reticence," the Count expounded, sententious—and enjoying himself hugely—"isn't possible in the human relations. Sooner or later one is doomed to share one's secrets, however reluctantly, even unconsciously, with a wife, a mistress, a child, or with some trusted friend. And a secret between two is—a prolific breeder of platitudes! Granted this line of reasoning, the Lone Wolf is of necessity not only unmarried but practically friendless. Other attributes of his will obviously comprise youth, courage, imagination, a rather high order of intelligence, and a social position—let us say, rather, an ostensible business—enabling him to travel at will hither and yon without exciting comment. So far, good! My friend the Chief of the Sûreté forthwith commissioned his agents to seek such an one, and by this means several fine fish were enmeshed in the net of suspicion, carefully scrutinized, and one by one let go—all except one, the veritable man. Him they sedulously watched, shadowing him across Europe and back again. He was in Berlin at the time of the famous Rheinart robbery, though he compassed that coup without detection; he was in Vienna when the British embassy there was looted, but escaped by a clever ruse and managed to dispose of his plunder before the agents of the Sûreté could lay hands on him; recently he has been in London, and there he made love to, and ran away with, the diamonds of a certain lady of some eminence. You have heard of Madame Omber, eh?" Now by Roddy's expression it was plain that, if Madame Omber's name wasn't strange in his hearing, at least he found this news about her most surprising. He was frankly staring, with a slackened jaw and with stupefaction in his blank blue eyes.

Lanyard gently pinched the small end of a cigar, dipped it into his coffee, and lighted it with not so much as a suspicion of tremor. His brain, however, was working rapidly in effort to determine whether De Morbihan meant this for warning, or was simply narrating an amusing yarn founded on advance information and amplified by an ingenious imagination. For by now the news of the Omber affair must have thrilled many a Continental telegraph-wire...

"Madame Omber—of course!" the American agreed thoughtfully. "Everyone has heard of her wonderful jewels. The real marvel is that the Lone Wolf neglected so shining a mark as long as he did."

"But truly so, monsieur!"

"And they caught him at it, eh?"

"Not precisely: but he left a clue—and London, to boot—with such haste as would seem to indicate he knew his cunning hand had, for once, slipped."

"Then they'll nab him soon?"

"Ah, monsieur, one must say no more!" De Morbihan protested. "Rest assured the Chief of the Sûreté has laid his plans: his web is spun, and so artfully that I think our unsociable outlaw will soon be making friends in the Prison of the Santé... But now we must adjourn. One is sorry. It has been so very pleasant..."

A waiter conjured the bill from some recess of his waistcoat and served it on a clean plate to the American. Another ran bawling for the vestiaire. Roddy glued his gaze afresh to the Daily Mail. The party rose.

Lanyard noticed that the American signed instead of settling the bill with cash, indicating that he resided at Troyon's as well as dined there. And the adventurer found time to reflect that it was odd for such as he to seek that particular establishment in preference to the palatial modern hostelries of the Rive Droit—before De Morbihan, ostensibly for the first time espying Lanyard, plunged across the room with both hands outstretched and a cry of joyous surprise not really justified by their rather slight acquaintanceship.

"Ah! Ah!" he clamoured vivaciously. "It is Monsieur Lanyard, who knows all about paintings! But this is delightful, my friend—one grand pleasure! You must know my friends... But come!"

And seizing Lanyard's hands, when that one somewhat reluctantly rose in response to this surprisingly over-exuberant greeting, he dragged him willy-nilly from behind his table.

"And you are American, too. Certainly you must know one another.

Mademoiselle Bannon—with your permission—my friend, Monsieur Lanyard.

And Monsieur Bannon—an old, dear friend, with whom you will share a passion for the beauties of art."

The hand of the American, when Lanyard clasped it, was cold, as cold as ice; and as their eyes met that abominable cough laid hold of the man, as it were by the nape of his neck, and shook him viciously. Before it had finished with him, his sensitively coloured face was purple, and he was gasping, breathless—and infuriated.

"Monsieur Bannon," De Morbihan explained disconnectedly—"it is most distressing—I tell him he should not stop in Paris at this season—"

"It is nothing!" the American interposed brusquely between paroxysms.

"But our winter climate, monsieur—it is not fit for those in the prime of health—"

"It is I who am unfit!" Bannon snapped, pressing a handkerchief to his lips—"unfit to live!" he amended venomously.

Lanyard murmured some conventional expression of sympathy. Through it all he was conscious of the regard of the girl. Her soft brown eyes met his candidly, with a look cool in its composure, straightforward in its enquiry, neither bold nor mock-demure. And if they were the first to fall, it was with an effect of curiosity sated, without hint of discomfiture... And somehow the adventurer felt himself measured, classified, filed away.

Between amusement and pique he continued to stare while the elderly American recovered his breath and De Morbihan jabbered on with unfailing vivacity; and he thought that this closer scrutiny discovered in her face contours suggesting maturity of thought beyond her apparent years—which were somewhat less than the sum of Lanyard's—and with this the suggestion of an elusive, provoking quality of wistful languor, a hint of patient melancholy...

"We are off for a glimpse of Montmartre," De Morbihan was explaining—"Monsieur Bannon and I. He has not seen Paris in twenty years, he tells me. Well, it will be amusing to show him what changes have taken place in all that time. One regrets mademoiselle is too fatigued to accompany us. But you, my friend—now if you would consent to make our third, it would be most amiable of you."

"I'm sorry," Lanyard excused himself; "but as you see, I am only just in from the railroad, a long and tiresome journey. You are very good, but I—"

"Good!" De Morbihan exclaimed with violence. "I? On the contrary, I am a very selfish man; I seek but to afford myself the pleasure of your company. You lead such a busy life, my friend, romping about Europe, here one day, God-knows-where the next, that one must make one's best of your spare moments. You will join us, surely?"

"Really I cannot tonight. Another time perhaps, if you'll excuse me."

"But it is always this way!" De Morbihan explained to his friends with a vast show of mock indignation. "'Another time, perhaps'—his invariable excuse! I tell you, not two men in all Paris have any real acquaintance with this gentleman whom all Paris knows! His reserve is proverbial—'as distant as Lanyard,' we say on the boulevards!" And turning again to the adventurer, meeting his cold stare with the De Morbihan grin of quenchless effrontery—"As you will, my friend!" he granted. "But should you change your mind—well, you'll have no trouble finding us. Ask any place along the regular route. We see far too little of one another, monsieur—and I am most anxious to have a little chat with you."

"It will be an honour," Lanyard returned formally...

In his heart he was pondering several most excruciating methods of murdering the man. What did he mean? How much did he know? If he knew anything, he must mean ill, for assuredly he could not be ignorant of Roddy's business, or that every other word he uttered was rivetting suspicion on Lanyard of identity with the Lone Wolf, or that Roddy was listening with all his ears and staring into the bargain!

Decidedly something must be done to silence this animal, should it turn out he really did know anything!

It was only after profound reflection over his liqueur (while Roddy devoured his Daily Mail and washed it down with a third bottle of Bass) that Lanyard summoned the maitre-d'hôtel and asked for a room.

It would never do to fix the doubts of the detective by going elsewhere that night. But, fortunately, Lanyard knew that warren which was Troyon's as no one else knew it; Roddy would find it hard to detain him, should events seem to advise an early departure.

IV

A STRATAGEM

When the maitre-d'hôtel had shown him all over the establishment (innocently enough, en route, furnishing him with a complete list of his other guests and their rooms: memoranda readily registered by a retentive memory) Lanyard chose the bedchamber next that occupied by Roddy, in the second storey.

The consideration influencing this selection was—of course—that, so situated, he would be in position not only to keep an eye on the man from Scotland Yard but also to determine whether or not Roddy were disposed to keep an eye on him.

In those days Lanyard's faith in himself was a beautiful thing. He could not have enjoyed the immunity ascribed to the Lone Wolf as long as he had without gaining a power of sturdy self-confidence in addition to a certain amount of temperate contempt for spies of the law and all their ways.

Against the peril inherent in this last, however, he was self-warned, esteeming it the most fatal chink in the armour of the lawbreaker, this disposition to underestimate the acumen of the police: far too many promising young adventurers like himself were annually laid by the heels in that snare of their own infatuate weaving. The mouse has every right, if he likes, to despise the cat for a heavy-handed and bloodthirsty beast, lacking wit and imagination, a creature of simple force-majeure; but that mouse will not advisedly swagger in cat-haunted territory; a blow of the paw is, when all's said and done, a blow of the paw—something to numb the wits of the wiliest mouse.

Considering Roddy, he believed it to be impossible to gauge the limitations of that essentially British intelligence—something as self-contained as a London flat. One thing only was certain: Roddy didn't always think in terms of beef and Bass; he was nobody's facile fool; he could make a shrewd inference as well as strike a shrewd blow.

Reviewing the scene in the restaurant, Lanyard felt measurably warranted in assuming not only that Roddy was interested in De Morbihan, but that the Frenchman was well aware of that interest. And he resented sincerely his inability to feel as confident that the Count, with his gossip about the Lone Wolf, had been merely seeking to divert Roddy's interest to putatively larger game. It was just possible that De Morbihan's identification of Lanyard with that mysterious personage, at least by innuendo, had been unintentional. But somehow Lanyard didn't believe it had.

The two questions troubled him sorely: Did De Morbihan *know*, did he merely suspect, or had he only loosed an aimless shot which chance had sped to the right goal? Had the mind of Roddy proved fallow to that suggestion, or had it, with its simple national tenacity, been impatient of such side issues, or incredulous, and persisted in focusing its processes upon the personality and activities of Monsieur le Comte Remy de Morbihan? However, one would surely learn something illuminating before very long. The business of a sleuth is to sleuth, and sooner or later Roddy must surely make some move to indicate the quarter wherein his real interest lay.

Just at present, reasoning from noises audible through the bolted door that communicated with the adjoining bedchamber, the business of a sleuth seemed to comprise going to bed. Lanyard, shaving and dressing, could distinctly hear a tuneless voice contentedly humming "Sally in our Alley," a rendition punctuated by one heavy thump and then another and then by a heartfelt sigh of relief—as Roddy kicked off his boots—and followed by the tapping of a pipe against grate-bars, the squeal of a window lowered for ventilation, the click of an electric-light, and the creaking of bed-springs.

Finally, and before Lanyard had finished dressing, the man from Scotland Yard began placidly to snore.

Of course, he might well be bluffing; for Lanyard had taken pains to let Roddy know that they were neighbours, by announcing his selection in loud tones close to the communicating door.

But this was a question which the adventurer meant to have answered before he went out...

It was hard upon twelve o'clock when the mirror on the dressing-table assured him that he was at length point-device in the habit and apparel of a gentleman of elegant nocturnal leisure. But if he approved the figure he cut, it was mainly because clothes interested him and he reckoned his own impeccable. Of their tenant he was feeling just then a bit less sure than he had half-an-hour since; his regard was louring and mistrustful. He was, in short, suffering reaction from the high spirits engendered by his cross-Channel exploits, his successful getaway, and the unusual circumstances attendant upon his return to this memory-haunted mausoleum of an unhappy childhood. He even shivered a trifle, as if under premonition of misfortune, and asked himself heavily: Why not?

For, logically considered, a break in the run of his luck was due. Thus far he had played, with a success almost too uniform, his dual role, by day the amiable amateur of art, by night the nameless mystery that prowled unseen and preyed unhindered. Could such success be reasonably expected to attend him always? Should he count De Morbihan's yarn a warning? Black must turn up every so often in a run of red: every gambler knows as much. And what was Michael Lanyard but a common gambler, who persistently staked life and liberty against the blindly impartial casts of Chance?

With one last look round to make certain there was nothing in the calculated disorder of his room to incriminate him were it to be searched in his absence, Lanyard enveloped himself in a long full-skirted coat, clapped on an opera hat, and went out, noisily locking the door. He might as well have left it wide, but it would do no harm to pretend he didn't know the bedchamber keys at Troyon's were interchangeable—identically the same keys, in fact, that had been in service in the days of Marcel the wretched.

A single half-power electric bulb now modified the gloom of the corridor; its fellow made a light blot on the darkness of the courtyard. Even the windows of the conciergerie were black.

Nonetheless, Lanyard tapped them smartly.

"*Cordon!*" he demanded in a strident voice. "*Cordon, s'il vous plait!*"

"*Eh?*" A startled grunt from within the lodge was barely audible. Then the latch clicked loudly at the end of the passageway.

Groping his way in the direction of this last sound, Lanyard found the small side door ajar. He opened it, and hesitated a moment, looking out as though questioning the weather; simultaneously his deft fingers wedged the latch back with a thin slip of steel.

No rain, in fact, had fallen within the hour; but still the sky was dense with a sullen rack, and still the sidewalks were inky wet.

The street was lonely and indifferently lighted, but a swift searching reconnaissance discovered nothing that suggested a spy skulking in the shelter of any of the nearer shadows.

Stepping out, he slammed the door and strode briskly round the corner, as if making for the cab-rank that lines up along the Luxembourg Gardens side of the rue de Medicis; his boot-heels made a cheerful racket in that quiet hour; he was quite audibly going away from Troyon's.

But instead of holding on to the cab-rank, he turned the next corner, and then the next, rounding the block; and presently, reapproaching the entrance to Troyon's, paused in the recess of a dark doorway and, lifting one foot after another, slipped rubber caps over his heels. Thereafter his progress was practically noiseless.

The smaller door yielded to his touch without a murmur. Inside, he closed it gently, and stood a moment listening with all his senses—not with his ears alone but with every nerve and fibre of his being—with his imagination, to boot. But there was never a sound or movement in all the house that he could detect.

And no shadow could have made less noise than he, slipping cat-footed across the courtyard and up the stairs, avoiding with super-developed sensitiveness every lift that might complain beneath his tread. In a trice he was again in the corridor leading to his bedchamber.

It was quite as gloomy and empty as it had been five minutes ago, yet with a difference, a something in its atmosphere that made him nod briefly in confirmation of that suspicion which had brought him back so stealthily.

For one thing, Roddy had stopped snoring. And Lanyard smiled over the thought that the man from Scotland Yard might profitably have copied that trick of poor Bourke's, of snoring like the Seven Sleepers when most completely awake...

It was naturally no surprise to find his bedchamber door unlocked and slightly ajar. Lanyard made sure of the readiness of his automatic, strode into the room, and shut the door quietly but by no means soundlessly.

He had left the shades down and the hangings drawn at both windows; and since these had not been disturbed, something nearly approaching complete darkness reigned in the room. But though promptly on entering his fingers closed upon the wall-switch near the door, he refrained from turning up the lights immediately, with a fancy of impish inspiration that it would be amusing to learn what move Roddy would make when the tension became too much even for his trained nerves.

Several seconds passed without the least sound disturbing the stillness.

Lanyard himself grew a little impatient, finding that his sight failed to grow accustomed to the darkness because that last was too absolute, pressing against his staring eyeballs like a black fluid impenetrably opaque, as unbroken as the hush.

Still, he waited: surely Roddy wouldn't be able much longer to endure such suspense...

And, surely enough, the silence was abruptly broken by a strange and moving sound, a hushed cry of alarm that was half a moan and half a sob.

Lanyard himself was startled: for that was never Roddy's voice!

There was a noise of muffled and confused footsteps, as though someone had started in panic for the door, then stopped in terror.

Words followed, the strangest he could have imagined, words spoken in a gentle and tremulous voice:

"In pity's name! who are you and what do you want?"

Thunderstruck, Lanyard switched on the lights.

At a distance of some six paces he saw, not Roddy, but a woman, and not a woman merely, but the girl he had met in the restaurant.

V

ANTICLIMAX

The surprise was complete; none, indeed, was ever more so; but it's a question which party thereto was the more affected.

Lanyard stared with the eyes of stupefaction. To his fancy, this thing passed the compass of simple incredulity: it wasn't merely improbable, it was preposterous; it was anticlimax exaggerated to the proportions of the grotesque.

He had come prepared to surprise and bully rag the most astute police detective of whom he had any knowledge; he found himself surprised and discountenanced by *this*...!

Confusion no less intense informed the girl's expression; her eyes were fixed to his with a look of blank enquiry; her face, whose colouring had won his admiration two hours since, was colourless; her lips were just ajar; the fingers of one hand touched her cheek, indenting it.

The other hand caught up before her the long skirts of a pretty robe-de-chambre, beneath whose edge a hand's-breadth of white silk shimmered and the toe of a silken mule was visible. Thus she stood, poised for flight, attired only in a dressing-gown over what, one couldn't help suspecting, was her night-dress: for her hair was down, and she was unquestionably all ready for her bed...But Bourke's patient training had been wasted if this man proved one to remain long at loss. Rallying his wits quickly from their momentary rout, he reasserted command over them, and if he didn't in the least understand, made a brave show of accepting this amazing accident as a commonplace.

"I beg your pardon, Miss Bannon—" he began with a formal bow.

She interrupted with a gasp of wondering recognition: "Mr Lanyard!"

He inclined his head a second time: "Sorry to disturb you—"

"But I don't understand—"

"Unfortunately," he proceeded smoothly, "I forgot something when I went out, and had to come back for it."

"But—but—"

"Yes?"

Suddenly her eyes, for the first time detached from his, swept the room with a glance of wild dismay.

"This room," she breathed—"I don't know it—"

"It is mine."

"Yours! But—"

"That is how I happened to—interrupt you."

The girl shrank back a pace—two paces—uttering a low-toned monosyllable of understanding, an "*O!*" abruptly gasped. Simultaneously her face and throat flamed scarlet.

"*Your* room, Mr Lanyard!"

Her tone so convincingly voiced shame and horror that his heart misgave him. Not that alone, but the girl was very good to look upon. "I'm sure," he began soothingly; "it doesn't matter. You mistook a door—"

"But you don't understand!" She shuddered... "This dreadful habit! And I was hoping I had outgrown it! How can I ever explain—?"

"Believe me, Miss Bannon, you need explain nothing."

"But I must... I wish to... I can't bear to let you think...But surely you can make allowances for sleepwalking!"

To this appeal he could at first return nothing more intelligent than a dazed repetition of the phrase.

So that was how…Why hadn't he thought of it before? Ever since he had turned on the lights, he had been subjectively busy trying to invest her presence there with some plausible excuse. But somnambulism had never once entered his mind. And in his stupidity, at pains though he had been to render his words inoffensive, he had been guilty of constructive incivility.

In his turn, Lanyard coloured warmly.

"I beg your pardon," he muttered.

The girl paid no attention; she seemed self-absorbed, thinking only of herself and the anomalous position into which her infirmity had tricked her. When she did speak, her words came swiftly:

"You see…I was so frightened! I found myself suddenly standing up in darkness, just as if I had jumped out of bed at some alarm; and then I heard somebody enter the room and shut the door stealthily…Oh, please understand me!"

"But I do, Miss Bannon—quite."

"I am so ashamed—"

"Please don't consider it that way."

"But now that you know—you don't think—"

"My dear Miss Bannon!"

"But it must be so hard to credit! Even I… Why, it's more than a year since this last happened. Of course, as a child, it was almost a habit; they had to watch me all the time. Once… But that doesn't matter. I *am* so sorry."

"You really mustn't worry," Lanyard insisted. "It's all quite natural—such things do happen—are happening all the time—"

"But I don't want you—"

"I am nobody, Miss Bannon. Besides I shan't mention the matter to a soul. And if ever I am fortunate enough to meet you again, I shall have forgotten it completely—believe me."

There was convincing sincerity in his tone. The girl looked down, as though abashed.

"You are very good," she murmured, moving toward the door.

"I am very fortunate."

Her glance of surprise was question enough.

"To be able to treasure this much of your confidence," he explained with a tentative smile.

She was near the door; he opened it for her, but cautioned her with a gesture and a whispered word: "Wait. I'll make sure nobody's about."

He stepped noiselessly into the hall and paused an instant, looking right and left, listening.

The girl advanced to the threshold and there checked, hesitant, eyeing him anxiously.

He nodded reassurance: "All right—coast's clear!"

But she delayed one moment more.

"It's you who are mistaken," she whispered, colouring again beneath his regard, in which admiration could not well be lacking, "It is I who am fortunate—to have met a—gentleman."

Her diffident smile, together with the candour of her eyes, embarrassed him to such extent that for the moment he was unable to frame a reply.

"Goodnight," she whispered—"and thank you, thank you!"

Her room was at the far end of the corridor. She gained its threshold in one swift dash, noiseless save for the silken whisper of her garments, turned, flashed him a final look that left him with the thought that novelists did not always exaggerate, that eyes could shine like stars...

Her door closed softly.

Lanyard shook his head as if to dissipate a swarm of annoying thoughts, and went back into his own bedchamber.

He was quite content with the explanation the girl had given, but being the slave of a methodical and pertinacious habit of mind, spent five busy minutes examining his room and all that it contained with a perseverance that would have done credit to a Frenchman searching for a mislaid sou.

If pressed, he would have been put to it to name what he sought or thought to find. What he did find was that nothing had been tampered with and nothing more—not even so much as a dainty, lace-trimmed wisp of sheer linen bearing the lady's monogram and exhaling a faint but individual perfume.

Which, when he came to consider it, seemed hardly playing the game by the book.

As for Roddy, Lanyard wasted several minutes, off and on, listening attentively at the communicating door; but if the detective had stopped snoring, his respiration was loud enough in that quiet hour, a sound of harsh monotony.

True, that proved nothing; but Lanyard, after the fiasco of his first attempt to catch his enemy awake, was no more disposed to be hypercritical; he had his fill of being ingenious and profound. And when presently he again left Troyon's (this time without troubling the repose of the concierge) it was with the reflection that, if Roddy were really playing 'possum, he was welcome to whatever he could find of interest in the quarters of Michael Lanyard.

VI

THE PACK GIVES TONGUE

Lanyard's first destination was that convenient little rez-de-chaussée apartment near the Trocadéro, at the junction of the rue Roget and the avenue de l'Alma; but his way thither was so roundabout that the best part of an hour was required for what might have been less than a twenty-minute taxicab course direct from Troyon's. It was past one when he arrived, afoot, at the corner.

Not that he grudged the time; for in Lanyard's esteem Bourke's epigram had come to have the weight and force of an axiom: "The more trouble you make for yourself, the less the good public will make for you."

Paradoxically, he hadn't the least intention of attempting to deceive anybody as to his permanent address in Paris, where Michael Lanyard, connoisseur of fine paintings, was a figure too conspicuous to permit his making a secret of his residence. De Morbihan, moreover, through recognizing him at Troyon's, had rendered it impossible for Lanyard to adopt a nom-de-guerre there, even had he thought that ruse advisable.

But he had certain businesses to attend to before dawn, affairs demanding privacy; and while by no means sure he was followed, one can seldom be sure of anything, especially in Paris, where nothing is impossible; and it were as well to lose a spy first as last. And his mind could not be at ease with respect to Roddy, thanks to De Morbihan's gasconade in the presence of the detective and also to that hint which the Count had dropped concerning some fatal blunder in the course of Lanyard's British campaign.

The adventurer could recall leaving no step uncovered. Indeed, he had prided himself on conducting his operations with a degree of circumspection unusually thorough-going, even for him. Yet he was unable to rid himself of those misgivings roused by De Morbihan's declaration that the theft of the Omber jewels had been accomplished only at cost of a clue to the thief's identity.

Now the Count's positive information concerning the robbery proved that the news thereof had anticipated the arrival of its perpetrator in Paris; yet Roddy unquestionably had known nothing of it prior to its mention in his presence, after dinner. Or else the detective was a finer actor than Lanyard credited.

But how could De Morbihan have come by his news?

Lanyard was really and deeply perturbed...

Pestered to distraction by such thoughts, he fitted key to latch and quietly let himself into his flat by a private street-entrance which, in addition to the usual door opening on the court and under the eye of the concierge, distinguished this from the ordinary Parisian apartment and rendered it doubly suited to the adventurer's uses.

Then he turned on the lights and moved quickly from room to room of the three comprising his quarters, with comprehensive glances reviewing their condition.

But, indeed, he hadn't left the reception-hall for the salon without recognizing that things were in no respect as they ought to be: a hat he had left on the hall rack had been moved to another peg; a chair had been shifted six inches from its ordained position; and the door of a clothes-press, which he had locked on leaving, now stood ajar.

Furthermore, the state of the salon, which he had furnished as a lounge and study, and of the tiny dining-room and the bedchamber adjoining, bore out these testimonies to the fact that alien hands had thoroughly ransacked the apartment, leaving no square inch unscrutinized.

Yet the proprietor missed nothing. His rooms were a private gallery of valuable paintings and antique furniture to poison with envy the mind of any collector, and housed into the bargain a small museum of rare books, manuscripts, and articles of exquisite workmanship whose individuality, aside from intrinsic worth, rendered them priceless. A burglar of discrimination might have carried off in one coat-pocket loot enough to foot the bill for a twelve-month of profligate existence. But nothing had been removed, nothing at least that was apparent in the first tour of inspection; which, if sweeping, was by no means superficial.

Before checking off more elaborately his mental inventory, Lanyard turned attention to the protective device, a simple but exhaustive system of burglar-alarm wiring so contrived that any attempt to enter the apartment save by means of a key which fitted both doors and of which no duplicate existed would alarm both the concierge and the burglar protective society. Though it seemed to have been in no way tampered with, to test the apparatus he opened a window on the court.

The lodge of the concierge was within earshot. If the alarm had been in good order, Lanyard could have heard the bell from his window. He heard nothing.

With a shrug, he shut the window. He knew well—none better—how such protection could be rendered valueless by a thoughtful and fore-handed housebreaker.

Returning to the salon, where the main body of his collection was assembled, he moved slowly from object to object, ticking off items and noting their condition; with the sole result of justifying his first conclusion, that whereas nothing had escaped handling, nothing had been removed.

By way of a final test, he opened his desk (of which the lock had been deftly picked) and went through its pigeon-holes.

His scanty correspondence, composed chiefly of letters exchanged with art dealers, had been scrutinized and replaced carelessly, in disorder: and here again he missed nothing; but in the end, removing a small drawer and inserting a hand in its socket, he dislodged a rack of pigeon-holes and exposed the secret cabinet that is almost inevitably an attribute of such pieces of period furniture.

A shallow box, this secret space contained one thing only, but that one of considerable value, being the leather bill-fold in which the adventurer kept a store of ready money against emergencies.

It was mostly for this, indeed, that he had come to his apartment; his London campaign having demanded an expenditure far beyond his calculations, so that he had landed in Paris with less than one hundred francs in pocket. And Lanyard, for all his pride of spirit, acknowledged one haunting fear that of finding himself strapped in the face of emergency.

The fold yielded up its hoard to a sou: Lanyard counted out five notes of one thousand francs and ten of twenty pounds: their sum, upwards of two thousand dollars.

But if nothing had been abstracted, something had been added: the back of one of the Bank of England notes had been used as a blank for memorandum.

Lanyard spread it out and studied it attentively.

The handwriting had been traced with no discernible attempt at disguise, but was quite strange to him. The pen employed had been one of those needle-pointed nibs so popular in France; the hand was that of an educated Frenchman. The import of the memorandum translated substantially as follows:

"To the Lone Wolf—" "The Pack sends Greetings"and extends its invitation "to participate in the benefits" of its Fraternity. "One awaits him always at "L'Abbaye Thêléme."

A date was added, the date of that very day…

Deliberately, having conned this communication, Lanyard produced his cigarette-case, selected a cigarette, found his briquet, struck a light, twisted the note of twenty pounds into a rude spill, set it afire, lighted his cigarette there from and, rising, conveyed the burning paper to a cold and empty fireplace wherein he permitted it to burn to a crisp black ash.

When this was done, his smile broke through his clouding scowl.

"Well, my friend!" he apostrophized the author of that document which now could never prove incriminating—"at all events, I have you to thank for a new sensation. It has long been my ambition to feel warranted in lighting a cigarette with a twenty-pound note, if the whim should ever seize me!"

His smile faded slowly; the frown replaced it: something far more valuable to him than a hundred dollars had just gone up in smoke...

VII

L'ABBAYE

His secret uncovered, that essential incognito of his punctured, his vanity touched to the quick—all that laboriously constructed edifice of art and chicane which yesterday had seemed so substantial, so impregnable a wall between the Lone Wolf and the World, today rent, torn asunder, and cast down in ruins about his feet—Lanyard wasted time neither in profitless lamentation or any other sort of repining.

He had much to do before morning: to determine, as definitely as might in discretion be possible, who had fathomed his secret and how; to calculate what chance he still had of pursuing his career without exposure and disaster; and to arrange, if investigation verified his expectations, which were of the gloomiest, to withdraw in good order, with all honours of war, from that dangerous field.

Delaying only long enough to revise plans disarranged by the discoveries of this last bad quarter of an hour, he put out the lights and went out by the courtyard door; for it was just possible that those whose sardonic whim it had been to name themselves "the Pack" might have stationed agents in the street to follow their dissocial brother in crime. And now more than ever Lanyard was firmly bent on going his own way unwatched. His own way first led him stealthily past the door of the conciergerie and through the court to the public hall in the main body of the building. Happily, there were no lights to betray him had anyone been awake to notice. For thanks to Parisian notions of economy even the best apartment houses dispense with elevator-boys and with lights that burn up real money every hour of the night. By pressing a button beside the door on entering, however, Lanyard could have obtained light in the hallways for five minutes, or long enough to enable any tenant to find his front-door and the key-hole therein; at the end of which period the lamps would automatically have extinguished themselves. Or by entering a narrow-chested box of about the dimensions of a generous coffin, and pressing a button bearing the number of the floor at which he wished to alight, he could have been comfortably wafted aloft without sign of more human agency. But he prudently availed himself of neither of these conveniences. Afoot and in complete darkness he made the ascent of five flights of winding stairs to the door of an apartment on the sixth floor. Here a flash from a pocket lamp located the key-hole; the key turned without sound; the door swung on silent hinges.

Once inside, the adventurer moved more freely, with less precaution against noise. He was on known ground, and alone; the apartment, though furnished, was untenanted, and would so remain as long as Lanyard continued to pay the rent from London under an assumed name.

It was the convenience of this refuge and avenue of retreat, indeed which had dictated his choice of the rez-de-chaussée; for the sixth-floor flat possessed one invaluable advantage—a window on a level with the roof of the adjoining building.

Two minutes' examination sufficed to prove that here at least the Pack had not trespassed...

Five minutes later Lanyard picked the common lock of a door opening from the roof of an apartment house on the farthest corner of the block, found his way downstairs, tapped the door of the conciergerie, chanted that venerable Open Sesame of Paris, "*Cordon, s'il vous plait!*" and was made free of the street by a worthy guardian too sleepy to challenge the identity of this late-departing guest.

He walked three blocks, picked up a taxicab, and in ten minutes more was set down at the Gare des Invalides.

Passing through the station without pause, he took to the streets afoot, following the boulevard St. Germain to the rue du Bac; a brief walk up this time-worn thoroughfare brought him to the ample, open and unguarded porte-cochére of a court walled with beetling ancient tenements.

When he had made sure that the courtyard was deserted, Lanyard addressed himself to a door on the right; which to his knock swung promptly ajar with a clicking latch. At the same time the adventurer whipped from beneath his cloak a small black velvet visor and adjusted it to mask the upper half of his face. Then entering a narrow and odorous corridor, whose obscurity was emphasized by a lonely guttering candle, he turned the knob of the first door and walked into a small, ill-furnished room.

A spare-bodied young man, who had been reading at a desk by the light of an oil-lamp with a heavy green shade, rose and bowed courteously.

"Good morning, monsieur," he said with the cordiality of one who greets an acquaintance of old standing. "Be seated," he added, indicating an arm-chair beside the desk. "It seems long since one has had the honour of a call from monsieur."

"That is so," Lanyard admitted, sitting down.

The young man followed suit. The lamplight, striking across his face beneath the greenish penumbra of the shade, discovered a countenance of Hebraic cast.

"Monsieur has something to show me, eh?"

"But naturally."

Lanyard's reply just escaped a suspicion of curtness: as who should say, what did you expect? He was puzzled by something strange and new in the attitude of this young man, a trace of reserve and constraint...

They had been meeting from time to time for several years, conducting their secret and lawless business according to a formula invented by Bourke and religiously observed by Lanyard. A note or telegram of innocent superficial intent, addressed to a certain member of a leading firm of jewellers in Amsterdam, was the invariable signal for conferences such as this; which were invariably held in the same place, at an hour indeterminate between midnight and dawn, between on the one hand this intelligent, cultivated and well-mannered young Jew, and on the other hand the thief in his mask.

In such wise did the Lone Wolf dispose of his loot, at all events of the bulk thereof; other channels were, of course, open to him, but none so safe; and with no other receiver of stolen goods could he hope to make such fair and profitable deals.

Now inevitably in the course of this long association, though each remained in ignorance of his confederate's identity, these two had come to feel that they knew each other fairly well. Not infrequently, when their business had been transacted, Lanyard would linger an hour with the agent, chatting over cigarettes: both, perhaps, a little thrilled by the piquancy of the situation; for the young Jew was the only man who had ever wittingly met the Lone Wolf face to face...

Why then this sudden awkwardness and embarrassment on the part of the agent?

Lanyard's eyes narrowed with suspicion.

In silence he produced a jewel-case of morocco leather and handed it over to the Jew, then settled back in his chair, his attitude one of lounging, but his mind as quick with distrust as the fingers that, under cover of his cloak, rested close to a pocket containing his automatic.

Accepting the box with a little bow, the Jew pressed the catch and discovered its contents. But the richness of the treasure thus disclosed did not seem to surprise him; and, indeed, he had more than once been introduced with no more formality to plunder of far greater value. Fitting a jeweller's glass to his eye, he took up one after another of the pieces and examined them under the lamplight. Presently he replaced the last, shut down the cover of the box, turned a thoughtful countenance to Lanyard, and made as if to speak, but hesitated.

"Well?" the adventurer demanded impatiently.

"This, I take it," said the Jew absently, tapping the box, "is the jewellery of Madame Omber."

"*I* took it," Lanyard retorted good-naturedly—"not to put too fine a point upon it!"

"I am sorry," the other said slowly.

"Yes?"

"It is most unfortunate..."

"May one enquire what is most unfortunate?"

The Jew shrugged and with the tips of his fingers gently pushed the box toward his customer. "This makes me very unhappy," he admitted: "but I have no choice in the matter, monsieur. As the agent of my principals I am instructed to refuse you an offer for these valuables."

"Why?"

Again the shrug, accompanied by a deprecatory grimace: "That is difficult to say. No explanation was made me. My instructions were simply to keep this appointment as usual, but to advise you it will be impossible for my principals to continue their relations with you as long as your affairs remain in their present status."

"Their present status?" Lanyard repeated. "What does that mean, if you please?"

"I cannot say monsieur. I can only repeat that which was said to me."

After a moment Lanyard rose, took the box, and replaced it in his pocket. "Very well," he said quietly. "Your principals, of course, understand that this action on their part definitely ends our relations, rather than merely interrupts them at their whim?"

"I am desolated, monsieur, but... one must assume that they have considered everything. You understand, it is a matter in which I am wholly without discretion, I trust?"

"O quite!" Lanyard assented carelessly. He held out his hand. "Goodbye, my friend."

The Jew shook hands warmly.

"Goodnight, monsieur—and the best of luck!"

There was significance in his last words that Lanyard did not trouble to analyze. Beyond doubt, the man knew more than he dared admit. And the adventurer told himself he could shrewdly surmise most of that which the other had felt constrained to leave unspoken.

Pressure from some quarter had been brought to bear upon that eminently respectable firm of jewel dealers in Amsterdam to induce them to discontinue their clandestine relations with the Lone Wolf, profitable though these must have been.

Lanyard believed he could name the quarter whence this pressure was being exerted, but before going further or coming to any momentous decision, he was determined to know to a certainty who were arrayed against him and how much importance he need attach to their antagonism. If he failed in this, it would be the fault of the other side, not his for want of readiness to accept its invitation.

In brief, he didn't for an instant contemplate abandoning either his rigid rule of solitude or his chosen career without a fight; but he preferred not to fight in the dark.

Anger burned in him no less hotly than chagrin. It could hardly be otherwise with one who, so long suffered to go his way without let or hindrance, now suddenly, in the course of a few brief hours, found himself brought up with a round turn—hemmed in and menaced on every side by secret opposition and hostility.

He no longer feared to be watched; and the very fact that, as far as he could see, he wasn't watched, only added fuel to his resentment, demonstrating as it did so patently the cynical assurance of the Pack that they had him cornered, without alternative other than to supple himself to their will.

To the driver of the first taxicab he met, Lanyard said "L'Abbaye," then shutting himself within the conveyance, surrendered to the most morose reflections.

Nothing of this mood was, however, apparent in his manner on alighting. He bore a countenance of amiable insouciance through the portals of this festal institution whose proudest boast and—incidentally—sole claim to uniquity is that it never opens its doors before midnight nor closes them before dawn.

He had moved about with such celerity since entering his flat on the rue Roget that it was even now only two o'clock; an hour at which revelry might be expected to have reached its apogee in this, the soi-disant "smartest" place in Paris.

A less sophisticated adventurer might have been flattered by the cordiality of his reception at the hands of that arbiter elegantiarum the maitre-d'hôtel.

"Ah-h, Monsieur Lanya_rrr_! But it is long since we have been so favoured. However, I have kept your table for you."

"Have you, though?"

"Could it be otherwise, after receipt of your honoured order?"

"No," said Lanyard coolly, "I presume not, if you value your peace of mind."

"Monsieur is alone?" This with an accent of disappointment.

"Temporarily, it would seem so."

"But this way, if you please..."

In the wake of the functionary, Lanyard traversed that frowsy anteroom where doubtful wasters are herded on suspicion in company with the corps of automatic Bacchanalians and figurantes, to the main restaurant, the inner sanctum toward which the naïve soul of the travel-bitten Anglo-Saxon aspires so ardently.

It was not a large room; irregularly octagonal in shape, lined with wall-seats behind a close-set rank of tables; better lighted than most Parisian restaurants, that is to say, less glaringly; abominably ventilated; the open space in the middle of the floor reserved for a handful of haggard young professional dancers, their stunted bodies more or less costumed in brilliant colours, footing it with all the vivacity to be expected of five-francs per night per head; the tables occupied by parties Anglo-Saxon and French in the proportion of five to one, attended by a company of bored and apathetic waiters; a string orchestra ragging incessantly; a vicious buck-nigger on a dais shining with self-complacence while he vamped and shouted "*Waitin' foh th' Robuht E. Lee*"...

Lanyard permitted himself to be penned in a corner behind a table, ordered champagne not because he wanted it but because it was etiquette, suppressed a yawn, lighted a cigarette, and reviewed the assemblage with a languid but shrewd glance.

He saw only the company of every night; for even in the off-season there are always enough English-speaking people in Paris to make it possible for L'Abbaye Thêléme to keep open with profit: the inevitable assortment of respectable married couples with friends, the men chafing and wondering if possibly all this might seem less unattractive were they foot-loose and fancy-free, the women contriving to appear at ease with varying degrees of success, but one and all flushed with dubiety; the sprinkling of demi-mondaines not in the least concerned about *their* social status; the handful of people who, having brought their fun with them, were having the good time they would have had anywhere; the scattering of plain drunks in evening dress... Nowhere a face that Lanyard recognized definitely: no Mr Bannon, no Comte Remy de Morbihan...

He regarded this circumstance, however, with more vexation than surprise: De Morbihan would surely show up in time; meanwhile, it was annoying to be obliged to wait, to endure this martyrdom of ennui.

He sipped his wine sparingly, without relish, considering the single subsidiary fact which did impress him with some wonder—that he was being left severely to himself; something which doesn't often fall to the lot of the unattached male at L'Abbaye. Evidently an order had been issued with respect to him. Ordinarily he would have been grateful: tonight he was merely irritated: such neglect rendered him conspicuous...

The fixed round of delirious divertissement unfolded as per schedule. The lights were lowered to provide a melodramatic atmosphere for that startling novelty, the Apache Dance. The coon shouted stridently. The dancers danced bravely on their poor, tired feet. An odious dwarf creature in a miniature outfit of evening clothes toddled from table to table, offensively soliciting stray francs—but shied from the gleam in Lanyard's eyes. Lackeys made the rounds, presenting each guest with a handful of coloured, feather-weight celluloid balls, with which to bombard strangers across the room. The inevitable shamefaced Englishman departed in tow of an overdressed Frenchwoman with pride of conquest in her smirk. The equally inevitable alcoholic was dug out from under his table and thrown into a cab. An American girl insisted on climbing upon a table to dance, but swayed and had to be helped down, giggling foolishly. A Spanish dancing girl was afforded a clear floor for her specialty, which consisted in singing several verses understood by nobody, the choruses emphasized by frantic assaults on the hair of several variously surprised, indignant, and flattered male guests—among them Lanyard, who submitted with resignation...

And then, just when he was on the point of consigning the Pack to the devil for inflicting upon him such cruel and inhuman punishment, the Spanish girl picked her way through the mob of dancers who invaded the floor promptly on her withdrawal, and paused beside his table.

"You're not angry, mon coco?" she pleaded with a provocative smile.

Lanyard returned a smiling negative.

"Then I may sit down with you and drink a glass of your wine?"

"Can't you see I've been saving the bottle for you?"

The woman plumped herself promptly into the chair opposite the adventurer. He filled her glass.

"But you are not happy tonight?" she demanded, staring over the brim as she sipped.

"I am thoughtful," he said.

"And what does that mean?"

"I am saddened to contemplate the infirmities of my countrymen, these Americans who can't rest in Paris until they find some place as deadly as any Broadway boasts, these English who adore beautiful Paris solely because here they may continue to get drunk publicly after half-past twelve!"

"Ah, then it's la barbe, is it not?" said the girl, gingerly stroking her faded, painted cheek.

"It is true: I am bored."

"Then why not go where you're wanted?" She drained her glass at a gulp and jumped up, swirling her skirts. "Your cab is waiting, monsieur—and perhaps you will find it more amusing with that Pack!"

Flinging herself into the arms of another girl, she swung away, grinning impishly at Lanyard over her partner's shoulder.

VIII

THE HIGH HAND

Evidently his first move toward departure was signalled; for as he passed out through L'Abbaye's doors the carriage-porter darted forward and saluted.

"Monsieur Lanyarr'?"

"Yes?"

"Monsieur's car is waiting."

"Indeed?" Lanyard surveyed briefly a handsome black limousine that, at pause beside the curb, was champing its bits in the most spirited fashion. Then he smiled appreciatively. "All the same, I thank you for the compliment," he said, and forthwith tipped the porter.

But before entrusting himself to this gratuitous conveyance, he put himself to the trouble of inspecting the chauffeur—a capable-looking mechanic togged out in a rich black livery which, though relieved by a vast amount of silk braiding, was like the car guiltless of any sort of insignia.

"I presume you know where I wish to go, my man?"

The chauffeur touched his cap: "But naturally, monsieur."

"Then take me there, the quickest way you know."

Nodding acknowledgement of the porter's salute, Lanyard sank gratefully back upon uncommonly luxurious upholstery. The fatigue of the last thirty-six hours was beginning to tell on him a bit, though his youth was still so vital, so instinct with strength and vigour, that he could go as long again without sleep if need be.

Nonetheless he was glad of this opportunity to snatch a few minutes' rest by way of preparation against the occult culmination of this adventure. No telling what might ensue of this violation of all those principles which had hitherto conserved his welfare! And he entertained a gloomy suspicion that he would be inclined to name another ass, who proposed as he did to beard this Pack in its den with nothing more than his wits and an automatic pistol to protect ten thousand-francs, the jewels of Madame Omber, the Huysman plans, and (possibly) his life.

However, he stood committed to his folly, if folly it were: he would play the game as it lay.

As for curiosity concerning his immediate destination, there was little enough of that in his temper; a single glance round on leaving the car would fix his whereabouts beyond dispute, so thorough was his knowledge of Paris.

He contemplated briefly, with admiration, the simplicity with which that affair at L'Abbaye had been managed, finding no just cause to suspect anyone there of criminal complicity in the plans of the Pack: a forged order for a table to the maitre-d'hotel, ten francs to the carriage-porter and twenty more to the dancing woman to play parts in a putative practical joke—and the thing had been arranged without implicating a soul...!

Of a sudden, ending a ride much shorter than Lanyard would have liked, the limousine swung in toward a curb.

Bending forward, he unlatched the door and, glancing through the window, uttered a grunt of profound disgust.

If this were the best that Pack could do...!

He had hoped for something a trifle more original from men with wit and imagination enough to plot the earlier phases of this intrigue.

The car had pulled up in front of an institution which he knew well—far too well, indeed, for his own good.

Nonetheless, he consented to get out.

"Sure you've come to the right place?" he asked the chauffeur.

Two fingers touching the visor of his cap: "But certainly, monsieur!"

"Oh, all right!" Lanyard grumbled resignedly; and tossing the man a five-franc piece, applied his knuckles to the door of an outwardly commonplace hôtel particulier in the rue Chaptal between the impasse of the Grand Guignol and the rue Pigalle.

Now the neophyte needs the introduction of a trusted sponsor before he can win admission to the club-house of the exclusive Circle of Friends of Humanity; but Lanyard's knock secured him prompt and unquestioned right of way. The unfortunate fact is, he was a member in the best of standing; for this society of pseudo-altruistic aims was nothing more nor less than one of those several private gambling clubs of Paris which the French Government tolerates more or less openly, despite adequate restrictive legislation; and gambling was Lanyard's ruling passion—a legacy from Bourke no less than the rest of his professional equipment.

To every man his vice (the argument is Bourke's, in defence of his failing). And perhaps the least mischievous vice a professional cracksman can indulge is that of gambling, since it can hardly drive him to lengths more desperate than those whereby he gains a livelihood.

In the esteem of Paris, Count Remy de Morbihan himself was scarcely a more light-hearted plunger than Monsieur Lanyard.

Naturally, with this reputation, he was always free of the handsome salons wherein the Friends of Humanity devoted themselves to roulette, auction bridge, baccarat and chemin-de-fer: and of this freedom he now proceeded to avail himself, with his hat just a shade aslant on his head, his hands in his pockets, a suspicion of a smile on his lips and a glint of the devil in his eyes—in all an expression accurately reflecting the latest phase of his humour, which was become largely one of contemptuous toleration, thanks to what he chose to consider an exhibition of insipid stupidity on the part of the Pack.

Nor was this humour in any way modified when, in due course, he confirmed anticipation by discovering Monsieur le Comte Remy de Morbihan lounging beside one of the roulette tables, watching the play, and now and again risking a maximum on his own account.

A flash of animation crossed the unlovely mask of the Count when he saw Lanyard approaching, and he greeted the adventurer with a gay little flirt of his pudgy dark hand.

"Ah, my friend!" he cried. "It is you, then, who have changed your mind! But this is delightful!"

"And what has become of your American friend?" Asked the adventurer.

"He tired quickly, that one, and packed himself off to Troyon's. Be sure I didn't press him to continue the grand tour!"

"Then you really did wish to see me tonight?" Lanyard enquired innocently.

"Always—always, my dear Lanyard!" the Count declared, jumping up. "But come," he insisted: "I've a word for your private ear, if these gentlemen will excuse us."

"Do!" Lanyard addressed in a confidential manner those he knew at the table, before turning away to the tug of the Count's hand on his arm—"I think he means to pay up twenty pounds he owes me!"

Some derisive laughter greeted this sally.

"I mean that, however," Lanyard informed the other cheerfully as they moved away to a corner where conversation without an audience was possible—"you ruined that Bank of England note, you know."

"Cheap at the price!" the Count protested, producing his bill-fold.

"Five hundred francs for an introduction to Monsieur the Lone Wolf!"

"Are you joking?" Lanyard asked blankly—and with a magnificent gesture abolished the proffered banknote.

"Joking? I! But surely you don't mean to deny—"

"My friend," Lanyard interrupted, "before we assert or deny anything, let us gather the rest of the players round the table and deal from a sealed deck. Meantime, let us rest on the understanding that I have found, at one end, a message scrawled on a bank-note hidden in a secret place, at the other end, yourself, Monsieur le Comte. Between and beyond these points exists a mystery, of which one anticipates elucidation."

"You shall have it," De Morbihan promised. "But first, we must go to those others who await us."

"Not so fast!" Lanyard interposed. "What am I to understand? That you wish me to accompany you to the—ah—den of the Pack?"

"Where else?" De Morbihan grinned.

"But where is that?"

"I am not permitted to say—"

"Still, one has one's eyes. Why not satisfy me here?"

"Your eyes, by your leave, monsieur, will be blindfolded."

"Impossible."

"Pardon—it is an essential—"

"Come, come, my friend: we are not in the Middle Ages!"

"I have no discretion, monsieur. My confrères—"

"I insist: there will be trust on both sides or no negotiations."

"But I assure you, my dear friend—"

"My dear Count, it is useless: I am determined. Blindfold? I should say not! This is not—need I remind you again?—the Paris of Balzac and that wonderful Dumas of yours!"

"What do you propose, then?" De Morbihan enquired, worrying his moustache.

"What better place for the proposed conference than here?"

"But not here!"

"Why not? Everybody comes here: it will cause no gossip. I am here—I have come halfway; your friends must do as much on their part."

"It is not possible..."

"Then, I beg you, tender them my regrets."

"Would you give us away?"

"Never that: one makes gifts to one's friends only. But my interest in yours is depreciating so rapidly that, should you delay much longer, it will be on sale for the sum of two sous."

"O—damn!" the Count complained peevishly.

"With all the pleasure in life... But now," Lanyard went on, rising to end the interview, "you must forgive me for reminding you that the morning wanes apace. I shall be going home in another hour."

De Morbihan shrugged. "Out of my great affection for you," he purred venomously, "I will do my possible. But I promise nothing."

"I have every confidence in your powers of moral suasion, monsieur," Lanyard assured him cheerfully. "Au revoir!"

And with this, not at all ill-pleased with himself, he strutted off to a table at which a high-strung session of chemin-de-fer was in process, possessed himself of a vacant chair, and in two minutes was so engrossed in the game that the Pack was quite forgotten.

In fifteen minutes he had won thrice as many thousands of francs. Twenty minutes or half an hour later, a hand on his shoulder broke the grip of his besetting passion.

"Our table is made up, my friend," De Morbihan announced with his inextinguishable grin. "We're waiting for you."

"Quite at your service."

Settling his score and finding himself considerably better off than he had imagined, he resigned his place gracefully, and suffered the Count to link arms and drag him away up the main staircase to the second storey, where smaller rooms were reserved for parties who preferred to gamble privately.

"So it appears you succeeded!" he chaffed his conductor good-humouredly.

"I have brought you the mountain," De Morbihan assented.

"One is grateful for small miracles..."

But De Morbihan wouldn't laugh at his own expense; for a moment, indeed, he seemed inclined to take umbrage at Lanyard's levity. But the sudden squaring of his broad shoulders and the hardening of his features was quickly modified by an uneasy sidelong glance at his companion. And then they were at the door of the cabinet particulier.

De Morbihan rapped, turned the knob, and stood aside, bowing politely.

With a nod acknowledging the courtesy, Lanyard consented to precede him, and entered a room of intimate proportions, furnished chiefly with a green-covered card-table and five easy-chairs, of which three were occupied—two by men in evening dress, the third by one in a well-tailored lounge suit of dark grey.

Now all three men wore visors of black velvet.

Lanyard looked from one to the other and chuckled quietly.

With an aggrieved air De Morbihan launched into introductions:

"Messieurs, I have the honour to present to you our confrère, Monsieur Lanyard, best known as 'The Lone Wolf.' Monsieur Lanyard—the Council of our Association, known to you as 'The Pack.'"

The three rose and bowed ceremoniously, Lanyard returned a cool, good-natured nod. Then he laughed again and more openly:

"A pack of knaves!"

"Monsieur doubtless feels at ease?" one retorted acidly.

"In your company, Popinot? But hardly!" Lanyard returned in light contempt.

The fellow thus indicated, a burly rogue of a Frenchman in rusty and baggy evening clothes, started and flushed scarlet beneath his mask; but the man next him dropped a restraining hand upon his arm, and Popinot, with a shrug, sank back into his chair.

"Upon my word!" Lanyard declared gracelessly, "it's as good as a play! Are you sure, Monsieur le Comte, there's no mistake—that these gay masqueraders haven't lost their way to the stage of the Grand Guignol?"

"Damn!" muttered the Count. "Take care, my friend! You go too far!"

"You really think so? But you amaze me! You can't in reason expect me to take you seriously, gentlemen!"

"If you don't, it will prove serious business for you!" growled the one he had called Popinot.

"You mean that? But you are magnificent, all of you! We lack only the solitary illumination of a candle-end—a grinning skull—a cup of blood upon the table—to make the farce complete! But as it is... Messieurs, you must be rarely uncomfortable, and feeling as foolish as you look, into the bargain! Moreover, I'm no child... Popinot, why not disembarrass your amiable features? And you, Mr Wertheimer, I'm sure, will feel more at ease with an open countenance—as the saying runs," he said, nodding to the man beside Popinot. "As for this gentleman," he concluded, eyeing the third, "I haven't the pleasure of his acquaintance."

With a short laugh, Wertheimer unmasked and exposed a face of decidedly English type, fair and well-modelled, betraying only the faintest traces of Semitic cast to account for his surname. And with this example, Popinot snatched off his own black visor—and glared at Lanyard: in his shabby dress, the incarnate essence of bourgeoisie outraged. But the third, he of the grey lounge suit, remained motionless; only his eyes clashed coldly with the adventurer's.

He seemed a man little if at all Lanyard's senior, and built upon much the same lines. A close-clipped black moustache ornamented his upper lip. His chin was square and strong with character. The cut of his clothing was conspicuously neither English nor Continental.

"I don't know you, sir," Lanyard continued slowly, puzzled to account for a feeling of familiarity with this person, whom he could have sworn he had never met before.

"But you won't let your friends here outdo you in civility, I trust?"

"If you mean you want me to unmask, I won't," the other returned brusquely, in fair French but with a decided transatlantic intonation.

"American, eh?"

"Native-born, if it interests you."

"Have I ever met you before?"

"You have not."

"My dear Count," Lanyard said, turning to De Morbihan, "do me the favour to introduce this gentleman."

"Your dear Count will do nothing like that, Mr Lanyard. If you need a name to call me by, Smith's good enough."

The incisive force of his enunciation assorted consistently with the general habit of the man. Lanyard recognized a nature no more pliable than his own. Idle to waste time bickering with this one...

"It doesn't matter," he said shortly; and drawing back a chair, sat down. "If it did, I should insist—or else decline the honour of receiving the addresses of this cosmopolitan committee. Truly, messieurs, you flatter me. Here we have Mr Wertheimer, representing the swell-mobsmen across Channel; Monsieur le Comte standing for the gratin of Paris; Popinot, spokesman for our friends the Apaches; and the well-known Mr Goodenough Smith, ambassador of the gunmen of New York—no doubt. I presume one is to understand you wait upon me as representing the fine flower of the European underworld?"

"You're to understand that I, for one, don't relish your impudence," the stout Popinot snapped.

"Sorry... But I have already indicated my inability to take you seriously."

"Why not?" the American demanded ominously. "You'd be sore enough if we took you as a joke, wouldn't you?"

"You misapprehend, Mr.—ah—Smith: it is my first aim and wish that you do not take me in any manner, shape or form. It is you, remember, who requested this interview and—er—dressed your parts so strikingly!"

"What are we to understand by that?" De Morbihan interposed.

"This, messieurs—if you must know." Lanyard dropped for the moment his tone of raillery and bent forward, emphasizing his points by tapping the table with a forefinger. "Through some oversight of mine or cleverness of yours—I can't say which—perhaps both—you have succeeded in penetrating my secret. What then? You become envious of my success. In short, I stand in your light: I'm always getting away with something you might have lifted if you'd only had wit enough to think of it first. As your American accomplice, Mr Mysterious Smith, would say, I 'cramp your style'."

"You learned that on Broadway," the American commented shrewdly.

"Possibly... To continue: so you get together, and bite your nails until you concoct a plan to frighten me into my profits. I've no doubt you're prepared to allow me to retain one-half the proceeds of my operations, should I elect to ally myself with you?"

"That's the suggestion we are empowered to make," De Morbihan admitted.

"In other words, you need me. You say to yourselves: 'We'll pretend to be the head of a criminal syndicate, such as the silly novelists are forever writing about, and we'll threaten to put him out of business unless he comes to our terms.' But you overlook one important fact: that you are not mentally equipped to get away with this amusing impersonation! What! Do you expect me to accept you as leading spirits of a gigantic criminal system—you, Popinot, who live by standing between the police and your murderous rats of Belleville, or you, Wertheimer, sneak-thief and black-mailer of timid women, or you, De Morbihan, because you eke out your income by showing a handful of second-storey men where to seek plunder in the homes of your friends!"

He made a gesture of impatience, and lounged back to wait the answer to this indictment. His gaze, ranging the four faces, encountered but one that was not darkly flushed with resentment; and this was the American's.

"Aren't you overlooking me?" this last suggested gently.

"On the contrary: I refuse to recognize you as long as you lack courage to show your face."

"As you will, my friend," the American chuckled. "Make your profit out of that any way you like."

Lanyard sat up again: "Well, I've stated your case, messieurs. It amounts to simple, clumsy blackmail. I'm to split my earnings with you, or you'll denounce me to the police. That's about it, isn't it?"

"Not of necessity," De Morbihan softly purred, twisting his moustache.

"For my part," Popinot declared hotly, "I engage that Monsieur of the High Hand, here, will either work with us or conduct no more operations in Paris."

"Or in New York," the American amended.

"England is yet to be heard from," Lanyard suggested mockingly.

To this Wertheimer replied, almost with diffidence: "If you ask me, I don't think you'd find it so jolly pleasant over there, if you mean to cut up nasty at this end."

"Then what am I to infer? If you're afraid to lay an information against me—and it wouldn't be wise, I admit—you'll merely cause me to be assassinated, eh?"

"Not of necessity," the Count murmured in the same thoughtful tone and manner—as one holding a hidden trump.

"There are so many ways of arranging these matters," Wertheimer ventured.

"Nonetheless, if I refuse, you declare war?"

"Something like that," the American admitted.

"In that case—I am now able to state my position definitely." Lanyard got up and grinned provokingly down at the group. "You can—all four of you—go plumb to hell!"

"My dear friend!" the Count cried, shocked—"you forget—"

"I forget nothing!" Lanyard cut in coldly—"and my decision is final. Consider yourselves at liberty to go ahead and do your damnedest! But don't forget that it is you who are the aggressors. Already you've had the insolence to interfere with my arrangements: you began offensive operations before you declared war. So now if you're hit beneath the belt, you mustn't complain: you've asked for it!"

"Now just what *do* you mean by that?" the American drawled ironically.

"I leave you to figure it out for yourselves. But I will say this: I confidently expect you to decide to live and let live, and shall be sorry, as you'll certainly be sorry, if you force my hand."

He opened the door, turned, and saluted them with sarcastic punctilio.

"I have the honour to bid adieu to Messieurs the Council of—'The Pack'!"

IX

DISASTER

Having fulfilled his purpose of making himself acquainted with the personnel of the opposition, Lanyard slammed the door in its face, thrust his hands in his pockets, and sauntered downstairs, chuckling, his nose in the air, on the best of terms with himself.

True, the fat was in the fire and well ablaze: he had to look to himself now, and go warily in the shadow of their enmity. But it was something to have faced down those four, and he wasn't seriously impressed by any one of them.

Popinot, perhaps, was the most dangerous in Lanyard's esteem; a vindictive animal, that Popinot; and the creatures he controlled, a murderous lot, drug-ridden, drink bedevilled, vicious little rats of Belleville, who'd knife a man for the price of an absinthe. But Popinot wouldn't move without leave from De Morbihan, and unless Lanyard's calculations were seriously miscast, De Morbihan would restrain both himself and his associates until thoroughly convinced Lanyard was impregnable against every form of persuasion. Murder was something a bit out of De Morbihan's line—something, at least, which he might be counted on to hold in reserve. And by the time he was ready to employ it, Lanyard would be well beyond his reach. Wertheimer, too, would deprecate violence until all else failed; his half-caste type was as cowardly as it was blackguard; and cowards kill only impulsively, before they've had time to weigh consequences. There remained "Smith," enigma; a man apparently gifted with both intelligence and character... But if so, what the deuce was *he* doing in such company?

Still, there he was: and the association damned him beyond consideration. His sorts were all of a piece, beneath the consideration of men of spirit...

At this point, the self-complacence bred of his contempt for Messrs. de Morbihan et Cie. bred in its turn a thought that brought the adventurer up standing.

The devil! Who was he, Michael Lanyard, that held himself above such vermin, yet lived in such a way as practically to invite their advances? What right was his to resent their opening the door to confraternity, as long as he trod paths so closely parallel to theirs that only a sophist might discriminate them? What comforting distinction was to be drawn between on the one hand a blackmailer like Wertheimer, a chevalier-d'industrie like De Morbihan, or a patron of Apaches like Popinot, and on the other himself whose bread was eaten in the sweat of thievery?

He drew a long face; whistled softly; shook his head; and smiled a wry smile.

"Glad I didn't think of that two minutes ago, or I'd never have had the cheek..."

Without warning, incongruously and, in his understanding, inexplicably, he found himself beset by recurrent memory of the girl, Lucia Bannon.

For an instant he saw her again, quite vividly, as last he had seen her: turning at the door of her bedchamber to look back at him, a vision of perturbing charm in her rose-silk dressing-gown, with rich hair loosened, cheeks softly glowing, eyes brilliant with an emotion illegible to her one beholder...

What had been the message of those eyes, flashed down the dimly lighted length of that corridor at Troyon's, ere she vanished?

Adieu? Or au revoir?...

She had termed him, naïvely enough, and a gentleman.

But if she knew—suspected—even dreamed—that he was what he was?...

He shook his head again, but now impatiently, with a scowl and a grumble:

"What's the matter with me anyway? Mooning over a girl I never saw before tonight! As if it matters a whoop in Hepsidam what she thinks!... Or is it possible I'm beginning to develop a rudimentary conscience, at this late day? Me...!"

If there were anything in this hypothesis, the growing-pains of that late-blooming conscience were soon enough numbed by the hypnotic spell of clattering chips, an ivory ball singing in an ebony race, and croaking croupiers.

For Lanyard's chair at the table of chemin-de-fer had been filled by another and, too impatient to wait a vacancy, he wandered on to the salon dedicated to roulette, tested his luck by staking a note of five hundred francs on the black, won, and incontinently subsided into a chair and an oblivion that endured for the space of three-quarters of an hour.

At the end of that period he found himself minus his heavy winnings at chemin-de-fer and ten thousand francs of his reserve fund to boot.

By way of lining for his pockets there remained precisely the sum which he had brought into Paris that same evening, less subsequent general disbursements.

The experience was nothing novel in his history. He rose less resentful than regretful that his ill-luck obliged him to quit just when play was most interesting, and resignedly sought the cloak-room for his coat and hat.

And there he found De Morbihan—again!—standing all garmented for the street, mouthing a huge cigar and wearing a look of impatient discontent.

"At last!" he cried in an aggrieved tone as Lanyard appeared in the offing. "You do take your time, my friend!"

Lanyard smothered with a smile whatever emotion was his of the moment.

"I didn't imagine you really meant to wait for me," he parried with double meaning, both to humour De Morbihan and hoodwink the attendant.

"What do you think?" retorted the Count with asperity—"that I'm willing to stand by and let you moon round Paris at this hour of the morning, hunting for a taxicab that isn't to be found and running God-knows-what risk of being stuck up by some misbegotten Apache? But I should say not! I mean to take you home in my car, though it cost me a half-hour of beauty sleep not lightly to be forfeited at my age!"

The significance that underlay the semi-humourous petulance of the little man was not wasted.

"You're most amiable, Monsieur le Comte!" Lanyard observed thoughtfully, while the attendant produced his hat and coat. "So now, if you're ready, I won't delay you longer."

In another moment they were outside the club-house, its doors shut behind them, while before them, at the curb, waited that same handsome black limousine which had brought the adventurer from L'Abbaye.

Two swift glances, right and left, showed him an empty street, bare of hint of danger.

"One moment, monsieur!" he said, detaining the Count with a touch on his sleeve. "It's only right that I should advise you... I'm armed."

"Then you're less foolhardy than one feared. If such things interest you, I don't mind admitting I carry a life-preserver of my own. But what of that? Is one eager to go shooting at this time of night, for the sheer fun of explaining to sergents de ville that one has been attacked by Apaches?... Providing always one lives to explain!"

"It's as bad as that, eh?"

"Enough to make me loath to linger at your side in a lighted doorway!"

Lanyard laughed in his own discomfiture. "Monsieur le Comte," said he, "there's a dash in you of what your American pal, Mysterious Smith, would call sporting blood, that commands my unstinted admiration. I thank you for your offered courtesy, and beg leave to accept."

De Morbihan replied with a grunt of none too civil intonation, instructed the chauffeur "To Troyon's," and followed Lanyard into the car.

"Courtesy!" he repeated, settling himself with a shake. "That makes nothing. If I regarded my own inclinations, I'd let you go to the devil as quick as Popinot's assassins could send you there!"

"This is delightful!" Lanyard protested. "First you must see me home to save my life, and then you tell me your inclinations consign me to a premature grave. Is there an explanation, possibly?"

"On your person," said the Count, sententious.

"Eh?"

"You carry your reason with you, my friend—in the shape of the Omber loot."

"Assuming you are right—"

"You never went to the rue du Bac, monsieur, without those jewels: and I have had you under observation ever since."

"What conceivable interest," Lanyard pursued evenly, "do you fancy you've got in the said loot?"

"Enough, at least, to render me unwilling to kiss it adieu by leaving you to the mercies of Popinot. You don't imagine I'd ever hear of it again, when his Apaches had finished with you?"

"Ah!... So, after all, your so-called organization isn't founded on that reciprocal trust so essential to the prosperity of such—enterprises!"

"Amuse yourself as you will with your inferences, my friend," the Count returned, unruffled; "but don't forget my advice: pull wide of Popinot!"

"A vindictive soul, eh?"

"One may say that."

"You can't hold him?"

"That one? No fear! You were anything but wise to bait him as you did."

"Perhaps. It's purely a matter of taste in associates."

"If I were the fool you think me," mused the Count "I'd resent that innuendo. As it happens, I'm not. At least, I can wait before calling you to account."

"And meantime profit by your patience?"

"But naturally. Haven't I said as much?"

"Still, I'm perplexed. I can't imagine how you reckon to declare yourself in on the Omber loot."

"All in good time: if you were wise, you'd hand the stuff over to me here and now, and accept what I chose to give you in return. But inasmuch as you're the least wise of men, you must have your lesson."

"Meaning—?"

"The night brings counsel: you'll have time to think things over. By tomorrow you'll be coming to offer me those jewels in exchange for what influence I have in certain quarters."

"With your famous friend, the Chief of the Sûreté, eh?"

"Possibly. I am known also at La Tour Pointue."

"I confess I don't follow you, unless you mean to turn informer."

"Never that."

"It's a riddle, then?"

"For the moment only... But I will say this: it will be futile, your attempting to escape Paris; Popinot has already picketted every outlet. Your one hope resides in me; and I shall be at home to you until midnight tomorrow—today, rather."

Impressed in spite of himself, Lanyard stared. But the Count maintained an imperturbable manner, looking straight ahead. Such calm assurance would hardly be sheer bluff.

"I must think this over," Lanyard mused aloud.

"Pray don't let me hinder you," the Count begged with mild sarcasm. "I have my own futile thoughts..."

Lanyard laughed quietly and subsided into a reverie which, undisturbed by De Morbihan, endured throughout the brief remainder of their drive; for, thanks to the smallness of the hour, the streets were practically deserted and offered no obstacle to speed; while the chauffeur was doubtless eager for his bed.

As they drew near Troyon's, however, Lanyard sat up and jealously reconnoitered both sides of the way.

"Surely you don't expect to be kept out?" the Count asked dryly. "But that just shows how little you appreciate our good Popinot. He'll never object to your locking yourself up where he knows he can find you—but only to your leaving without permission!"

"Something in that, perhaps. Still, I make it a rule to give myself the benefit of every doubt."

There was, indeed, no sign of ambush that he could detect in any quarter, nor any indication that Popinot's Apaches were posted thereabouts. Nevertheless, Lanyard produced his automatic and freed the safety-catch before opening the door.

"A thousand thanks, my dear Count!"

"For what? Doing myself a service? But you make me feel ashamed!"

"I know," agreed Lanyard, depreciatory; "but that's the way I am—a little devil—you really can't trust me! Adieu, Monsieur le Comte."

"Au revoir, monsieur!"

Lanyard saw the car round the corner before turning to the entrance of Troyon's, keeping his weather-eye alert the while. But when the car was gone, the street seemed quite deserted and as soundless as though it had been the thoroughfare of some remote village rather than an artery of the pulsing old heart of Paris.

Yet he wasn't satisfied. He was as little susceptible to psychic admonition as any sane and normal human organism, but he was just then strongly oppressed by intuitive perception that there was something radically amiss in his neighbourhood. Whether or not the result of the Count's open intimations and veiled hints working upon a nature sensitized by excitement and fatigue, he felt as though he had stepped from the cab into an atmosphere impregnated to saturation with nameless menace. And he even shivered a bit, perhaps because of the chill in that air of early morning, perhaps because a shadow of premonition had fallen athwart his soul...

Whatever its cause, he could find no reason for this; and shaking himself impatiently, pressed a button that rang a bell by the ear of the concierge, heard the latch click, thrust the door wide, and re-entered Troyon's.

Here reigned a silence even more marked than that of the street, a silence as heavy and profound as the grave's, so that sheer instinct prompted Lanyard to tread lightly as he made his way down the passage and across the courtyard toward the stairway; and in that hush the creak of a greaseless hinge, when the concierge opened the door of his quarters to identify this belated guest, seemed little less than a profanity.

Lanyard paused and delved into his pockets, nodding genially to the blowsy, sleepy old face beneath the guardian's nightcap.

"Sorry to disturb monsieur," he said politely, further impoverishing himself in the sum of five francs in witness to the sincerity of his regret.

"I thank monsieur; but what need to consider me? It's my duty. And what is one interruption more or less? All night they come and go..."

"Goodnight, monsieur," Lanyard cut short the old man's garrulity; and went on up the stairs, now a little wearily, of a sudden newly conscious of his vast and enervating fatigue.

He thought longingly of bed, yawned involuntarily and, reaching his door, fumbled the key in a most unprofessional way; there were weights upon his eyelids, a heaviness in his brain...

But the key met with no resistance from the wards; and in a trice, appreciating this fact, Lanyard was wide awake again.

No question but that he had locked the door securely, on leaving after his adventure with the charming somnambulist...

Had she, then, taken a whim to his room?

Or was this but proof of what he had anticipated in the beginning—a bit of sleuthing on the part of Roddy?

He entertained little doubt as to the correctness of this latter surmise, as he threw the door open and stepped into the room, his first action being to grasp the electric switch and twist it smartly.

But no light answered.

"Hello!" he exclaimed softly, remembering that the lights could readily have been turned off at the bulbs. "What's the good of that?"

In the same breath he started violently, and swung about.

The door had closed behind him, swiftly but gently, eclipsing the faint light from the hall, leaving what amounted to stark darkness.

His first impression was that the intruder—Roddy or whoever—had darted past him and out, pulling the door to in that act.

Before he could consciously revise this misconception he was fighting for his life.

So unexpected, so swift and sudden fell the assault, that he was caught completely off guard: between the shutting of the door and an onslaught whose violence sent him reeling to the wall, the elapsed time could have been measured by the fluttering of an eyelash.

And then two powerful arms were round him, pinioning his hands to his sides, his feet were tripped up, and he was thrown with a force that fairly jarred his teeth, half-stunning him.

For a breath he lay dazed, struggling feebly; not long, but long enough to enable his antagonist to shift his hold and climb on top of his body, where he squatted, bearing down heavily with a knee on either of Lanyard's forearms, hands encircling his neck, murderous thumbs digging into his windpipe.

He revived momentarily, pulled himself together, and heaved mightily in futile effort to unseat the other.

The sole outcome of this was a tightening pressure on his throat.

The pain grew agonizing; Lanyard's breath was almost completely shut off; he gasped vainly, with a rattling noise in his gullet; his eyeballs started; a myriad coruscant lights danced and interlaced blindingly before them; in his ears there rang a roaring like the voice of heavy surf breaking upon a rock-bound coast.

And of a sudden he ceased to struggle and lay slack, passive in the other's hands.

Only an instant longer was the clutch on his throat maintained. Both hands left it quickly, one shifting to his head to turn and press it roughly cheek to floor. Simultaneously he was aware of the other hand fumbling about his neck, and then of a touch of metal and the sting of a needle driven into the flesh beneath his ear.

That galvanized him; he came to life again in a twinkling, animate with threefold strength and cunning. The man on his chest was thrown off as by a young earthquake; and Lanyard's right arm was no sooner free than it shot out with blind but deadly accuracy to the point of his assailant's jaw. A click of teeth was followed by a sickish grunt as the man lurched over...

Lanyard found himself scrambling to his feet, a bit giddy perhaps, but still sufficiently master of his wits to get his pistol out before making another move.

X

TURN ABOUT

The thought of Lanyard's pocket flash-lamp offering itself, immediately its wide circle of light enveloped his late antagonist.

That one was resting on a shoulder, legs uncouthly a-sprawl, quite without movement of any perceptible sort; his face more than half-turned to the floor, and masked into the bargain.

Incredulously Lanyard stirred the body with a foot, holding his weapon poised as though half-expecting it to quicken with instant and violent action; but it responded in no way.

With a nod of satisfaction, he shifted the light until it marked down the nearest electric bulb, which proved, in line with his inference, to have been extinguished by the socket key, while the heat of its bulb indicated that the current had been shut off only an instant before his entrance.

The light full up, he went back to the thug, knelt and, lifting the body, turned it upon its back.

Recognition immediately rewarded this manoeuvre: the masked face upturned to the glare was that of the American who had made a fourth in the concert of the Pack—"Mr Smith," Quickly unlatching the mask, Lanyard removed it; but the countenance thus exposed told little more than he knew; he could have sworn he had never seen it before. None the less, something in its evil cast persistently troubled his memory, with the same provoking and baffling effect that had attended their first encounter.

Already the American was struggling toward consciousness. His lips and eyelids twitched spasmodically, he shuddered, and his flexed muscles began to relax. In this process something fell from between the fingers of his right hand—something small and silver-bright that caught Lanyard's eye.

Picking it up, he examined with interest a small hypodermic syringe loaded to the full capacity of its glass cylinder, plunger drawn back—all ready for instant service.

It was the needle of this instrument that had pricked the skin of Lanyard's neck; beyond reasonable doubt it contained a soporific, if not exactly a killing dose of some narcotic drug—cocaine, at a venture.

So it appeared that this agent of the Pack had been commissioned to put the Lone Wolf to sleep for an hour or two or more—*perhaps* not permanently!—that he might be out of the way long enough for their occult purposes.

He smiled grimly, fingering the hypodermic and eyeing the prostrate man.

"Turn about," he reflected, "is said to be fair play... Well, why not?"

He bent forward, dug the needle into the wrist of the American and shot the plunger home, all in a single movement so swift and deft that the drug was delivered before the pain could startle the victim from his coma.

As for that, the man came to quickly enough; but only to have his clearing senses met and dashed by the muzzle of a pistol stamping a cold ring upon his temple.

"Lie perfectly quiet, my dear Mr Smith," Lanyard advised; "don't speak above a whisper! Give the good dope a chance: it'll only need a moment, or I'm no judge and you're a careless highbinder! I'd like to know, however—if it's all the same to you—"

But already the injection was taking effect; the look of panic, which had drawn the features of the American and flickered from his eyes with dawning appreciation of his plight, was clouding, fading, blending into one of daze and stupour. The eyelids flickered and lay still; the lips moved as if with urgent desire to speak, but were dumb; a long convulsive sigh shook the American's body; and he rested with the immobility of the dead, save for the slow but steady rise and fall of his bosom.

Lanyard thoughtfully reviewed these phenomena.

"Must kick like a mule, that dope!" he reflected. "Lucky it didn't get me before I guessed what was up! If I'd even suspected its strength, however, I'd have been less hasty: I could do with a little information from Mr Mysterious Stranger here!"

Suddenly conscious of a dry and burning throat, he rose and going to the washstand drank deep and thirstily from a water-bottle; then set himself resolutely to repair the disarray of his wits and consider what was best to be done.

In his abstraction he wandered to a chair over whose back hung a light dressing-gown of wine-coloured silk, which, because it would pack in small compass, was in the habit of carrying with him on his travels. Lanyard had left this thrown across his bed; and he was wondering subconsciously what use the man had thought to make of it, that he should have taken the trouble to shift it to the chair.

But even as he laid hold of it, Lanyard dropped the garment in sheer surprise to find it damp and heavy in his grasp, sodden with viscid moisture. And when, in a swift flash of intuition, he examined his fingers, he discovered them discoloured with a faint reddish stain.

Had the dye run? And how had the American come to dabble the garment in water—to what end?

Then the shape of an object on the floor near his feet arrested Lanyard's questing vision. He stared, incredulous, moved forward, bent over and picked it up, clipping it gingerly between fingertips.

It was one of his razors—a heavy hollow-ground blade—and it was foul with blood.

With a low cry, smitten with awful understanding, Lanyard wheeled and stared fearfully at the door communicating with Roddy's room.

It stood ajar an inch or two, its splintered lock accounted for by a small but extremely efficient jointed steel jimmy which lay near the threshold.

Beyond the door... darkness... silence...

Mustering up all his courage, the adventurer strode determinedly into the adjoining room.

The first flash of his hand-lamp discovered to him sickening verification of his most dreadful apprehensions.

Now he saw why his dressing-gown had been requisitioned—to protect a butcher's clothing.

After a moment he returned, shut the door, and set his back against it, as if to bar out that reeking shambles.

He was very pale, his face drawn with horror; and he was powerfully shaken with nausea.

The plot was damnably patent: Roddy proving a menace to the Pack and requiring elimination, his murder had been decreed as well as that the blame for it should be laid at Lanyard's door. Hence the attempt to drug him, that he might not escape before police could be sent to find him there.

He could no longer doubt that De Morbihan had been left behind at the Circle of Friends of Harmony solely to detain him, if need be, and afford Smith time to finish his hideous job and set the trap for the second victim.

And the plot had succeeded despite its partial failure, despite the swift reverse chance and Lanyard's cunning had meted out to the Pack's agent. It was *his* dressing-gown that was saturate with Roddy's blood, just as they were his gloves, pilfered from his luggage, which had measurably protected the killer's hands, and which Lanyard had found in the next room, stripped hastily off and thrown to the floor—twin crumpled wads of blood-stained chamois-skin.

He had now little choice; he must either flee Paris and trust to his wits to save him, or else seek De Morbihan and solicit his protection, his boasted influence in high quarters.

But to give himself into the hands, to become an associate, of one who could be party to so cowardly a Crime as this... Lanyard told himself he would sooner pay the guillotine the penalty...

Consulting his watch, he found the hour to be no later than half-past four: so swiftly (truly treading upon one another's heels) events had moved since the incident of the somnambulist.

This left at his disposal a fair two hours more of darkness: November nights are long and black in Paris; it would hardly be even moderately light before seven o'clock. But that were a respite none too long for Lanyard's necessity; he must think swiftly in contemplation of instant action were he to extricate himself without the Pack's knowledge and consent.

Granted, then, he must fly this stricken field of Paris. But how? De Morbihan had promised that Popinot's creatures would guard every outlet; and Lanyard didn't doubt him. An attempt to escape the city by any ordinary channel would be to invite either denunciation to the police on the charge of murder, or one of those fatally expeditious forms of assassination of which the Apaches are past-masters.

He must and would find another way; but his decision was frightfully hampered by lack of ready money; the few odd francs in his pocket were no store for the war-chest demanded by this emergency.

True, he had the Omber jewels; but they were not negotiable—not at least in Paris.

And the Huysman plans?

He pondered briefly the possibilities of the Huysman plans.

In his fretting, pacing softly to and fro, at each turn he passed his dressing-table, and chancing once to observe himself in its mirror, he stopped short, thunderstruck by something he thought to detect in the counterfeit presentment of his countenance, heavy with fatigue as it was, and haggard with contemplation of this appalling contretemps.

And instantly he was back beside the American, studying narrowly the contours of that livid mask. Here, then, was that resemblance which had baffled him; and now that he saw it, he could not deny that it was unflatteringly close: feature for feature the face of the murderer reproduced his face, coarsened perhaps but recognizably a replica of that Michael Lanyard who confronted him every morning in his shaving-glass, almost the only difference residing in the scrubby black moustache that shadowed the American's upper lip.

After all, there was nothing wonderful in this; Lanyard's type was not uncommon; he would never have thought himself a distinguished figure.

Before rising he turned out the pockets of his counterfeit. But this profited him little: the assassin had dressed for action with forethought to evade recognition in event of accident. Lanyard collected only a cheap American watch in a rolled-gold case of a sort manufactured by wholesale, a briquet, a common key that might fit any hotel door, a broken paper of Régie cigarettes, an automatic pistol, a few francs in silver—nothing whatever that would serve as a mark of identification; for though the grey clothing was tailor-made, the maker's labels had been ripped out of its pockets, while the man's linen and underwear alike lacked even a laundry's hieroglyphic.

With this harvest of nothing for his pains, Lanyard turned again to the wash-stand and his shaving kit, mixed a stiff lather, stropped another razor to the finest edge he could manage, fetched a pair of keen scissors from his dressing-case, and went back to the murderer.

He worked rapidly, at a high pitch of excitement—as much through sheer desperation as through any appeal inherent in the scheme either to his common sense or to his romantic bent.

In two minutes he had stripped the moustache clean away from that stupid, flaccid mask.

Unquestionably the resemblance was now most striking; the American would readily pass for Michael Lanyard.

This much accomplished, he pursued his preparations in feverish haste. In spite of this, he overlooked no detail. In less than twenty minutes he had exchanged clothing with the American in detail, even down to shirts, collars and neckties; had packed in his own pockets the several articles taken from the other, together with the jointed jimmy and a few of his personal effects, and was ready to bid adieu to himself, to that Michael Lanyard whom Paris knew.

The insentient masquerader on the floor had called himself "good-enough Smith"; he must serve now as good-enough Lanyard, at least for the Lone Wolf's purposes; the police at all events would accept him as such. And if the memory of Michael Lanyard must needs wear the stigma of brutal murder, he need not repine in his oblivion, since through this perfunctory decease the Lone Wolf would gain a freedom even greater than before.

The Pack had contrived only to eliminate Michael Lanyard, the amateur of fine paintings; remained the Lone Wolf with not one faculty impaired, but rather with a deadlier purpose to shape his occult courses...

Under the influence of his methodical preparations, his emotions had cooled appreciably, taking on a cast of cold malignant vengefulness.

He who never in all his criminal record had so much as pulled trigger in self-defence, was ready now to shoot to kill with the most cold-blooded intent—given one of three targets; while Popinot's creatures, if they worried him, he meant to exterminate with as little compunction as though they were rats in fact as well as in spirit...

Extinguishing the lights, he stepped quickly to a window and from one edge of its shade looked down into the street.

He was in time to see a stunted human silhouette detach itself from the shadow of a doorway on the opposite walk, move to the curb, and wave an arm—evidently signaling another sentinel on a corner out of Lanyard's range of vision.

Herein was additional proof, if any lacked, that De Morbihan had not exaggerated the disposition of Popinot. This animal in the street, momentarily revealed by the corner light as he darted across to take position by the door, this animal with sickly face and pointed chin, with dirty muffler round its chicken-neck, shoddy coat clothing its sloping shoulders, baggy corduroy trousers flapping round its bony shanks—this was Popinot's, and but one of a thousand differing in no essential save degree of viciousness.

It wasn't possible to guess how thoroughly Popinot had picketed the house, in co-operation with Roddy's murderer, by way of provision against mischance; but the adventurer was satisfied that, in his proper guise as himself, he needed only to open that postern door at the street end of the passage, to feel a knife slip in between his ribs—most probably in his back, beneath the shoulder-blade...

He nodded grimly, moved back from the window, and used the flash-lamp to light him to the door.

XI

FLIGHT

Now when Lanyard had locked the door, he told himself that the gruesome peace of those two bedchambers was ensured, barring mischance, for as long as the drug continued to hold dominion over the American; and he felt justified in reckoning that period apt to be tolerably protracted; while not before noon at earliest would any hôtelier who knew his business permit the rest of an Anglo-Saxon guest to be disturbed—lacking, that is, definite instructions to the contrary.

For a full minute after withdrawing the key the adventurer stood at alert attention; but the heavy silence of that sinister old rookery sang in his ears untroubled by any untoward sound...

That wistful shadow of his memories, that cowering Marcel of the so-dead yesterday in acute terror of the hand of Madame Troyon, had never stolen down that corridor more quietly: yet Lanyard had taken not five paces from his door when that other opened, at the far end, and Lucia Bannon stepped out.

He checked then, and shut his teeth upon an involuntary oath: truly it seemed as though this run of the devil's own luck would never end!

Astonishment measurably modified his exasperation.

What had roused the girl out of bed and dressed her for the street at that unholy hour? And why her terror at sight of him?

For that the surprise was no more welcome to her than to him was as patent as the fact that she was prepared to leave the hotel forthwith, enveloped in a business-like Burberry rainproof from her throat to the hem of a tweed walking-skirt, and wearing boots both stout and brown. And at sight of him she paused and instinctively stepped back, groping blindly for the knob of her bedchamber door; while her eyes, holding to his with an effect of frightened fascination, seemed momentarily to grow more large and dark in her face of abnormal pallor.

But these were illegible evidences, and Lanyard was intent solely on securing her silence before she could betray him and ruin incontinently that grim alibi which he had prepared at such elaborate pains. He moved toward her swiftly, with long and silent strides, a lifted hand enjoining rather than begging her attention, aware as he drew nearer that a curious change was colouring the complexion of her temper: she passed quickly from dread to something oddly like relief, from repulsion to something strangely like welcome; and dropping the hand that had sought the doorknob, in her turn moved quietly to meet him.

He was grateful for this consideration, this tacit indulgence of the wish he had as yet to voice; drew a little hope and comfort from it in an emergency which had surprised him without resource other than to throw himself upon her generosity. And as soon as he could make himself heard in the clear yet concentrated whisper that was a trick of his trade, a whisper inaudible to ears a yard distant from those to which it was pitched, he addressed her in a manner at once peremptory and apologetic.

"If you please, Miss Bannon—not a word, not a whisper!"

She paused and nodded compliance, questioning eyes steadfast to his.

Doubtfully, wondering that she betrayed so little surprise, he pursued as one committed to a forlorn hope:

"It's vitally essential that I leave this hotel without it becoming known. If I may count on you to say nothing—"

She gave him reassurance with a small gesture. "But how?" she breathed in the least of whispers. "The concierge—!"

"Leave that to me—I know another way. I only need a chance—"

"Then won't you take me with you?"

"Eh?" he stammered, dashed.

Her hands moved toward him in a flutter of entreaty: "I too must leave unseen—I *must*! Take me with you—out of this place—and I promise you no one shall ever know—"

He lacked time to weigh the disadvantages inherent in her proposition; though she offered him a heavy handicap, he had no choice but to accept it without protest.

"Come, then," he told her—"and not a sound—"

She signified assent with another nod; and on this he turned to an adjacent door, opened it gently, whipped out his flash-lamp, and passed through. Without sign of hesitancy, she followed; and like two shadows they dogged the dancing spot-light of the flash-lamp, through a linen-closet and service-room, down a shallow well threaded by a spiral of iron steps and, by way of the long corridor linking the kitchen-offices, to a stout door secured only by huge, old-style bolts of iron.

Thus, in less than two minutes from the instant of their encounter, they stood outside Troyon's back door, facing a cramped, malodorous alleyway—a dark and noisome souvenir of that wild mediaeval Paris whose effacement is an enduring monument to the fame of the good Baron Haussmann.

Now again it was raining, a thick drizzle that settled slowly, lacking little of a fog's opacity; and the faint glimmer from the street lamps of that poorly lighted quarter, reflected by the low-swung clouds, lent Lanyard and the girl little aid as they picked their way cautiously, and always in complete silence, over the rude and slimy cobbles of the foul back way. For the adventurer had pocketed his lamp, lest its beams bring down upon them some prowling creature of Popinot's; though he felt passably sure that the alley had been left unguarded in the confidence that he would never dream of its existence, did he survive to seek escape from Troyon's.

For all its might and its omniscience, Lanyard doubted if the Pack had as yet identified Michael Lanyard with that ill-starred Marcel who once had been as intimate with this forgotten way as any skulking tom of the quarter.

But with the Lone Wolf confidence was never akin to foolhardiness; and if on leaving Troyon's he took the girl's hand without asking permission and quite as a matter-of-course, and drew it through his arm—it was his left arm that he so dedicated to gallantry; his right hand remained unhampered, and never far from the grip of his automatic.

Nor was he altogether confident of his companion. The weight of her hand upon his arm, the fugitive contacts of her shoulder, seemed to him, just then, the most vivid and interesting things in life; the consciousness of her personality at his side was like a shaft of golden light penetrating the darkness of his dilemma. But as minutes passed and their flight was unchallenged, his mood grew dark with doubts and quick with distrust. Reviewing it all, he thought to detect something too damnably adventitious in the way she had nailed him, back there in the corridor of Troyon's. It was a bit too coincidental—"a bit thick!"—like that specious yarn of somnambulism she had told to excuse her presence in his room. Come to examine it, that excuse had been far too clumsy to hoodwink any but a man bewitched by beauty in distress.

Who was she, anyway? And what her interest in him? What had she been after in his room?—this American girl making a first visit to Paris in company with her venerable ruin of a parent? Who, for that matter, was Bannon? If her story of sleepwalking were untrue, then Bannon must have been at the bottom of her essay in espionage—Bannon, the intimate of De Morbihan, and an American even as the murderer of poor Roddy was an American!

Was this singularly casual encounter, then, but a cloak for further surveillance? Had he in his haste and desperation simply played into her hands, when he burdened himself with the care of her?

But it seemed absurd; to think that she... a girl like her, whose every word and gesture was eloquent of gentle birth and training...!

Yet—what *had* she wanted in his room? Somnambulists are sincere indeed in the indulgence of their failing when they time their expeditions so opportunely—and arm themselves with keys to fit strange doors. Come to think of it, he had been rather willfully blind to that flaw in her excuse... Again, why should she be up and dressed and so madly bent on leaving Troyon's at half-past four in the morning? Why couldn't she wait for daylight at least? What errand, reasonable duty or design could have roused her out into the night and the storm at that weird hour? He wondered!

And momentarily he grew more jealously heedful of her, critical of every nuance in her bearing. The least trace of added pressure on his arm, the most subtle suggestion that she wasn't entirely indifferent to him or regarded him in any way other than as the chance-found comrade of an hour of trouble, would have served to fix his suspicions. For such, he told himself, would be the first thought of one bent on beguiling—to lead him on by some intimation, the more tenuous and elusive the more provocative, that she found his person not altogether objectionable.

But he failed to detect anything of this nature in her manner.

So, what was one to think? That she was mentally enough to appreciate how ruinous to her design would be any such advances?...

In such perplexity he brought her to the end of the alley and there pulled up for a look round before venturing out into the narrow, dark, and deserted side street that then presented itself.

At this the girl gently disengaged her hand and drew away a pace or two; and when Lanyard had satisfied himself that there were no Apaches in the offing, he turned to see her standing there, just within the mouth of the alley, in a pose of blank indecision.

Conscious of his regard, she turned to his inspection a face touched with a fugitive, uncertain smile.

"Where are we?" she asked.

He named the street; and she shook her head. "That doesn't mean much to me," she confessed; "I'm so strange to Paris, I know only a few of the principal streets. Where is the boulevard St. Germain?"

Lanyard indicated the direction: "Two blocks that way."

"Thank you." She advanced a step or two, but paused again. "Do you know, possibly, just where I could find a taxicab?"

"I'm afraid you won't find any hereabouts at this hour," he replied. "A fiacre, perhaps—with luck: I doubt if there's one disengaged nearer than Montmartre, where business is apt to be more brisk."

"Oh!" she cried in dismay. "I hadn't thought of that... I thought Paris never went to sleep!"

"Only about three hours earlier than most of the world's capitals... But perhaps I can advise you—"

"If you would be so kind! Only, I don't like to be a nuisance—"

He smiled deceptively: "Don't worry about that. Where do you wish to go?"

"To the Gare du Nord."

That made him open his eyes. "The Gare du Nord!" he echoed. "But—I beg your pardon—"

"I wish to take the first train for London," the girl informed him calmly.

"You'll have a while to wait," Lanyard suggested. "The first train leaves about half-past eight, and it's now not more than five."

"That can't be helped. I can wait in the station."

He shrugged: that was her own lookout—if she were sincere in asserting that she meant to leave Paris; something which he took the liberty of doubting.

"You can reach it by the Métro," he suggested—"the Underground, you know; there's a station handy—St. Germain des Prés. If you like, I'll show you the way."

Her relief seemed so genuine, he could have almost believed in it. And yet—!

"I shall be very grateful," she murmured.

He took that for whatever worth it might assay, and quietly fell into place beside her; and in a mutual silence—perhaps largely due to her intuitive sense of his bias—they gained the boulevard St. Germain. But here, even as they emerged from the side street, that happened which again upset Lanyard's plans: a belated fiacre hove up out of the mist and ranged alongside, its driver loudly soliciting patronage.

Beneath his breath Lanyard cursed the man liberally, nothing could have been more inopportune; he needed that uncouth conveyance for his own purposes, and if only it had waited until he had piloted the girl to the station of the Métropolitain, he might have had it. Now he must either yield the cab to the girl or—share it with her... But why not? He could readily drop out at his destination, and bid the driver continue to the Gare du Nord; and the Métro was neither quick nor direct enough for his design—which included getting under cover well before daybreak.

Somewhat sulkily, then, if without betraying his temper, he signalled the cocher, opened the door, and handed the girl in.

"If you don't mind dropping me en route..."

"I shall be very glad," she said... "anything to repay, even in part, the courtesy you've shown me!"

"Oh, please don't fret about that..."

He gave the driver precise directions, climbed in, and settled himself beside the girl. The whip cracked, the horse sighed, the driver swore; the aged fiacre groaned, stirred with reluctance, crawled wearily off through the thickening drizzle.

Within its body a common restraint held silence like a wall between the two.

The girl sat with face averted, reading through the window what corner signs they passed: rue Bonaparte, rue Jacob, rue des Saints Pères, Quai Malquais, Pont du Carrousel; recognizing at least one landmark in the gloomy arches of the Louvre; vaguely wondering at the inept French taste in nomenclature which had christened that vast, louring, echoing quadrangle the place du Carrousel, unliveliest of public places in her strange Parisian experience.

And in his turn, Lanyard reviewed those well-remembered ways in vast weariness of spirit—disgusted with himself in consciousness that the girl had somehow divined his distrust...

"The Lone Wolf, eh?" he mused bitterly. "Rather, the Cornered Rat—if people only knew! Better still, the Errant—no!—the Arrant Ass!"

They were skirting the Palais Royal when suddenly she turned to him in an impulsive attempt at self-justification.

"What *must* you be thinking of me, Mr Lanyard?"

He was startled: "I? Oh, don't consider me, please. It doesn't matter what I think—does it?"

"But you've been so kind; I feel I owe you at least some explanation—"

"Oh, as for that," he countered cheerfully, "I've got a pretty definite notion you're running away from your father."

"Yes. I couldn't stand it any longer—"

She caught herself up in full voice, as though tempted but afraid to say more. He waited briefly before offering encouragement.

"I hope I haven't seemed impertinent..."

"No, no!"

Than this impatient negative his pause of invitation evoked no other recognition. She had subsided into her reserve, but—he fancied—not altogether willingly.

Was it, then, possible that he had misjudged her?

"You've friends in London, no doubt?" he ventured.

"No—none."

"But—"

"I shall manage very well. I shan't be there more than a day or two—till the next steamer sails."

"I see." There had sounded in her tone a finality which signified desire to drop the subject. Nonetheless, he pursued mischievously: "Permit me to wish you bon voyage, Miss Bannon... and to express my regret that circumstances have conspired to change your plans."

She was still eyeing him askance, dubiously, as if weighing the question of his acquaintance with her plans, when the fiacre lumbered from the rue Vivienne into the place de la Bourse, rounded that frowning pile, and drew up on its north side before the blue lights of the all-night telegraph bureau.

"With permission," Lanyard said, unlatching the door, "I'll stop off here. But I'll direct the cocher very carefully to the Gare du Nord. Please don't even tip him—that's my affair. No—not another word of thanks; to have been permitted to be of service—it is a unique pleasure, Miss Bannon. And so, goodnight!"

With an effect that seemed little less than timid, the girl offered her hand.

"Thank you, Mr Lanyard," she said in an unsteady voice. "I am sorry—"

But she didn't say what it was she regretted; and Lanyard, standing with bared head in the driving mist, touched her fingers coolly, repeated his farewells, and gave the driver both money and instructions, and watched the cab lurch away before he approached the telegraph bureau...

But the enigma of the girl so deeply intrigued his imagination that it was only with difficulty that he concocted a non-committal telegram to Roddy's friend in the Prefecture—that imposing personage who had watched with the man from Scotland Yard at the platform gates in the Gare du Nord.

It was couched in English, when eventually composed and submitted to the telegraph clerk with a fervent if inaudible prayer that he might be ignorant of the tongue.

"Come at once to my room at Troyon's. Enter via adjoining room prepared for immediate action on important development. Urgent. Roddy."

Whether or not this were Greek to the man behind the wicket, it was accepted with complete indifference—or, rather, with an interest that apparently evaporated on receipt of the fees. Lanyard couldn't see that the clerk favoured him with as much as a curious glance before he turned away to lose himself, to bury his identity finally and forever under the incognito of the Lone Wolf.

He couldn't have rested without taking that one step to compass the arrest of the American assassin; now with luck and prompt action on the part of the Préfecture, he felt sure Roddy would be avenged by Monsieur de Paris... But it was very well that there should exist no clue whereby the author of that mysterious telegram might be traced...

It was, then, not an ill-pleased Lanyard who slipped oft into the night and the rain; but his exasperation was elaborate when the first object that met his gaze was that wretched fiacre, back in place before the door, Lucia Bannon leaning from its lowered window, the cocher on his box brandishing an importunate whip at the adventurer.

He barely escaped choking on suppressed profanity; and for two sous would have swung on his heel and ignored the girl deliberately. But he didn't dare: close at hand stood a sergent de ville, inquisitive eyes bright beneath the dripping visor of his kepi, keenly welcoming this diversion of a cheerless hour.

With at least outward semblance of resignation, Lanyard approached the window.

"I have been guilty of some stupidity, perhaps?" he enquired with lip-civility that had no echo in his heart. "But I am sorry—"

"The stupidity is mine," the girl interrupted in accents tense with agitation. "Mr Lanyard, I—I—"

Her voice faltered and broke off in a short, dry sob, and she drew back with an effect of instinctive distaste for public emotion. Lanyard smothered an impulse to demand roughly "Well, what now?" and came closer to the window.

"Something more I can do, Miss Bannon?"

"I don't know... I've just found it out—I came away so hurriedly I never thought to make sure; but I've no money—not a franc!"

After a little pause he commented helpfully: "That does complicate matters, doesn't it?"

"What am I to do? I can't go back—I won't! Anything rather. You may judge how desperate I am, when I prefer to throw myself on your generosity—and already I've strained your patience—"

"Not much," he interrupted in a soothing voice. "But—half a moment—we must talk this over."

Directing the cocher to drive to the place Pigalle, he reentered the cab, suspicion more than ever rife in his mind. But as far as he could see—with that confounded sergo staring!—there was nothing else for it. He couldn't stand there in the rain forever, gossiping with a girl half-hysterical—or pretending to be.

"You see," she explained when the fiacre was again under way, "I thought I had a hundred-franc note in my pocketbook; and so I have—but the pocketbook's back there, in my room at Troyon's."

"A hundred francs wouldn't see you far toward New York," he observed thoughtfully.

"Oh, I hope you don't think—!"

She drew back into her corner with a little shudder of humiliation.

As if he hadn't noticed, Lanyard turned to the window, leaned out, and redirected the driver sharply: "Impasse Stanislas!"

Immediately the vehicle swerved, rounded a corner, and made back toward the Seine with a celerity which suggested that the stables were on the Rive Gauche.

"Where?" the girl demanded as Lanyard sat back. "Where are you taking me?"

"I'm sorry," Lanyard said with every appearance of sudden contrition;

"I acted impulsively—on the assumption of your complete confidence. Which, of course, was unpardonable. But, believe me; you have only to say no and it shall be as you wish."

"But," she persisted impatiently—"you haven't answered me: what is this impasse Stanislas?"

"The address of an artist I know—Solon, the painter. We're going to take possession of his studio in his absence. Don't worry; he won't mind. He is under heavy obligation to me—I've sold several canvasses for him; and when he's away, as now, in the States, he leaves me the keys. It's a sober-minded, steady-paced neighbourhood, where we can rest without misgivings and take our time to think things out."

"But—" the girl began in an odd tone.

"But permit me," he interposed hastily, "to urge the facts of the case upon your consideration."

"Well?" she said in the same tone, as he paused.

"To begin with—I don't doubt you've good reason for running away from your father."

"A very real, a very grave reason," she affirmed quietly.

"And you'd rather not go back—"

"That is out of the question!"—with a restrained passion that almost won his credulity.

"But you've no friends in Paris—?"

"Not one!"

"And no money. So it seems, if you're to elude your father, you must find some place to hide pro tem. As for myself, I've not slept in forty-eight hours and must rest before I'll be able to think clearly and plan ahead...And we won't accomplish much riding round forever in this ark. So I offer the only solution I'm capable of advancing, under the circumstances."

"You are quite right," the girl agreed after a moment. "Please don't think me unappreciative. Indeed, it makes me very unhappy to think I know no way to make amends for your trouble."

"There may be a way," Lanyard informed her quietly; "but we'll not discuss that until we've rested up a bit."

"I shall be only too glad—" she began, but fell silent and, in a silence that seemed almost apprehensive, eyed him speculatively throughout the remainder of the journey.

It wasn't a long one; in the course of the next ten minutes they drew up at the end of a shallow pocket of a street, a scant half-block in depth; where alighting, Lanyard helped the girl out, paid and dismissed the cocher, and turned to an iron gate in a high stone wall crowned with spikes.

The grille-work of that gate afforded glimpses of a small, dark garden and a little house of two storeys. Blank walls of old tenements shouldered both house and garden on either side.

Unlocking the gate, Lanyard refastened it very carefully, repeated the business at the front door of the house, and when they were securely locked and bolted within a dark reception-hall, turned on the electric light.

But he granted the girl little more than time for a fugitive survey of this ante-room to an establishment of unique artistic character.

"These are living-rooms, downstairs here," he explained hurriedly. "Solon's unmarried, and lives quite alone—his studio-devil and femme-de-ménage come in by the day only—and so he avoids that pest a concierge. With your permission, I'll assign you to the studio—up here."

And leading the way up a narrow flight of steps, he made a light in the huge room that was the upper storey.

"I believe you'll be comfortable," he said—"that divan yonder is as easy a couch as one could wish—and there's this door you can lock at the head of the staircase; while I, of course, will be on guard below... And now, Miss Bannon… unless there's something more I can do—?"

The girl answered with a wan smile and a little broken sigh. Almost involuntarily, in the heaviness of her fatigue, she had surrendered to the hospitable arms of a huge lounge-chair.

Her weary glance ranged the luxuriously appointed studio and returned to Lanyard's face; and while he waited he fancied something moving in those wistful eyes, so deeply shadowed with distress, perplexity, and fatigue.

"I'm very tired indeed," she confessed—"more than I guessed. But I'm sure I shall be comfortable... And I count myself very fortunate, Mr Lanyard. You've been more kind than I deserved. Without you, I don't like to think what might have become of me..."

"Please don't!" he pleaded and, suddenly discountenanced by consciousness of his duplicity, turned to the stairs. "Goodnight, Miss Bannon," he mumbled; and was halfway down before he heard his valediction faintly echoed.

As he gained the lower floor, the door was closed at the top of the stairs and its bolt shot home with a soft thud.

But turning to lock the lower door, he stayed his hand in transient indecision.

"Damn it!" he growled uneasily—"there can't be any harm in that girl! Impossible for eyes like hers to lie!... And yet... And yet!... Oh, what's the matter with me? Am I losing my grip? Why stick at ordinary precaution against treachery on the part of a woman who's nothing to me and of whom I know nothing that isn't conspicuously questionable?... All because of a pretty face and an appealing manner!"

And so he secured that door, if very quietly; and having pocketed the key and made the round of doors and windows, examining their locks, he stumbled heavily into the bedroom of his friend the artist.

Darkness overwhelmed him then: he was stricken down by sleep as an ox falls under the pole.

XII

AWAKENING

It was late afternoon when Lanyard wakened from sleep so deep and dreamless that nothing could have induced it less potent than sheer systemic exhaustion, at once nervous, muscular and mental.

A profound and stifling lethargy benumbed his senses. There was stupor in his brain, and all his limbs ached dully. He opened dazed eyes upon blank darkness. In his ears a vast silence pulsed.

And in that strange moment of awakening he was conscious of no individuality: it was, for the time, as if he had passed in slumber from one existence to another, sloughing en passant all his three-fold personality as Marcel Troyon, Michael Lanyard, and the Lone Wolf. Had any one of these names been uttered in his hearing just then it would have meant nothing to him—or little more than nothing: he was for the time being merely *himself*, a shell of sensations enclosing dull embers of vitality.

For several minutes he lay without moving, curiously intrigued by this riddle of identity: it was but slowly that his mind, like a blind hand groping round a dark chamber, picked up the filaments of memory.

One by one the connections were renewed, the circuits closed...

But, singularly enough in his understanding, his first thought was of the girl upstairs in the studio, unconsciously his prisoner and hostage—rather than of himself, who lay there, heavy with loss of sleep, languidly trying to realize himself.

For he was no more as he had been. Wherein the difference lay he couldn't say, but that a difference existed he was persuaded—that he had changed, that some strange reaction in the chemistry of his nature had taken place during slumber. It was as if sleep had not only repaired the ravages of fatigue upon the tissues of his brain and body, but had mended the tissues of his soul as well. His thoughts were fluent in fresh channels, his interests no longer the interests of the Michael Lanyard he had known, no longer self-centred, the interests of the absolute ego. He was concerned less for himself, even now when he should be most gravely so, than for another, for the girl Lucia Bannon, who was nothing to him, whom he had yet to know for twenty-four hours, but of whom he could not cease to think if he would.

It was her plight that perturbed him, from which he sought an outlet—never his own.

Yet his own was desperate enough...

Baffled and uneasy, he at length bethought him of his watch. But its testimony seemed incredible: surely the hour could not be five in the afternoon!—surely he could not have slept so close upon a full round of the clock!

And if it were so, what of the girl? Had she, too, so sorely needed sleep that the brief November day had dawned and waned without her knowledge?

That question was one to rouse him: in an instant he was up and groping his way through the gloom that enshrouded bedchamber and dining-room to the staircase door in the hall. He found this fast enough, its key still safe in his pocket, and unlocking it quietly, shot the beam of his flash-lamp up that dark well to the door at the top; which was tight shut.

For several moments he attended to a taciturn silence broken by never a sound to indicate that he wasn't a lonely tenant of the little dwelling, then irresolutely lifted a foot to the first step—and withdrew it. If she continued to sleep, why disturb her? He had much to do in the way of thinking things out; and that was a process more easily performed in solitude.

Leaving the door ajar, then, he turned to one of the front windows, parted its draperies, and peered out, over the little garden and through the iron ribs of the gate, to the street, where a single gas-lamp, glimmering within a dull golden halo of mist, made visible the scant length of the impasse Stanislas, empty, rain-swept, desolate.

The rain persisted with no hint of failing purpose...

Something in the dreary emptiness of that brief vista deepened the shadow in his mood and knitted a careworn frown into his brows.

Abstractedly he sought the kitchen and, making a light, washed up at the tap, then foraged for breakfast. Persistence turned up a spirit-stove, a half-bottle of methylated, a packet of tea, a tin or two of biscuit, as many more of potted meats: leftovers from the artist's stock, dismally scant and uninviting in array. With these he made the discovery that he was half-famished, and found no reason to believe that the girl would be in any better case. An expedition to the nearest charcuterie was indicated; but after he had searched for and found an old raincoat of Solon's, Lanyard decided against leaving the girl alone. Pending her appearance, he filled the spirit-stove, put the kettle on to boil, and lighting a cigarette, sat himself down to watch the pot and excogitate his several problems.

In a fashion uncommonly clear-headed, even for him, he assembled all the facts bearing upon their predicament, his and Lucia Bannon's, jointly and individually, and dispassionately pondered them...

But insensibly his thoughts reverted to their exotic phase of his awakening, drifting into such introspection as he seldom indulged, and led him far from the immediate riddle, by strange ways to a revelation altogether unpresaged and a resolve still more revolutionary.

A look of wonder flickered in his brooding eyes; and clipped between two fingers, his cigarette grew a long ash, let it fall, and burned down to a stump so short that the coal almost scorched his flesh. He dropped it and crushed out the fire with his heel, all unwittingly.

Slowly but irresistibly his world was turning over beneath his feet...

The sound of a footfall recalled him as from an immeasurable remove; he looked up to see Lucia at pause upon the threshold, and rose slowly, with effort recollecting himself and marshalling his wits against the emergency foreshadowed by her attitude.

Tense with indignation, quick with disdain, she demanded, without any preface whatever: "Why did you lock me in?"

He stammered unhappily: "I beg your pardon—"

"Why did you lock me in?"

"I'm sorry—"

"Why did you—"

But she interrupted herself to stamp her foot emphatically; and he caught her up on the echo of that:

"If you must know, because I wasn't trusting you."

Her eyes darkened ominously: "Yet you insisted I should trust you!"

"The circumstances aren't parallel: you're not a notorious malefactor, wanted by the police of every capital in Europe, hounded by rivals to boot—fighting for life, liberty and"—he laughed shortly—"the pursuit of happiness!"

She caught her breath sharply—whether with dismay or mere surprise at his frankness he couldn't tell.

"Are you?" she demanded quickly.

"Am I what?"

"What you've just said—"

"A crook—and all that? Miss Bannon, you know it!"

"The Lone Wolf?"

"You've known it all along. De Morbihan told you—or else your father. Or, it may be, you were shrewd enough to guess it from De Morbihan's bragging in the restaurant. At all events, it's plain enough, nothing but desire to find proof to identify me with the Lone Wolf took you to my room last night—whether for your personal satisfaction or at the instigation of Bannon—just as nothing less than disgust with what was going on made you run away from such intolerable associations... Though, at that, I don't believe you even guessed how unspeakably vicious those were!"

He paused and waited, anticipating furious denial or refutation; such would, indeed, have been the logical development of the temper in which she had come down to confront him.

Rather than this, she seemed calmed and sobered by his charge; far from resenting it, disposed to concede its justice; anger deserted her expression, leaving it intent and grave. She came quietly into the room and faced him squarely across the table.

"You thought all that of me—that I was capable of spying on you—yet were generous enough to believe I despised myself for doing it?"

"Not at first... At first, when we met back there in the corridor, I was sure you were bent on further spying. Only since waking up here, half an hour ago, did I begin to understand how impossible it would be for you to lend yourself to such villainy as last night's."

"But if you thought that of me then, why did you—?"

"It occurred to me that it would be just as well to prevent your reporting back to headquarters."

"But now you've changed your mind about me?"

He nodded: "Quite."

"But why?" she demanded in a voice of amazement. "Why?"

"I can't tell you," he said slowly—"I don't know why. I can only presume it must be because—I can't help believing in you."

Her glance wavered: her colour deepened. "I don't understand…" she murmured.

"Nor I," he confessed in a tone as low...

A sudden grumble from the teakettle provided welcome distraction. Lanyard lifted it off the flames and slowly poured boiling water on a measure of tea in an earthenware pot.

"A cup of this and something to eat'll do us no harm," he ventured, smiling uneasily—"especially if we're to pursue this psychological enquiry into the whereforeness of the human tendency to change one's mind!"

XIII

CONFESSIONAL

And then, when the girl made no response, but remained with troubled gaze focused on some remote abstraction, "You will have tea, won't you?" he urged.

She recalled her thoughts, nodded with the faintest of smiles—"Yes, thank you!"—and dropped into a chair.

He began at once to make talk in effort to dissipate that constraint which stood between them like an unseen alien presence: "You must be very hungry?"

"I am."

"Sorry I've nothing better to offer you. I'd have run out for something more substantial, only—"

"Only—?" she prompted, coolly helping herself to biscuit and potted ham.

"I didn't think it wise to leave you alone."

"Was that before or after you'd made up your mind about me—the latest phase, I mean?" she persisted with a trace of malice.

"Before," he returned calmly—"likewise, afterwards. Either way you care to take it, it wouldn't have been wise to leave you here. Suppose you had waked up to find me gone, yourself alone in this strange house—"

"I've been awake several hours," she interposed—"found myself locked in, and heard no sound to indicate that you were still here."

"I'm sorry: I was overtired and slept like a log... But assuming the case: you would have gone out, alone, penniless—"

"Through a locked door, Mr Lanyard?"

"I shouldn't have left it locked," he explained patiently... "You would have found yourself friendless and without resources in a city to which you are a stranger."

She nodded: "True. But what of that?"

"In desperation you might have been forced to go back—"

"And report the outcome of my investigation!"

"Pressure might have been brought to induce admissions damaging to me," Lanyard submitted pleasantly. "Whether or no, you'd have been obliged to renew associations you're well rid of."

"You feel sure of that?"

"But naturally."

"How can you be?" she challenged. "You've yet to know me twenty-four hours."

"But perhaps I know the associations better. In point of fact, I do. Even though you may have stooped to play the spy last night, Miss Bannon—you couldn't keep it up. You had to fly further contamination from that pack of jackals."

"Not—you feel sure—merely to keep you under observation?"

"I do feel sure of that. I have your word for it."

The girl deliberately finished her tea, and sat back, regarding him steadily beneath level brows. Then she said with an odd laugh: "You have your own way of putting one on honour!"

"I don't need to—with you."

She analyzed this with gathering perplexity. "What do you mean by that?"

"I mean, I don't need to put you on your honour—because I'm sure of you. Even were I not, still I'd refrain from exacting any pledge, or attempting to." He paused and shrugged before continuing: "If I thought you were still to be distrusted, Miss Bannon, I'd say: 'There's a free door; go when you like, back to the Pack, turn in your report, and let them act as they see fit.'... Do you think I care for them? Do you imagine for one instant that I fear anyone—or all—of that gang?"

"That rings suspiciously of egoism!"

"Let it," he retorted. "It's pride of caste, if you must know. I hold myself a grade better than such cattle; I've intelligence, at least... I can take care of myself!"

If he might read her countenance, it expressed more than anything else distress and disappointment.

"Why do you boast like this—to me?"

"Less through self-satisfaction than in contempt for a pack of murderous mongrels—impatience that I have to consider such creatures as Popinot, Wertheimer, De Morbihan and—all their crew."

"And Bannon," she corrected calmly—"you meant to say!"

"Wel-l—" he stammered, discountenanced.

"It doesn't matter," she assured him. "I quite understand, and strange as it may sound, I've very little feeling in the matter." And then she acknowledged his stupefied stare with a weary smile. "I know what I know," she added, with obscure significance...

"I'd give a good deal to know how much you know," he muttered in his confusion.

"But what do *you* know?" she caught him up—"against Mr Bannon—against my father, that is—that makes you so ready to suspect both him and me?"

"Nothing," he confessed—"I know nothing; but I suspect everything and everybody... And the more I think of it, the more closely I examine that brutal business of last night, the more I seem to sense his will behind it all—as one might glimpse a face in darkness through a lighted lattice... Oh, laugh if you like! It sounds high-flown, I know. But that's the effect I get... What took you to my room, if not his orders? Why does he train with De Morbihan, if he's not blood-kin to that breed? Why are you running away from him if not because you've found out his part in that conspiracy?"

His pause and questioning look evoked no answer; the girl sat moveless and intent, meeting his gaze inscrutably. And something in her impassive attitude worked a little exasperation into his temper.

"Why," he declared hotly—"if I dare trust to intuition—forgive me if I pain you—"

She interrupted with impatience: "I've already begged you not to consider my feelings, Mr Lanyard! If you dared trust to your intuition—what then?"

"Why, then, I could believe that Mr Bannon, your father... I could believe it was his order that killed poor Roddy!"

There could be no doubting her horrified and half-incredulous surprise.

"Roddy?" she iterated in a whisper almost inaudible, with face fast blanching. "Roddy—!"

"Inspector Roddy of Scotland Yard," he told her mercilessly, "was murdered in his sleep last night at Troyon's. The murderer broke into his room by way of mine—the two adjoin. He used my razor, wore my dressing-gown to shield his clothing, did everything he could think of to cast suspicion on me, and when I came in assaulted me, meaning to drug and leave me insensible to be found by the police. Fortunately—I was beforehand with him. I had just left him drugged, insensible in my place, when I met you in the corridor... You didn't know?"

"How can you ask?" the girl moaned.

Bending forward, an elbow on the table, she worked her hands together until their knuckles shone white through the skin—but not as white as the face from which her eyes sought his with a look of dumb horror, dazed, pitiful, imploring.

"You're not deceiving me? But no—why should you?" she faltered. "But how terrible, how unspeakably awful!..."

"I'm sorry," Lanyard mumbled—"I'd have held my tongue if I hadn't thought you knew—"

"You thought I knew—and didn't lift a finger to save the man?" She jumped up with a blazing face. "Oh, how could you?"

"No—not that—I never thought that. But, meeting you then and there, so opportunely—I couldn't ignore the coincidence; and when you admitted you were running away from your father, considering all the circumstances, I was surely justified in thinking it was realization, in part at least, of what had happened that was driving you away." She shook her head slowly, her indignation ebbing as quickly as it had risen. "I understand," she said; "you had some excuse, but you were mistaken. I ran away—yes—but not because of that. I never dreamed..."

She fell silent, sitting with bowed head and twisting her hands together in a manner he found it painful to watch.

"But please," he implored, "don't take it so much to heart, Miss Bannon. If you knew nothing, you couldn't have prevented it."

"No," she said brokenly—"I could have done nothing... But I didn't know. It isn't that—it's the horror and pity of it. And that you could think—!"

"But I didn't!" he protested—"truly I did not. And for what I did think, for the injustice I did do you, believe me, I'm truly sorry."

"You were quite justified," she said—"not only by circumstantial evidence but to a degree in fact. You must know... now I must tell you..."

"Nothing you don't wish to!" he interrupted. "The fact that I practically kidnapped you under pretence of doing you a service, and suspected you of being in the pay of that Pack, gives me no title to your confidence."

"Can I blame you for thinking what you did?" She went on slowly, without looking up—gaze steadfast to her interlaced fingers: "Now for my own sake I want you to know what otherwise, perhaps, I shouldn't have told you—not yet, at all events. I'm no more Bannon's daughter than you're his son. Our names sound alike—people frequently make the same mistake. My name is Shannon—Lucy Shannon. Mr Bannon called me Lucia because he knew I didn't like it, to tease me; for the same reason he always kept up the pretence that I was his daughter when people misunderstood."

"But—if that is so—then what—?"

"Why—it's very simple." Still she didn't look up. "I'm a trained nurse. Mr Bannon is consumptive—so far gone, it's a wonder he didn't die years ago: for months I've been haunted by the thought that it's only the evil in him keeps him alive. It wasn't long after I took the assignment to nurse him that I found out something about him... He'd had a haemorrhage at his desk; and while he lay in coma, and I was waiting for the doctor, I happened to notice one of the papers he'd been working over when he fell. And then, just as I began to appreciate the sort of man I was employed by, he came to, and saw—and knew. I found him watching me with those dreadful eyes of his, and though he was unable to speak, knew my life wasn't safe if ever I breathed a word of what I had read. I would have left him then, but he was too cunning for me, and when in time I found a chance to escape—I was afraid I'd not live long if ever I left him. He went about it deliberately; to keep me frightened, and though he never mentioned the matter directly, let me know plainly, in a hundred ways, what his power was and what would happen if I whispered a word of what I knew. It's nearly a year now—nearly a year of endless terror and…"

Her voice fell; she was trembling with the recrudescent suffering of that year-long servitude. And for a little Lanyard felt too profoundly moved to trust himself to speak; he stood aghast, staring down at this woman, so intrinsically and gently feminine, so strangely strong and courageous; and vaguely envisaging what anguish must have been hers in enforced association with a creature of Bannon's ruthless stamp, he was rent with compassion and swore to himself he'd stand by her and see her through and free and happy if he died for it—or ended in the Santé!

"Poor child!" he heard himself murmuring—"poor child!"

"Don't pity me!" she insisted, still with face averted. "I don't deserve it. If I had the spirit of a mouse, I'd have defied him; it needed only courage enough to say one word to the police—"

"But who is he, then?" Lanyard demanded. "What is he, I mean?"

"I hardly know how to tell you. And I hardly dare: I feel as if these walls would betray me if I did... But to me he's the incarnation of all things evil..." She shook herself with a nervous laugh. "But why be silly about it? I don't really know what or who he is: I only suspect and believe that he is a man whose life is devoted to planning evil and ordering its execution through his lieutenants. When the papers at home speak of 'The Man Higher Up' they mean Archer Bannon, though they don't know it—or else I'm merely a hysterical woman exaggerating the impressions of a morbid imagination... And that's all I know of him that matters."

"But why, if you believe all this—how did you at length find courage—?"

"Because I no longer had courage to endure; because I was more afraid to stay than to go—afraid that my own soul would be forfeit. And then, last night, he ordered me to go to your room and search it for evidence that you were the Lone Wolf. It was the first time he'd ever asked anything like that of me. I was afraid, and though I obeyed, I was glad when you interrupted—glad even though I had to lie the way I did... And all that worked on me, after I'd gone back to my room, until I felt I could stand it no longer; and after a long time, when the house seemed all still, I got up, dressed quietly and... That is how I came to meet you—quite by accident."

"But you seemed so frightened at first when you saw me—"

"I was," she confessed simply; "I thought you were Mr Greggs."

"Greggs?"

"Mr Bannon's private secretary—his right-hand man. He's about your height and has a suit like the one you wear, and in that poor light—at the distance I didn't notice you were clean-shaven—Greggs wears a moustache—"

"Then it was Greggs murdered Roddy and tried to drug me!... By George, I'd like to know whether the police got there before Bannon, or somebody else, discovered the substitution. It was a telegram to the police, you know, I sent from the Bourse last night!"

In his excitement Lanyard began to pace the floor rapidly; and now that he was no longer staring at her, the girl lifted her head and watched him closely as he moved to and fro, talking aloud—more to himself than to her.

"I wish I knew!... And what a lucky thing, you did meet me! For if you'd gone on to the Gare du Nord and waited there... Well, it isn't likely Bannon didn't discover your flight before eight o'clock this morning, is it?"

"I'm afraid not..."

"And they've drawn the deadline for me round every conceivable exit from Paris: Popinot's Apaches are picketed everywhere. And if Bannon had found out about you in time, it would have needed only a word..."

He paused and shuddered to think what might have ensued had that word been spoken and the girl been found waiting for her train in the Gare du Nord.

"Mercifully, we've escaped that. And now, with any sort of luck, Bannon ought to be busy enough, trying to get his precious Mr Greggs out of the Santé, to give us a chance. And a fighting chance is all I ask."

"Mr Lanyard"—the girl bent toward him across the table with a gesture of eager interest—"have you any idea why he—why Mr Bannon hates you so?"

"But does he? I don't know!"

"If he doesn't, why should he plot to cast suspicion of murder on you, and why be so anxious to know whether you were really the Lone Wolf? I saw his eyes light up when De Morbihan mentioned that name, after dinner; and if ever I saw hatred in a man's face, it was in his as he watched you, when you weren't looking."

"As far as I know, I never heard of him before," Lanyard said carelessly. "I fancy it's nothing more than the excitement of a manhunt. Now that they've found me out, De Morbihan and his crew won't rest until they've got my scalp."

"But why?"

"Professional jealousy. We're all crooks, all in the same boat, only I won't row to their stroke. I've always played a lone hand successfully; now they insist on coming into the game and sharing my winnings. And I've told them where they could go."

"And because of that, they're willing to—"

"There's nothing they wouldn't do, Miss Shannon, to bring me to my knees or see me put out of the way, where my operations couldn't hurt their pocketbooks. Well... all I ask is a fighting chance, and they shall have their way!"

Her brows contracted. "I don't understand... You want a fighting chance—to surrender—to give in to their demands?"

"In a way—yes. I want a fighting chance to do what I'd never in the world get them to credit—give it all up and leave them a free field."

And when still she searched his face with puzzled eyes, he insisted: "I mean it; I want to get away—clear out—chuck the game for good and all!"

A little silence greeted this announcement. Lanyard, at pause near the table, resting a hand on it, bent to the girl's upturned face a grave but candid regard. And the deeps of her eyes that never swerved from his were troubled strangely in his vision. He could by no means account for the light he seemed to see therein, a light that kindled while he watched like a tiny flame, feeble, fearful, vacillant, then as the moments passed steadied and grew stronger but ever leaped and danced; so that he, lost in the wonder of it and forgetful of himself, thought of it as the ardent face of a happy child dancing in the depths of some brown autumnal woodland...

"You," she breathed incredulously—"you mean, you're going to stop—?"

"I *have* stopped, Miss Shannon. The Lone Wolf has prowled for the last time. I didn't know it until I woke up, an hour or so ago, but I've turned my last job."

He remarked her hands were small, in keeping with the slightness of her person, but somehow didn't seem so—wore a look of strength and capability, befitting hands trained to a nurse's duties; and saw them each tight-fisted but quivering as they rested on the table, as though their mistress struggled to suppress the manifestation of some emotion as powerful as unfathomable to him.

"But why?" she demanded in bewilderment. "But why do you say that? What can have happened to make you—?"

"Not fear of that Pack!" he laughed—"not that, I promise you."

"Oh, I know!" she said impatiently—"I know that very well. But still I don't understand..."

"If it won't bore you, I'll try to explain." He drew up his chair and sat down again, facing her across the littered table. "I don't suppose you've ever stopped to consider what an essentially stupid animal a crook must be. Most of them are stupid because they practise clumsily one of the most difficult professions imaginable, and inevitably fail at it, yet persist. They wouldn't think of undertaking a job of civil engineering with no sort of preparation, but they'll tackle a dangerous proposition in burglary without a thought, and pay for failure with years of imprisonment, and once out try it again. That's one kind of criminal—the ninety-nine per-cent class—incurably stupid! There's another class, men whose imagination forewarns them of dangers and whose mental training, technical equipment and sheer manual dexterity enable them to attack a formidable proposition like a modern safe—by way of illustration—and force its secret. They're the successful criminals, like myself—but they're no less stupid, no less failures, than the other ninety-nine in our every hundred, because they never stop to think. It never occurs to them that the same intelligence, applied to any one of the trades they must be masters of, would not only pay them better, but leave them their self-respect and rid them forever of the dread of arrest that haunts us all like the memory of some shameful act... All of which is much more of a lecture than I meant to inflict upon you, Miss Shannon, and sums up to just this: *I*'ve stopped to think..."

With this he stopped for breath as well, and momentarily was silent, his faint, twisted smile testifying to self-consciousness; but presently, seeing that she didn't offer to interrupt, but continued to give him her attention so exclusively that it had the effect of fascination, he stumbled on, at first less confidently. "When I woke up it was as if, without my will, I had been thinking all this out in my sleep. I saw myself for the first time clearly, as

I have been ever since I can remember—a crook, thoughtless, vain, rapacious, ruthless, skulking in shadows and thinking myself an amazingly fine fellow because, between coups, I would play the gentleman a bit, venture into the light and swagger in the haunts of the gratin! In my poor, perverted brain I thought there was something fine and thrilling and romantic in the career of a great criminal and myself a wonderful figure—an enemy of society!"

"Why do you say this to me?" she demanded abruptly, out of a phase of profound thoughtfulness.

He lifted an apologetic shoulder. "Because, I fancy, I'm no longer self-sufficient. *I* was all of that, twenty-four hours ago; but now I'm as lonesome as a lost child in a dark forest. I haven't a friend in the world. I'm like a stray pup, grovelling for sympathy. And you are unfortunate enough to be the only person I can declare myself to. It's going to be a fight—I know that too well!—and without something outside myself to struggle toward, I'll be heavily handicapped. But if..." He faltered, with a look of wistful earnestness. "If I thought that you, perhaps, were a little interested, that I had your faith to respect and cherish... if I dared hope that you'd be glad to know I had won out against odds, it would mean a great deal to me, it might mean my salvation!"

Watching her narrowly, hanging upon her decision with the anxiety of a man proscribed and hoping against hope for pardon, he saw her eyes cloud and shift from his, her lips parted but hesitant; and before she could speak, hastily interposed:

"Please don't say anything yet. First let me demonstrate my sincerity. So far I've done nothing to persuade you but—talk and talk and talk! Give me a chance to prove I mean what I say."

"How"—she enunciated only with visible effort and no longer met his appeal with an open countenance—"how can you do that?"

"In the long run, by establishing myself in some honest way of life, however modest; but now, and principally, by making reparation for at least one crime I've committed that's not irreparable."

He caught her quick glance of enquiry, and met it with a confident nod as he placed between them the morocco-bound jewel-case.

"In London, yesterday," he said quietly, "I brought off two big coups. One was deliberate, the other the inspiration of a moment. The one I'd planned for months was the theft of the Omber jewels—here."

He tapped the case and resumed in the same manner: "The other job needs a diagram: Not long ago a Frenchman named Huysman, living in Tours, was mysteriously murdered—a poor inventor, who had starved himself to perfect a stabilizator, an attachment to render aeroplanes practically foolproof. His final trials created a sensation and he was on the eve of selling his invention to the Government when he was killed and his plans stolen. Circumstantial evidence pointed to an international spy named Ekstrom—Adolph Ekstrom, once Chief of the Aviation Corps of the German Army, cashiered for general blackguardism with a suspicion of treason to boot. However, Ekstrom kept out of sight; and presently the plans turned up in the German War Office. That was a big thing for Germany; already supreme with her dirigibles, the acquisition of the Huysman stabilizator promised her ten years' lead over the world in the field of aeroplanes... Now yesterday Ekstrom came to the surface in London with those self-same plans to sell to England. Chance threw him my way, and he mistook me for the man he'd expected to meet—Downing Street's secret agent. Well—no matter how—I got the plans from him and brought them over with me, meaning to turn them over to France, to whom by rights they belong."

"Without consideration?" the girl enquired shrewdly.

"Not exactly. I had meant to make no profit of the affair—I'm a bit squeamish about tainted money!—but under present conditions, if France insists on rewarding me with safe conduct out of the country, I shan't refuse it... Do you approve?"

She nodded earnestly: "It would be worse than criminal to return them to Ekstrom..."

"That's my view of the matter."

"But these?" The girl rested her hand upon the jewel-case.

"Those go back to Madame Omber. She has a home here in Paris that I know very well. In fact, the sole reason why I didn't steal them here was that she left for England unexpectedly, just as I was all set to strike. Now I purpose making use of my knowledge to restore the jewels without risk of falling into the hands of the police. That will be an easy matter... And that brings me to a great favour I would beg of you."

She gave him a look so unexpectedly kind that it staggered him. But he had himself well in hand.

"You can't now leave Paris before morning—thanks to my having overslept," he explained. "There's no honest way I know to raise money before the pawn-shops open. But I'm hoping that won't be necessary; I'm hoping I can arrange matters without going to that extreme. Meanwhile, you agree that these jewels must be returned?"

"Of course," she affirmed gently.

"Then... will you accompany me when I replace them? There won't be any danger: I promise you that. Indeed, it would be more hazardous for you to wait for me elsewhere while I attended to the matter alone. And I'd like you to be convinced of my good faith."

"Don't you think you can trust me for that as well?" she asked, with a flash of humour.

"Trust you!"

"To believe... Mr Lanyard," she told him gently but earnestly, "I do believe."

"You make me very happy," he said... "but I'd like you to see for yourself... And I'd be glad not to have to fret about your safety in my absence. As a bureau of espionage, Popinot's brigade of Apaches is without a peer in Europe. I am positively afraid to leave you alone..."

She was silent.

"Will you come with me, Miss Shannon?" "That is your sole reason for asking this of me?" she insisted, eyeing him steadily.

"That I wish you to believe in me—yes."

"Why?" she pursued, inexorable.

"Because... I've already told you."

"That you want someone's good opinion to cherish... But why, of all people, me—whom you hardly know, of whom what little you do know is hardly reassuring?"

He coloured, and boggled his answer... "I can't tell you," he confessed in the end.

"Why can't you tell me?"

He stared at her miserably... "I've no right..."

"In spite of all I've said, in spite of the faith you so generously promise me, in your eyes I must still figure as a thief, a liar, an impostor—self-confessed. Men aren't made over by mere protestations, nor even by their own efforts, in an hour, or a day, or a week. But give me a year: if I can live a year in honesty, and earn my bread, and so prove my strength—then, perhaps, I might find the courage, the—the effrontery to tell you why I want your good opinion... Now I've said far more than I meant or had any right to. I hope," he ventured pleadingly—"you're not offended."

Only an instant longer could she maintain her direct and unflinching look. Then, his meaning would no more be ignored. Her lashes fell; a tide of crimson flooded her face; and with a quick movement, pushing her chair a little from the table, she turned aside. But she said nothing.

He remained as he had been, bending eagerly toward her. And in the long minute that elapsed before either spoke again, both became oddly conscious of the silence brooding in that lonely little house, of their isolation from the world, of their common peril and mutual dependence.

"I'm afraid," Lanyard said, after a time—"I'm afraid I know what you must be thinking. One can't do your intelligence the injustice to imagine that you haven't understood me—read all that was in my mind and"—his voice fell—"in my heart. I own I was wrong to speak so transparently, to suggest my regard for you, at such a time, under such conditions. I am truly sorry, and beg you to consider unsaid all that I should not have said... After all, what earthly difference can it make to you if one thief more decides suddenly to reform?"

That brought her abruptly to her feet, to show him a face of glowing loveliness and eyes distractingly dimmed and softened.

"No!" she implored him breathlessly—"please—you mustn't spoil it! You've paid me the finest of compliments, and one I'm glad and grateful for... and would I might think I deserved!... You say you need a year to prove yourself? Then—I've no right to say this—and you must please not ask me what I mean—then I grant you that year. A year I shall wait to hear from you from the day we part, here in Paris... And tonight, I will go with you, too, and gladly, since you wish it!"

And then as he, having risen, stood at loss, thrilled, and incredulous, with a brave and generous gesture she offered him her hand.

"Mr Lanyard, I promise..."

To every woman, even the least lovely, her hour of beauty: it had not entered Lanyard's mind to think this woman beautiful until that moment. Of her exotic charm, of the allure of her pensive, plaintive prettiness, he had been well aware; even as he had been unable to deny to himself that he was all for her, that he loved her with all the strength that was his; but not till now had he understood that she was the one woman whose loveliness to him would darken the fairness of all others.

And for a little, holding her tremulous hand upon his finger-tips as though he feared to bruise it with a ruder contact, he could not take his eyes from her.

Then reverently he bowed his head and touched his lips to that hand... and felt it snatched swiftly away, and started back, aghast, the idyll roughly dissipated, the castle of his dreams falling in thunders round his ears.

In the studio-skylight overhead a pane of glass had fallen in with a shattering crash as ominous as the Trump of Doom.

XIV

RIVE DROIT

Falling without presage upon the slumberous hush enveloping the little house marooned in that dead backwater of Paris, the shock of that alarm drove the girl back from the table to the nearest wall, and for a moment held her there, transfixed in panic.

To the wide, staring eyes that questioned his so urgently, Lanyard promptly nodded grave reassurance. He hadn't stirred since his first, involuntary and almost imperceptible start, and before the last fragment of splintered glass had tinkled on the floor above, he was calming her in the most matter-of-fact manner.

"Don't be alarmed," he said. "It's nothing—merely Solon's skylight gone smash!"

"You call that nothing!" she cried gustily. "What caused it, then?"

"My negligence," he admitted gloomily. "I might have known that wide spread of glass with the studio electrics on, full-blaze, would give the show away completely. The house is known to be unoccupied; and it wasn't to be expected that both the police and Popinot's crew would overlook so shining a mark... And it's all my fault, my oversight: I should have thought of it before... High time I was quitting a game I've no longer the wit to play by the rules!"

"But the police would never...!"

"Certainly not. This is Popinot's gentle method of letting us know he's on the job. But I'll just have a look, to make sure... No: stop where you are, please. I'd rather go alone."

He swung alertly through to the hall window, pausing there only long enough for an instantaneous glance through the draperies—a fugitive survey that discovered the impasse Stanislas no more abandoned to the wind and rain, but tenanted visibly by one at least who lounged beneath the lonely lamp-post, a shoulder against it: a featureless civilian silhouette with attention fixed to the little house.

But Lanyard didn't doubt this one had a dozen fellows stationed within call...

Springing up the stairs, he paused prudently at the topmost step, one quick glance showing him the huge rent gaping black in the skylight, the second the missile of destruction lying amid a litter of broken glass—a brick wrapped in newspaper, by the look of it.

Swooping forward, he retrieved this, darted back from the exposed space beneath the shattered skylight, and had no more than cleared the threshold than a second something fell through the gap and buried itself in the parquetry. This was a bullet fired from the roof of one of the adjoining buildings: confirming his prior reasoning that the first missile must have fallen from a height, rather than have been thrown up from the street, to have wrought such destruction with those tough, thick panes of clouded glass...

Swearing softly to himself, he descended to the kitchen.

"As I thought," he said coolly, exhibiting his find.

"They're on the roof of the next house—though they've posted a sentry in the street, of course."

"But that second thump—?" the girl demanded.

"A bullet," he said, placing the bundle on the table and cutting the string that bound it: "they were on the quivive and fired when I showed myself beneath the skylight."

"But I heard no report," she objected.

"A Maxim silencer on the gun, I fancy," he explained, unwrapping the brick and smoothing out the newspaper... "Glad you thought to put on your hat before you came down," he added, with an approving glance for the girl; "it won't be safe to go up to the studio again—of course."

His nonchalance was far less real than it seemed, but helped to steady one who was holding herself together with a struggle, on the verge of nervous collapse.

"But what are we to do now?" she stammered. "If they've surrounded the house—!"

"Don't worry: there's more than one way out," he responded, frowning at the newspaper; "I wouldn't have picked this place out, otherwise. Nor would Solon have rented it in the first instance had it lacked an emergency exit, in event of creditors... Ah—thought so!"

"What—?"

"Troyon's is gone," he said, without looking up. "This is tonight's Presse...'*Totally destroyed by a fire which started at six-thirty this morning and in less than half an hour had reduced the ancient structure to a heap of smoking ashes*'...!" He ran his eye quickly down the column, selecting salient phrases: "'*Believed to have been of incendiary origin though the premises were uninsured*'—that's an intelligent guess!... 'Narrow escape of guests in their '*whatyemaycallems...*' Three lives believed to have been lost... one body recovered charred almost beyond recognition'—but later identified as Roddy—poor devil...! '*Two guests missing, Monsieur Lanyard, the well-known connoisseur of art, who occupied the room adjoining that of the unfortunate detective, and Mademoiselle Bannon, daughter of the American millionaire, who himself escaped only by a miracle with his secretary Monsieur Greggs, the latter being overcome by fumes'*—what a shame...! *'Police and firemen searching the ruins'*—hm-hm—' *extraordinary interest manifested by the Préfecture indicates a suspicion that the building may have been fired to conceal some crime of a political nature.'"*

Crushing the newspaper between his hands, he tossed it into a corner. "That's all of importance. Thoughtful of Popinot to let me know, this way! The Préfecture, of course, is humming like a wasp's nest with the mystery of that telegram, signed with Roddy's name and handed in at the Bourse an hour or so before he was 'burned to death.' Too bad I didn't know then what I do now; if I'd even remotely suspected Greggs' association with the Pack was via Bannon... But what's the use? I did my possible, knowing the odds were heavy against success."

"What was written on the paper?" the girl demanded obliquely.

He made his eyes blank: "Written on the paper—?"

"I saw something in red ink at the head of the column. You tried to hide it from me, but I saw... What was it?"

"Oh—that!" he laughed contemptuously: "just Popinot's impudence—an invitation to come out and be a good target."

She shook her head impatiently: "You're not telling me the truth. It was something else, or you wouldn't have been so anxious to hide it."

"Oh, but I assure you—!"

"You can't. Be honest with me, Mr Lanyard. It was an offer to let you off if you'd give me up to Bannon—wasn't it?"

"Something like that," he assented sheepishly—"too absurd for consideration... But now we're due to clear out of this before they find a way in. Not that they're likely to risk a raid until they've tried starving us out; but it would be as well to put a good distance between us before they find out we've decamped."

He shrugged into his borrowed raincoat, buttoned it to his chin, and turned down the brim of his felt hat; but when he looked up at the girl again, he found she hadn't moved; rather, she remained as one spellbound, staring less at than through him, her expression inscrutable.

"Well," he ventured—"if you're quite ready, Miss Shannon—?"

"Mr Lanyard," she demanded almost sharply—"what was the full wording of that message?"

"If you must know—"

"I must!"

He lifted a depreciative shoulder. "If you like, I'll read it to you—or, rather, translate it from the thieves' argot Popinot complimented me by using."

"Not necessary," she said tersely. "I'll take your word for it... But you must tell me the truth."

"As you will... Popinot delicately suggested that if I leave you here, to be reunited to your alleged parent—if I'll trust to his word of honour, that is, and walk out of the house alone, he'll give me twenty-four hours in which to leave Paris."

"Then only I stand between you and—"

"My dear young woman!" he protested hastily. "Please don't run away with any absurd notion like that. Do you imagine I'd consent to treat with such canaille under any circumstances?"

"All the same," she continued stubbornly, "I'm the stumbling-block. You're risking your life for me—"

"I'm not," he insisted almost angrily.

"You are," she returned with quiet conviction.

"Well!" he laughed—"have it your own way!..."

"But it's *my* life, isn't it? I really don't see how you're going to prevent my risking it for anything that may seem to me worth the risk!"

But she wouldn't laugh; only her countenance, suddenly bereft of its mutinous expression, softened winningly—and her eyes grew very kind to him.

"As long as it's understood I understand—very well," she said quietly; "I'll do as you wish, Mr Lanyard."

"Good!" he cried cheerfully. "I wish, by your leave, to take you out to dinner... This way, please!"

Leading through the scullery, he unbarred a low, arched door in one of the walls, discovering the black mouth of a narrow and tunnel-like passageway.

With a word of caution, flash-lamp in his left hand, pistol in right, Lanyard stepped out into the darkness.

In two minutes he was back, with a look of relief.

"All clear," he reported; "I felt pretty sure Popinot knew nothing of this way out—else we'd have entertained uninvited guests long since. Now, half a minute..."

The electric meter occupied a place on the wall of the scullery not far from the door. Prying open its cover, he unscrewed and removed the fuse plug, plunging the entire house in complete darkness.

"That'll keep 'em guessing a while!" he explained with a chuckle. "They'll hesitate a long time before rushing a dark house infested by a desperate armed man—if I know anything about that mongrel lot...! Besides, when they do get their courage up, the lack of light will stave off discovery of this way of escape... And now, one word more."

A flash of the lamp located her hand. Calmly he possessed himself of it, if without opposition.

"I've brought you into trouble enough, as it is, through my stupidity," he said; "but for that, this place should have been a refuge to us until we were quite ready to leave Paris. So now we mustn't forget, before we go out to run God-only-knows-what gauntlet, to fix a rendezvous in event of separation... Popinot, for instance, may have drawn a cordon around the block; we can't tell until we're in the street; if he has, you must leave me to entertain them until you're safe beyond their reach... Oh, don't worry: I'm perfectly well able to take care of myself... But afterwards, we must know where to find each other. Hotels, cafés and restaurants are out of the question: in the first place, we've barely money enough for our dinner; besides, they'll be watched closely; as for our embassies and consulates, they aren't open at all hours, and will likewise be watched. There remain—unless you can suggest something—only the churches; and I can think of none better suited to our purposes than the Sacré-Cour."

Her fingers tightened gently upon his.

"I understand," she said quietly; "if we're obliged to separate, I'm to go direct to the Sacré-Cour and await you there."

"Right!...But let's hope there'll be no such necessity."

Hand-in-hand like frightened children, these two stole down the tunnel-like passageway, through a forlorn little court cramped between two tall old tenements, and so came out into the gloomy, sinuous and silent rue d'Assas.

Here they encountered few wayfarers; and to these, preoccupied with anxiety to gain shelter from the inclement night, they seemed, no doubt, some student of the Quarter with his sweetheart—Lanyard in his shabby raincoat, striding rapidly, head and shoulders bowed against the driving mist, the girl in her trim Burberry clinging to his arm...

Avoiding the nearer stations as dangerous, Lanyard steered a roundabout course through by-ways to the rue de Sèvres station of the Nord-Sud subway; from which in due course they came to the surface again at the place de la Concorde, walked several blocks, took a taxicab, and in less than half an hour after leaving the impasse Stanislas were comfortably ensconced in a cabinet particulier of a little restaurant of modest pretensions just north of Les Halles.

They feasted famously: the cuisine, if bourgeois, was admirable and, better still, well within the resources of Lanyard's emaciated purse. Nor did he fret with consciousness that, when the bill had been paid and the essential tips bestowed, there would remain in his pocket hardly more than cab fare. Supremely self-confident, he harboured no doubts of a smiling future—now that the dark pages in his record had been turned and sealed by a resolution he held irrevocable.

His spirits had mounted to a high pitch, thanks to their successful evasion. He was young, he was in love, he was hungry, he was—in short—very much alive. And the consciousness of common peril knitted an enchanting intimacy into their communications. For the first time in his history Lanyard found himself in the company of a woman with whom he dared—and cared—to speak without reserve: a circumstance intrinsically intoxicating. And stimulated by her unquestionable interest and sympathy, he did talk without reserve of old Troyon's and its drudge, Marcel; of Bourke and his wanderings; of the education of the Lone Wolf and his career, less in pride than in relief that it was ended; of the future he must achieve for himself.

And sitting with chin cradled on the backs of her interlaced fingers, the girl listened with such indulgence as women find always for their lovers. Of herself she had little to say: Lanyard filled in to his taste the outlines of the simple history of a young woman of good family obliged to become self-supporting.

And if at times her grave eyes clouded and her attention wandered, it was less in ennui than because of occult trains of thought set astir by some chance word or phrase of Lanyard's.

"I'm boring you," he surmised once with quick contrition, waking up to the fact that he had monopolized the conversation for many minutes on end.

She shook a pensive head. "No, again... But I wonder, do you appreciate the magnitude of the task you've undertaken?"

"Possibly not," he conceded arrogantly; "but it doesn't matter. The heavier the odds, the greater the incentive to win."

"But," she objected, "you've told me a curious story of one who never had a chance or incentive to 'go straight'—as you put it. And yet you seem to think that an overnight resolution to reform is all that's needed to change all the habits of a lifetime. You persuade me of your sincerity of today; but how will it be with you tomorrow—and not so much tomorrow as six months from tomorrow, when you've found the going rough and know you've only to take one step aside to gain a smooth and easy way?"

"If I fail, then, it will be because I'm unfit—and I'll go under, and never be heard of again... But I shan't fail. It seems to me the very fact that I want to go straight is proof enough that I've something inherently decent in me to build on."

"I do believe that, and yet..." She lowered her head and began to trace a meaningless pattern on the cloth before she resumed. "You've given me to understand I'm responsible for your sudden awakening, that it's because of a regard conceived for me you're so anxious to become an honest man. Suppose... suppose you were to find out... you'd been mistaken in me?"

"That isn't possible," he objected promptly.

She smiled upon him wistfully—and leniently from her remote coign of superior intuitive knowledge of human nature.

"But if it were—?"

"Then—I think," he said soberly—"I think I'd feel as though there were nothing but emptiness beneath my feet!"

"And you'd backslide—?"

"How can I tell?" he expostulated. "It's not a fair question. I don't know what I'd do, but I do know it would need something damnable to shake my faith in you!"

"You think so now," she said tolerantly. "But if appearances were against me—"

"They'd have to be black!"

"If you found I had deceived you—?"

"Miss Shannon!" He threw an arm across the table and suddenly imprisoned her hand. "There's no use beating about the bush. You've got to know—"

She drew back suddenly with a frightened look and a monosyllable of sharp protest: "No!"

"But you must listen to me. I want you to understand... Bourke used to say to me: 'The man who lets love into his life opens a door no mortal hand can close—and God only knows what will follow in!' And Bourke was right... Now that door is open in my heart, and I think that whatever follows in won't be evil or degrading... Oh, I've said it a dozen different ways of indirection, but I may as well say it squarely now: I love you; it's love of you makes me want to go straight—the hope that when I've proved myself you'll maybe let me ask you to marry me... Perhaps you're in love with a better man today; I'm willing to chance that; a year brings many changes. Perhaps there's something I don't fathom in your doubting my strength and constancy. Only the outcome can declare that. But please understand this: if I fail to make good, it will be no fault of yours; it will be because I'm unfit and have proved it... All I ask is what you've generously promised me: opportunity to come to you at the end of the year and make my report... And then, if you will, you can say no to the question I'll ask you and I shan't resent it, and it won't ruin me; for if a man can stick to a purpose for a year, he can stick to it forever, with or without the love of the woman he loves."

She heard him out without attempt at interruption, but her answer was prefaced by a sad little shake of her head.

"That's what makes it so hard, so terribly hard," she said... "Of course I've understood you. All that you've said by indirection, and much besides, has had its meaning to me. And I'm glad and proud of the honour you offer me. But I can't accept it; I can never accept it—not now nor a year from now.

It wouldn't be fair to let you go on hoping I might some time consent to marry you... For that's impossible."

"You—forgive me—you're not already married?"

"No..."

"Or promised?"

"No..."

"Or in love with someone else?"

Again she told him, gently, "No."

His face cleared. He squared his shoulders. He even mustered up a smile.

"Then it isn't impossible. No human obstacle exists that time can't overthrow. In spite of all you say, I shall go on hoping with all my heart and soul and strength."

"But you don't understand—"

"Can you tell me—make me understand?"

After a long pause, she told him once more, and very sadly: "No."

XV

SHEER IMPUDENCE

Though it had been nearly eight when they entered the restaurant, it was something after eleven before Lanyard called for his bill.

"We've plenty of time," he had explained; "it'll be midnight before we can move. The gentle art of housebreaking has its technique, you know, its professional ethics: we can't well violate the privacy of Madame Omber's strongbox before the caretakers on the premises are sound asleep. It isn't *done*, you know, it isn't class, to go burglarizing when decent, law-abiding folk are wide awake... Meantime we're better off here than trapezing the streets..."

It's a silent web of side ways and a gloomy one by night that backs up north of Les Halles: old Paris, taciturn and sombre, steeped in its memories of grim romance. But for infrequent, flickering, corner lamps, the street that welcomed them from the doors of the warm and cosy restaurant was as dismal as an alley in some city of the dead. Its houses with their mansard roofs and boarded windows bent their heads together like mutes at a wake, black-cloaked and hooded; seldom one showed a light; never one betrayed by any sound the life that lurked behind its jealous blinds. Now again the rain had ceased and, though the sky remained overcast, the atmosphere was clear and brisk with a touch of frost, in grateful contrast to the dull and muggy airs that had obtained for the last twenty-four hours.

"We'll walk," Lanyard suggested—"if you don't mind—part of the way at least; it'll eat up time, and a bit of exercise will do us both good."

The girl assented quietly...

The drum of their heels on fast-drying sidewalks struck sharp echoes from the silence of that drowsy quarter, a lonely clamour that rendered it impossible to ignore their apparent solitude—as impossible as it was for Lanyard to ignore the fact that they were followed.

The shadow dogging them on the far side of the street, some fifty yards behind, was as noiseless as any cat; but for this circumstance—had it moved boldly with unmuffled footsteps—Lanyard would have been slow to believe it concerned with him, so confident had be felt, till that moment, of having given the Pack the slip.

And from this he diagnosed still another symptom of the Pack's incurable stupidity!

Supremely on the alert, he had discovered the pursuit before they left the block of the restaurant. Dissembling, partly to avoid alarming the girl, partly to trick the spy, he turned this way and that round several corners, until quite convinced that the shadow was dedicated to himself exclusively, then promptly revised his first purpose and, instead of sticking to darker back ways, struck out directly for the broad, well-lighted and lively boulevard de Sébastopol.

Crossing this without a backward glance, he turned north, seeking some café whose arrangements suited his designs; and, presently, though not before their tramp had brought them almost to the Grand Boulevards, found one to his taste, a cheerful and well-lighted establishment occupying a corner, with entrances from both streets. A hedge of forlorn fir-trees knee-deep in wooden tubs guarded its terrasse of round metal tables and spindle-shanked chairs; of which few were occupied. Inside, visible through the wide plate-glass windows, perhaps a dozen patrons sat round half as many tables—no more—idling over dominoes and gossip: steady-paced burghers with their wives, men in small ways of business of the neighbourhood.

Entering to this company, Lanyard selected a square marble-topped table against the back wall, entrenched himself with the girl upon the seat behind it, ordered coffee and writing materials, and proceeded to light a cigarette with the nonchalance of one to whom time is of no consequence.

"What is it?" the girl asked guardedly as the waiter scurried off to execute his commands. "You've not stopped in here for nothing!"

"True—but lower, please!" he begged. "If we speak English loud enough to be heard it will attract attention... The trouble is, we're followed. But as yet our faithful shadow doesn't know we know it—unless he's more intelligent than he seems. Consequently, if I don't misjudge him, he'll take a table outside, the better to keep an eye on us, as soon as he sees we're apparently settled for some time. More than that, I've got a note to write—and not merely as a subterfuge. This fellow must be shaken off, and as long as we stick together, that can't well be done."

He interrupted himself while the waiter served them, then added sugar to his coffee, arranged the ink bottle and paper to his satisfaction, and bent over his pen.

"Come closer," he requested—"as if you were interested in what I'm writing—and amused; if you can laugh a bit at nothing, so much the better. But keep a sharp eye on the windows. You can do that more readily than I, more naturally from under the brim of your hat... And tell me what you see..."

He had no more than settled into the swing of composition, than the girl—apparently following his pen with closest attention—giggled coquettishly and nudged his elbow.

"The window to the right of the door we came in," she said, smiling delightedly; "he's standing behind the fir trees, staring in."

"Can you make out who he is?" Lanyard asked without moving his lips.

"Nothing more than that he's tall," she said with every indication of enjoying a tremendous joke. "His face is all in shadow..."

"Patience!" counselled the adventurer. "He'll take heart of courage when convinced of our innocence."

He poised his pen, examined the ceiling for inspiration, and permitted a slow smile to lighten his countenance.

"You'll take this note, if you please," he said cheerfully, "to the address on the envelope, by taxi: it's some distance, near the Etoile... A long chance, but one we must risk; give me half an hour alone and I'll guarantee to discourage this animal one way or another. You understand?"

"Perfectly," she laughed archly.

He bent and for a few moments wrote busily.

"Now he's walking slowly round the corner, never taking his eyes from you," the girl reported, shoulder to his shoulder and head distractingly near his head.

"Good. Can you see him any better?"

"Not yet..."

"This note," he said, without stopping his pen or appearing to say anything "is for the concierge of a building where I rent stabling for a little motor-car. I'm supposed there to be a chauffeur in the employ of a crazy Englishman, who keeps me constantly travelling with him back and forth between Paris and London. That's to account for the irregularity with which I use the car. They know me, monsieur and madame of the conciergerie, as Pierre Lamier; and I *think* they're safe—not only trustworthy and of friendly disposition, but quite simple-minded; I don't believe they gossip much. So the chances are

De Morbihan and his gang know nothing of the arrangement. But that's all speculation—a forlorn hope!"

"I understand," the girl observed. "He's still prowling up and down outside the hedge."

"We're not going to need that car tonight; but the hôtel of Madame Omber is close by; and I'll follow and join you there within an hour at most. Meantime, this note will introduce you to the concierge and his wife—I hope you won't mind—as my fiancée. I'm telling them we became engaged in England, and I've brought you to Paris to visit my mother in Montrouge; but am detained by my employer's business; and will they please give you shelter for an hour."

"He's coming in," the girl announced quietly.

"In here?"

"No—merely inside the row of little trees."

"Which entrance?"

"The boulevard side. He's taken the corner table. Now a waiter's going out to him."

"You can see his face now?" Lanyard asked, sealing the note.

"Not well..."

"Nothing you recognize about him, eh?"

"Nothing..."

"You know Popinot and Wertheimer by sight?"

"No; they're only names to me; De Morbihan and Mr Bannon mentioned them last night."

"It won't be Popinot," Lanyard reflected, addressing the envelope; "he's tubby."

"This man is tall and slender."

"Wertheimer, possibly. Does he suggest an Englishman, any way?"

"Not in the least. He wears a moustache—blond—twisted up like the Kaiser's."

Lanyard made no reply; but his heart sank, and he shivered imperceptibly with foreboding. He entertained no doubt but that the worst had happened, that to the number of his enemies in Paris was added Ekstrom.

One furtive glance confirmed this inference. He swore bitterly, if privately and with a countenance of child-like blandness, as he sipped the coffee and finished his cigarette.

"Who is it, then?" she asked. "Do you know him?"

He reckoned swiftly against distressing her, recalling his mention of the fact that Ekstrom was credited with the Huysman murder.

"Merely a hanger-on of De Morbihan's," he told her lightly; "a spineless animal—no trouble about scaring him off... Now take this note, please, and we'll go. But as we reach the door, turn back—and go out the other. You'll find a taxi without trouble. And stop for nothing!"

He had shown foresight in paying when served, and was consequently able to leave abruptly, without giving Ekstrom time to shy. Rising smartly, he pushed the table aside. The girl was no less quick, and little less sensitive to the strain of the moment; but as she passed him her lashes lifted and her eyes were all his for the instant.

"Goodnight," she breathed—"goodnight... my dear!"

She could have guessed no more shrewdly what he needed to nerve him against the impending clash. He hadn't hesitated as to his only course, but till then he'd been horribly afraid, knowing too well the desperate cast of the outlawed German's nature. But now he couldn't fail.

He strode briskly toward the door to the boulevard, out of the corner of his eye aware that Ekstrom, taken by surprise, half-started from his chair, then sank back.

Two paces from the entrance the girl checked, murmured in French, "Oh, my handkerchief!" and turned briskly back. Without pause, as though he hadn't heard, Lanyard threw the door wide and swung out, turning directly to the spy. At the same time he dropped a hand into the pocket where nestled his automatic.

Fortunately Ekstrom had chosen a table in a corner well removed from any in use. Lanyard could speak without fear of being overheard.

But for a moment he refrained. Nor did Ekstrom speak or stir; sitting sideways at his table, negligently, with knees crossed, the German likewise kept a hand buried in the pocket of his heavy, dark ulster. Thus neither doubted the other's ill-will or preparedness. And through thirty seconds of silence they remained at pause, each striving with all his might to read the other's purpose in his eyes. But there was this distinction to be drawn between their attitudes, that whereas Lanyard's gaze challenged, the German's was sullenly defiant. And presently Lanyard felt his heart stir with relief: the spy's glance had winced.

"Ekstrom," the adventurer said quietly, "if you fire, I'll get you before I fall. That's a simple statement of fact."

The German hesitated, moistened the corners of his lips with a nervous tongue, but contented himself with a nod of acknowledgement.

"Take your hand off that gun," Lanyard ordered. "Remember—I've only to cry your name aloud to have you torn to pieces by these people. Your life's not worth a moment's purchase in Paris—as you should know."

The German hesitated, but in his heart knew that Lanyard didn't exaggerate. The murder of the inventor had exasperated all France; and though tonight's weather kept a third of Paris within doors, there was still a tide of pedestrians fluent on the sidewalk, beyond the flimsy barrier of firs, that would thicken to a ravening mob upon the least excuse.

He had mistaken his man; he had thought that Lanyard, even if aware of his pursuit, would seek to shake it off in flight rather than turn and fight—and fight here, of all places!

"Do you hear me?" Lanyard continued in the same level and unyielding tone. "Bring both hands in sight—upon the table!"

There was no more hesitation: Ekstrom obeyed, if with the sullen grace of a wild beast that would and could slay its trainer with one sweep of its paw—if only it dared.

For the first time since leaving the girl Lanyard relaxed his vigilant watch over the man long enough for one swift glance through the window at his side. But she was already vanished from the café.

He breathed more freely now.

"Come!" he said peremptorily. "Get up. We've got to talk, I presume—thrash this matter out—and we'll come to no decision here."

"Where do we go, then?" the German demanded suspiciously.

"We can walk."

Irresolutely the spy uncrossed his knees, but didn't rise.

"Walk?" he repeated, "walk where?"

"Up the boulevard, if you like—where the lights are brightest."

"Ah!"—with a malignant flash of teeth—"but I don't trust you."

Lanyard laughed: "You wear only one shoe of that pair, my dear captain! We're a distrustful flock, we birds of prey. Come along! Why sit there sulking, like a spoiled child? You've made an ass of yourself, following me to Paris; sadly though you bungled that job in London, I gave you credit for more wit than to poke your head into the lion's mouth here. But—admitting that—why not be graceful about it? Here am I, amiably treating you like an equal: you might at least show gratitude enough to accept my invitation to flâner yourself!"

With a grunt the spy got upon his feet, while Lanyard stood back, against the window, and made him free of the narrow path between the tree-tubs and the tables.

"After you, my dear Adolph...!"

The German paused, half turned towards him, choking with rage, his suffused face darkly relieving its white scars won at Heidelberg. At this, with a nod of unmistakable meaning, Lanyard advanced the muzzle of his pocketed weapon; and with an ugly growl the German moved on and out to the sidewalk, Lanyard respectfully an inch or two behind his elbow.

"To your right," he requested pleasantly—"if it's all the same to you: I've business on the Boulevards…"

Ekstrom said nothing for the moment, but sullenly yielded to the suggestion.

"By the way," the adventurer presently pursued, "you might be good enough to inform me how you knew where we were dining—eh?"

"If it interests you—"

"I own it does—tremendously!"

"Pure accident: I happened to be sitting in the café, and caught a glimpse of you through the door as you went upstairs. Therefore I waited till the waiter asked for your bill at the caisse, then stationed myself outside."

"But why? Can you tell me what you thought to accomplish?"

"You know well," Ekstrom muttered. "After what happened in London... it's your life or mine!"

"Spoken like a true villain! But it seems to me you overlooked a conspicuous chance to accomplish your hellish design, back there in the side streets."

"Would I be such a fool as to shoot you down before finding out what you've done with those plans?"

"You might as well have," Lanyard informed him lightly... "For you won't know otherwise."

With an infuriated oath the German stopped short: but he dared not ignore the readiness with which his tormentor imitated the manoeuvre and kept the pistol trained through the fabric of his raincoat.

"Yes—?" the adventurer enquired with an exasperating accent of surprise.

"Understand me," Ekstrom muttered vindictively: "next time I'll show you no mercy—"

"But if there *is* no next time? We're not apt to meet again, you know."

"That's something beyond your knowledge—"

"You think so?... But shan't we resume our stroll? People might notice us standing here—you with your teeth bared like an ill-tempered dog... Oh, thank you!"

And as they moved on, Lanyard continued: "Shall I explain why we're not apt to meet again?"

"If it amuses you."

"Thanks once more!... For the simple reason that Paris satisfies me; so here I stop."

"Well?" the spy asked with a blank sidelong look.

"Whereas you are leaving Paris tonight."

"What makes you think that?"

"Because you value your thick hide too highly to remain, my dear captain." Having gained the corner of the boulevard St. Denis, Lanyard pulled up. "One moment, by your leave. You see yonder the entrance to the Metro—don't you? And here, a dozen feet away, a perfectly able-bodied sergent de ville? Let this fateful conjunction impress you properly: for five minutes after you have descended to the Métro—or as soon as the noise of a train advises me you've had one chance to get away—I shall mention casually to the sergo—that I have seen Captain Ek—"

"Hush!" the German protested in a hiss of fright.

"But certainly: I've no desire to embarrass you: publicity must be terribly distasteful to one of your sensitive and retiring disposition... But I trust you understand me? On the one hand, there's the Métro; on the other, there's the flic; while here, you must admit, am I, as large as life and very much on the job!...

And inasmuch as I shall certainly mention my suspicions to the minion of the law—as aforesaid—I'd advise you to be well out of Paris before dawn!"

There was murder in the eyes of the spy as he lingered, truculently glowering at the smiling adventurer; and for an instant Lanyard was well-persuaded he had gone too far, that even there, even on that busy junction of two crowded thoroughfares, Ekström would let his temper get the better of his judgment and risk everything in an attempt upon the life of his despoiler.

But he was mistaken.

With a surly shrug the spy swung about and marched straight to the kiosk of the underground railway, into which, without one backward glance, he disappeared.

Two minutes later the earth beneath Lanyard's feet quaked with the crash and rumble of a north-bound train.

He waited three minutes longer; but Ekstrom didn't reappear; and at length convinced that his warning had proved effectual, Lanyard turned and made off.

XVI

RESTITUTION

For all that success had rewarded his effrontery, Lanyard's mind was far from easy during the subsequent hour that he spent before attempting to rejoin Lucy Shannon, dodging, ducking and doubling across Paris and back again, with design to confuse and confound any jackals of the Pack that might have picked up his trail as adventitiously as Ekstrom had.

His delight, indeed, in discomfiting his dupe was chilled by apprehension that it were madness, simply because the spy had proved unexpectedly docile, to consider the affaire Ekstrom closed. In the very fact of that docility inhered something strange and ominous, a premonition of evil which was hardly mitigated by finding the girl safe and sound under the wing of madame la concierge, in the little court of private stables, where he rented space for his car, off the rue des Acacias.

Monsieur le concierge, it appeared, was from home; and madame, thick-witted, warm-hearted, simple body that she was, discovered a phase of beaming incuriosity most grateful to the adventurer, enabling him as it did to dispense with embarrassing explanations, and to whisk the girl away as soon as he liked.

This last was just as soon as personal examination had reassured him with respect to his automobile—superficially an ordinary motor-cab of the better grade, but with an exceptionally powerful engine hidden beneath its hood. A car of such character, passing readily as the town-car of any family in modest circumstances, or else as what Paris calls a voiture de remise (a hackney car without taximeter) was a tremendous convenience, enabling its owner to scurry at will about cab-ridden Paris free of comment. But it could not be left standing in public places at odd hours, or for long, without attracting the interest of the police, and so was useless in the present emergency. Lanyard, however, entertained a shrewd suspicion that his plans might all miscarry and the command of a fast-travelling car soon prove essential to his salvation; and he cheerfully devoted a good half-hour to putting the motor in prime trim for the road.

With this accomplished—and the facts established through discreet interrogation of madame la concierge that no enquiries had been made for "Pierre Lamier," and that she had noticed no strange or otherwise questionable characters loitering in the neighbourhood of late—he was ready for his first real step toward rehabilitation...

It was past one in the morning when, with the girl on his arm, he issued forth into the dark and drowsy rue des Acacias and, moving swiftly, crossed the avenue de la Grande Armée. Thereafter, avoiding main-travelled highways, they struck southward through tangled side streets to aristocratic Passy, skirted the boulevards of the fortifications, and approached the private park of La Muette.

The hôtel particulier of that wealthy and amiable eccentric, Madame Hélène Omber, was a souvenir of those days when Passy had been suburban. A survival of the Revolution, a vast, dour pile that had known few changes since the days of its construction, it occupied a large, unkempt park, irregularly triangular in shape, bounded by two streets and an avenue, and rendered private by high walls crowned with broken glass. Carriage gates opened on the avenue, guarded by a porter's lodge; while of three posterns that pierced the walls on the side streets, one only was in general use by the servants of the establishment; the other two were presumed to be permanently sealed.

Lanyard, however, knew better.

When they had turned off from the avenue, he slackened pace and moved at caution, examining the prospect narrowly.

On the one hand rose the wall of the park, topped by naked, soughing limbs of neglected trees; on the other, across the way, a block of tall old dwellings, withdrawn behind jealous garden walls, showed stupid, sleepy faces and lightless eyes.

Within the perspective of the street but three shapes stirred; Lanyard and the girl in the shadow of the wall, and a disconsolate, misprized cat that promptly decamped like a terror-stricken ghost.

Overhead the sky was breaking and showing ebon patches and infrequent stars through a wind-harried wrack of cloud. The night had grown sensibly colder, and noisy with the rushing sweep of a new-sprung wind.

Several yards from the postern-gate, Lanyard paused definitely, and spoke for the first time in many minutes; for the nature of their errand had oppressed the spirits of both and enjoined an unnatural silence, ever since their departure from the rue des Acacias.

"This is where we stop," he said, with a jerk of his head toward the wall; "but it's not too late—"

"For what?" the girl asked quickly.

"I promised you no danger; but now I've thought it over, I can't promise that: there's always danger. And I'm afraid for you. It's not yet too late for you to turn back and wait for me in a safer place."

"You asked me to accompany you for a special purpose," she argued; "you begged me to come with you, in fact... Now that

I have agreed and come this far, I don't mean to turn back without good reason."

His gesture indicated uneasy acquiescence. "I should never have asked this of you. I think I must have been a little mad. If anything should come of this to injure you...!"

"If you mean to do what you promised—"

"Do you doubt my sincerity?"

"It was your own suggestion that you leave me no excuse for doubt..."

Without further remonstrance, if with a mind beset with misgivings, he led on to the gate—a blank door of wood, painted a dark green, deeply recessed in the wall.

In proof of his assertion that he had long since made every preparation to attack the premises, Lanyard had a key ready and in the lock almost before they reached it.

And the door swung back easily and noiselessly as though on well-greased hinges. As silently it shut them in.

They stood upon a weed-grown gravel path, hedged about with thick masses of shrubbery; but the park was as black as a pocket; and the heavy effluvia of wet mould, decaying weeds and rotting leaves that choked the air, seemed only to render the murk still more opaque.

But Lanyard evidently knew his way blindfold: though motives of prudence made him refrain from using his flash-lamp, he betrayed not the least incertitude in his actions.

Never once at loss for the right turning, he piloted the girl swiftly through a bewildering black labyrinth of paths, lawns and thickets...

In due course he pulled up, and she discovered that they had come out upon a clear space of lawn, close beside the featureless, looming bulk of a dark and silent building.

An admonitory grasp tightened upon her fingers, and she caught his singularly penetrating yet guarded whisper:

"This is the back of the house—the service-entrance. From this door a broad path runs straight to the main service gateway; you can't mistake it; and the gate itself has a spring lock, easy enough to open from the inside. Remember this in event of trouble. We might become separated in the darkness and confusion..."

Gently returning the pressure, "I understand," she said in a whisper.

Immediately he drew her on to the house, pausing but momentarily before a wide doorway; one half of which promptly swung open, and as soon as they had passed through, closed with no perceptible jar or click. And then Lanyard's flash-lamp was lancing the gloom on every hand, swiftly raking the bounds of a large, panelled servants' hall, until it picked out the foot of a flight of steps at the farther end. To this they moved stealthily over a tiled flooring.

The ascent of the staircase was accomplished, however, only with infinite care, Lanyard testing each rise before trusting it with his weight or the girl's. Twice he bade her skip one step lest the complaints of the ancient woodwork betray them. In spite of all this, no less than three hideous squeals were evoked before they gained the top; each indicating a pause and wait of several breathless seconds.

But it would seem that such servants as had been left in the house, in the absence of its chatelaine, either slept soundly or were accustomed to the midnight concert of those age-old timbers; and without mischance, at length, they entered the main reception-hall, revealed by the dancing spotlight as a room of noble proportions furnished with sombre magnificence.

Here the girl was left alone for a few minutes, while Lanyard darted above-stairs for a review of the state bedchambers and servants' quarters.

With a sensation of being crushed and suffocated by the encompassing dark mystery, she nerved herself against a protracted vigil. The obscurity on every hand seemed alive with stealthy footfalls, whisperings, murmurings, the passage of shrouded shapes of silence and of menace. Her eyes ached, her throat and temples throbbed, her skin crept, her scalp tingled. She seemed to hear a thousand different noises of alarm. The only sounds she did not hear were those—if any—that accompanied Lanyard's departure and return. Had he not been thoughtful enough, when a few feet distant, to give warning with the light, she might well have greeted with a cry of fright the consciousness of a presence near her: so silently he moved about. As it was, she was startled, apprehensive of some misadventure, to find him back so soon; for he hadn't been gone three minutes.

"It's quite all right," he announced in hushed accents—no longer whispering. "There are just five people in the house aside from ourselves—all servants, asleep in the rear wing. We've got a clear field—if no excuse for taking foolish chances! However, we'll be finished and off again in less than ten minutes. This way."

That way led to a huge and gloomy library at one extreme of a chain of great salons, a veritable treasure-gallery of exquisite furnishings and authentic old masters. As they moved slowly through these chambers Lanyard kept his flash-lamp busy; involuntarily, now and again, he checked the girl before some splendid canvas or extraordinary antique.

"I've always meant to happen in some day with a moving-van and loot this place properly!" he confessed with a little affected sigh. "Considered from the viewpoint of an expert practitioner in my—ah—late profession, it's a sin and a shame to let all this go neglected, when it's so poorly guarded. The old lady—Madame Omber, you know—has all the money there is, approximately, and when she dies all these beautiful things go to the Louvre; for she's without kith or kin."

"But how did she manage to accumulate them all?" the girl wondered. "It's the work of generations of passionate collectors," he explained. "The late Monsieur Omber was the last of his dynasty; he and his forebears brought together the paintings and the furniture; madame added the Orientals gathered together by her first husband, and her own collection of antique jewellery and precious stones—*her* particular fad..."

As he spoke the light of the flash-lamp was blotted out. An instant later the girl heard a little clashing noise, of curtain rings sliding along a pole; and this was thrice repeated.

Then, following another brief pause, a switch clicked; and streaming from the hood of a portable desk-lamp, a pool of light flooded the heart of a vast place of shadows, an apartment whose doors and windows alike were cloaked with heavy draperies that hung from floor to ceiling in long and shining folds. Immense black bookcases lined the walls, their shelves crowded with volumes in rich bindings; from their tops pallid marble masks peered down inquisitively, leering and scowling at the intruders. A huge mantelpiece of carved marble, supporting a great, dark mirror, occupied the best of one wall, beneath it a wide, deep fireplace yawned, partly shielded by a screen of wrought brass and crystal. In the middle of the room stood a library table of mahogany; huge leather chairs and couches encumbered the remainder of its space. And the corner to the right of the fireplace was shut off by a high Japanese screen of cinnabar and gold.

To this Lanyard moved confidently, carrying the lamp. Placing it on the floor, he grasped one wing of the screen with both hands, and at cost of considerable effort swung it aside, uncovering the face of a huge, old-style safe built into the wall.

For several seconds—but not for many—Lanyard studied this problem intently, standing quite motionless, his head lowered and thrust forward, hands resting on his hips. Then turning, he nodded an invitation to draw nearer.

"My last job," he said with a smile oddly lighted by the lamp at his feet—"and my easiest, I fancy. Sorry, too, for I'd rather have liked to show off a bit. But this old-fashioned tin bank gives no excuse for spectacular methods!"

"But," the girl objected, "You've brought no tools!"

"Oh, but I have!" And fumbling in a pocket, Lanyard produced a pencil. "Behold!" he laughed, brandishing it.

She knitted thoughtful brows: "I don't understand."

"All I need—except this."

Crossing to the desk, he found a sheet of note-paper and, folding it, returned.

"Now," he said, "give me five minutes..."

Kneeling, he gave the combination-knob a smart preliminary twirl, then rested a shoulder against the sheet of painted iron, his cheek to its smooth, cold cheek, his ear close beside the dial; and with the practised fingers of a master locksmith began to manipulate the knob.

Gently, tirelessly, to and fro he twisted, turned, raced, and checked the combination, caressing it, humouring it, wheedling it, inexorably questioning it in the dumb language his fingers spoke so deftly. And in his ear the click and whir and thump of shifting wards and tumblers murmured articulate response in the terms of their cryptic code.

Now and again, releasing the knob and sitting back on his heels, he would bend intent scrutiny to the dial; note the position of the combination, and with the pencil jot memoranda on the paper. This happened perhaps a dozen times, at intervals of irregular duration.

He worked diligently, in a phase of concentration that apparently excluded from his consciousness the near proximity of the girl, who stood—or rather stooped, half-kneeling—less than a pace from his shoulder, watching the process with interest hardly less keen than his own.

Yet when one faint, odd sound broke the slumberous silence of the salons, instantly he swung around and stood erect in a single movement, gaze to the curtains.

But it had only been a premonitory rumble in the throat of a tall old clock about to strike in the room beyond. And as its sonorous chimes heralded two deep-toned strokes, Lanyard laughed quietly, intimately, to the girl's startled eyes, and sank back before the safe.

And now his task was nearly finished. Within another minute he sat back with face aglow, uttered a hushed exclamation of satisfaction, studied his memoranda for a space, then swiftly and with assured movements threw the knob and dial into the several positions of the combination, grasped the lever-handle, turned it smartly, and swung the door wide open.

"Simple, eh?" he chuckled, with a glance aside to the girl's eager face, bewitchingly flushed and shadowed by the lamp's up-thrown glow—"when one knows the trick, of course! And now... if one were not an honest man!"

A wave of his hand indicated the pigeonholes with which the body of the safe was fitted: wide spaces and deep, stored tight with an extraordinary array of leather jewel-cases, packets of stout paper bound with tape and sealed, and boxes of wood and pasteboard of every shape and size.

"They were only her finest pieces, her personal jewels, that Madame Omber took with her to England," he explained; "she's mad about them... never separated from them... Perhaps the finest collection in the world, for size and purity of water... She had the heart to leave these—all this!"

Lifting a hand he chose at random, dislodged two leather cases, placed them on the floor, and with a blade of his pen-knife forced their fastenings.

From the first the light smote radiance in blinding, coruscant welter. Here was nothing but diamond jewellery, mostly in antique settings.

He took up a piece and offered it to the girl. She drew back her hand involuntarily.

"No!" she protested in a whisper of fright.

"But just look!" he urged. "There's no danger... and you'll never see the like of this again!"

Stubbornly she withheld her hand. "No, no!" she pleaded. "I—I'd rather not touch it. Put it back. Let's hurry. I—I'm frightened."

He shrugged and replaced the jewel; then yielded again to impulse of curiosity and lifted the lid of the second case.

It contained nothing but pieces set with coloured stones of the first order—emeralds, amethysts, sapphires, rubies, topaz, garnets, lapis-lazuli, jacinthes, jades, fashioned by master-craftsmen into rings, bracelets, chains, brooches, lockets, necklaces, of exquisite design: the whole thrown heedlessly together, without order or care.

For a moment the adventurer stared down soberly at this priceless hoard, his eyes narrowing, his breathing perceptibly quickened. Then with a slow gesture, he reclosed the case, took from his pocket that other which he had brought from London, opened it, and held it aside beneath the light, for the girl's inspection.

He looked not once either at its contents or at her, fearing lest his countenance betray the truth, that he had not yet succeeded completely in exorcising that mutinous and rebellious spirit, the Lone Wolf, from the tenement over which it had so long held sway; and content with the sound of her quick, startled sigh of amaze that what she now beheld could so marvellously outshine what had been disclosed by the other boxes, he withdrew it, shut it, found it a place in the safe, and without pause closed the door, shot the bolts, and twirled the dial until the tumblers fairly sang.

One final twist of the lever-handle convincing him that the combination was effectively dislocated, he rose, picked up the lamp, replaced it on the desk with scrupulous care to leave no sign that it had been moved, and looked round to the girl.

She was where he had left her, a small, tense, vibrant figure among the shadows, her eyes dark pools of wonder in a face of blazing pallor.

With a high head and his shoulders well back he made a gesture signifying more eloquently than any words: "All that is ended!"

"And now…?" she asked breathlessly.

"Now for our getaway," he replied with assumed lightness. "Before dawn we must be out of Paris... Two minutes, while I straighten this place up and leave it as I found it."

He moved back to the safe, restored the wing of the screen to the spot from which he had moved it, and after an instant's close examination of the rug, began to explore his pockets.

"What are you looking for?" the girl enquired.

"My memoranda of the combination—"

"I have it." She indicated its place in a pocket of her coat. "You left it on the floor, and I was afraid you might forget—"

"No fear!" he laughed. "No"—as she offered him the folded paper—"keep it and destroy it, once we're out of this. Now those portières…"

Extinguishing the desk-light, he turned attention to the draperies at doors and windows...

Within five minutes, they were once more in the silent streets of Passy.

They had to walk as far as the Trocadéro before Lanyard found a fiacre, which he later dismissed at the corner in the Faubourg St. Germain.

Another brief walk brought them to a gate in the garden wall of a residence at the junction of two quiet streets.

"This, I think, ends our Parisian wanderings," Lanyard announced. "If you'll be good enough to keep an eye out for busybodies—and yourself as inconspicuous as possible in this doorway..."

And he walked back to the curb, measuring the wall with his eye.

"What are you going to do?"

He responded by doing it so swiftly that she gasped with surprise: pausing momentarily within a yard of the wall, he gathered himself together, shot lithely into the air, caught the top curbing with both hands, and...

She heard the soft thud of his feet on the earth of the enclosure; the latch grated behind her; the door opened.

"For the last time," Lanyard laughed quietly, "permit me to invite you to break the law by committing an act of trespass!"

Securing the door, he led her to a garden bench secluded amid conventional shrubbery.

"If you'll wait here," he suggested—"well, it will be best. I'll be back as soon as possible, though I may be detained some time. Still, inasmuch as I'm about to break into this hôtel, my motives, which are most commendable, may be misinterpreted, and I'd rather you'd stop here, with the street at hand. If you hear a noise like trouble, you've only to unlatch the gate... But let's hope my purely benevolent intentions toward the French Republic won't be misconstrued!"

"I'll wait," she assured him bravely; "but won't you tell me—?"

With a gesture, he indicated the mansion back of the garden.

"I'm going to break in there to pay an early morning call and impart some interesting information to a person of considerable consequence—nobody less, in fact, than Monsieur Ducroy."

"And who is that?"

"The present Minister of War... We haven't as yet the pleasure of each other's acquaintance; still, I think he won't be sorry to see me... In brief, I mean to make him a present of the Huysman plans and bargain for our safeconduct from France."

Impulsively she offered her hand and, when he, surprised, somewhat diffidently took it, "Be careful!" she whispered brokenly, her pale sweet face upturned to his. "Oh, do be careful! I am afraid for you..."

And for a little the temptation to take her in his arms was stronger than any he had ever known...

But remembering his stipulated year of probation, he released her hand with an incoherent mumble, turned, and disappeared in the direction of the house.

XVII

THE FORLORN HOPE

Established behind his splendid mahogany desk in his office at the Ministère de la Guerre, or moving majestically abroad attired in frock coat and glossy topper, or lending the dignity of his presence to some formal ceremony in that beautiful uniform which appertained unto his office, Monsieur Hector Ducroy cut an imposing figure.

Abed... it was sadly otherwise.

Lanyard switched on the bedside light, turning it so that it struck full upon the face of the sleeper; and as he sat down, smiled.

The Minister of War lay upon his back, his distinguished corpulence severely dislocating the chaste simplicity of the bed-clothing. Athwart his shelving chest, fat hands were folded in a gesture affectingly naïve. His face was red, a noble highlight shone upon the promontory of his bald pate, his mouth was open. To the best of his unconscious ability he was giving a protracted imitation of a dog-fight; and he was really exhibiting sublime virtuosity: one readily distinguished individual howls, growls, yelps, against an undertone of blended voices of excited non-combatants…

As suddenly as though someone, wearying of the entertainment, had lifted the needle from that record, it was discontinued. The Minister of War stirred uneasily in his sleep, muttered a naughty word, opened one eye, scowled, opened the other.

He blinked furiously, half-blinded but still able to make out the disconcerting silhouette of a man seated just beyond the glare: a quiet presence that moved not but eyed him steadfastly; an apparition the more arresting because of its very immobility.

Rapidly the face of the Minister of War lost several shades of purple. He moistened his lips nervously with a thick, dry tongue, and convulsively he clutched the bed-clothing high and tight about his neck, as though labouring under the erroneous impression that the sanctity of his person was threatened.

"What do you want, monsieur?" he stuttered in a still, small voice which he would have been the last to acknowledge his own.

"I desire to discuss a matter of business with monsieur," replied the intruder after a small pause. "If you will be good enough to calm yourself—"

"I am perfectly calm—"

But here the Minister of War verified with one swift glance an earlier impression, to the effect that the trespasser was holding something that shone with metallic lustre; and his soul began to curl up round the edges.

"There are eighteen hundred francs in my pocketbook—about," he managed to articulate. "My watch is on the stand here. You will find the family plate in the dining-room safe, behind the buffet—the key is on my ring—and the jewels of madame my wife are in a small strongbox beneath the head of her bed. The combination—"

"Pardon: monsieur labours under a misapprehension," the housebreaker interposed drily. "Had one desired these valuables, one would readily have taken them without going to the trouble of disturbing the repose of monsieur... I have, however, already mentioned the nature of my errand."

"Eh?" demanded the Minister of War. "What is that? But give me of your mercy one chance to explain! I have never wittingly harmed you, monsieur, and if I have done so without my knowledge, rest assured you have but to petition me through the proper channels and I will be only too glad to make amends!"

"*Still* you do not listen!" the other insisted. "Come, Monsieur Ducroy—calm yourself. I have not robbed you, because I have no wish to rob you. I have not harmed you, for I have no wish to harm you. Nor have I any wish other than to lay before you, as representing Government, a certain matter of State business."

There was silence while the Minister of War permitted this exhortation to sink in. Then, apparently reassured, he sat up in bed and eyed his untimely visitor with a glare little short of truculent.

"Eh? What's that?" he demanded. "Business? What sort of business? If you wish to submit to my consideration any matter of business, how is it you break into my home at dead of night and rouse me in this brutal fashion"—here his voice faltered—"with a lethal weapon pointed at my head?"

"Monsieur will admit he speaks under an error," returned the burglar. "I have yet to point this pistol at him. I should be very sorry to feel obliged to do so. I display it, in fact, simply that monsieur may not forget himself and attempt to summon servants in his resentment of this (I admit) unusual method of introducing one's self to his attention. When we understand each other better there will be no need for such precautions, and then I shall put my pistol away, so that the sight of it may no longer annoy monsieur."

"It is true, I do not understand you," grumbled the Minister of War. "Why—if your errand be peaceable—break into my house?"

"Because it was urgently necessary to see monsieur instantly. Monsieur will reflect upon the reception one would receive did one ring the front doorbell and demand audience at three o'clock in the morning!"

"Well..." Monsieur Ducroy conceded dubiously. Then, on reflection, he iterated the monosyllable testily: "Well! What is it you want, then?"

"I can best explain by asking monsieur to examine—what I have to show him."

With this Lanyard dropped the pistol into his coat-pocket, from another produced a gold cigarette-case, and from the store of this last with meticulous care selected a single cigarette.

Regarding the Minister of War in a mystifying manner, he began to roll the cigarette briskly between his palms. A small shower of tobacco sifted to the floor: the rice-paper cracked and came away; and with the bland smile and gesture of a professional conjurer, Lanyard exhibited a small cylinder of stiff paper between his thumb and index-finger.

Goggling resentfully, Monsieur Ducroy spluttered:

"Eh—what impudence is this?"

His smile unchanged, Lanyard bent forward and silently dropped the cylinder into the Frenchman's hand. At the same time he offered him a pocket magnifying-glass. "What is this?" Ducroy persisted stupidly. "What—what—!"

"If monsieur will be good enough to unroll the papers and examine them with the aid of this glass—"

With a wondering grunt, the other complied, unrolling several small sheets of photographer's printing-out paper, to which several extraordinarily complicated and minute designs had been transferred—strongly resembling laborious efforts to conventionalize a spider's web.

But no sooner had Monsieur Ducroy viewed these through the glass, than he started violently, uttered an excited exclamation, and subjected them to an examination both prolonged and exacting.

"Monsieur is, no doubt, now satisfied?" Lanyard enquired when his patience would endure no longer.

"These are genuine?" the Minister of War demanded sharply, without looking up.

"Monsieur can readily discern notations made upon the drawings by the inventor, Georges Huysman, in his own hand. Furthermore, each plan has been marked in the lower left-hand corner with the word '*accepted*' followed by the initials of the German Minister of War. I think this establishes beyond dispute the authenticity of these photographs of the plan for Huysman's invention."

"Yes," the Minister of War agreed breathlessly. "You have the negatives from which these prints were made?"

"Here," Lanyard said, indicating a second cigarette.

And then, with a movement so leisurely and careless that his purpose was accomplished before the other in his preoccupation was aware of it, the adventurer leaned forward and swept up the prints from the counterpane in front of Monsieur Ducroy.

"Here!" the Frenchman exclaimed. "Why do you do that?"

"Monsieur no longer questions their authenticity?"

"I grant you that."

"Then I return to myself these prints, pending negotiations for their transfer to France."

"How did you come by them?" demanded Monsieur Ducroy, after a moment's thought.

"Need monsieur ask? Is France so ill-served by her spies that you do not already know of the misfortune one Captain Ekstrom recently suffered in London?"

Ducroy shook his head. Lanyard received this indication with impatience. It seemed hardly possible that the French Minister of War could be either so stupid or so ignorant...

But with a patient shrug, he proceeded to elucidate.

"Captain Ekstrom," he said, "but recently succeeded in photographing these plans and took them to London to sell to the English. Unfortunately for himself—unhappily for perfidious Albion!—Captain Ekstrom fell in with me and mistook me for Downing Street's representative. And here are the plans."

"You are—the Lone Wolf—then?"

"I am, as far as concerns you, monsieur, merely the person in possession of these plans, who offers them through you, to France, for a price."

"But why introduce yourself to me in this extraordinary fashion, for a transaction for which the customary channels—with which you must be familiar—are entirely adequate?"

"Simply because Ekstrom has followed me to Paris," Lanyard explained indulgently. "Did I venture to approach you in the usual way, my chances of rounding out a useful life thereafter would be practically nil. Furthermore, my circumstances are such that it has become necessary for me to leave France immediately—without an hour's delay—also secretly; else I might as well remain here to be butchered... Now you command the only means I know of, to accomplish my purpose. And that is the price, the only price, you will have to pay me for these plans."

"I don't understand you."

"It is on schedule, is it not, that Captain Vauquelin of the Aviation Corps is to attempt a non-stop flight from Paris to London this morning, with two passengers, in a new Parrott biplane?"

"That is so... Well?"

"I must be one of those passengers; and I have a companion, a young lady, who will take the place of the other."

"It isn't possible, monsieur. Those arrangements are already fixed."

"You will countermand them."

"There is no time—"

"You can get into telephonic communication with Port Aviation in two minutes."

"But the passengers have been promised—"

"You will disappoint them."

"The start is to be made in the first flush of daylight. How could you reach Port Aviation in time?"

"In your motor-car, monsieur."

"It cannot be done."

"It must! If the start must be delayed till we arrive, you will give orders that it shall be so delayed."

For a minute the Minister of War hesitated; then he shook his head definitely.

"The difficulties are insuperable—"

"There is no such thing, monsieur."

"I am sorry: it can't be done."

"That is your answer?"

"It is regrettable, monsieur..."

"Very well!" Lanyard bent forward again, took a match from the stand on the bedside table, and struck it. Very calmly he advanced the flame toward the cigarette containing the roll of inflammable films.

"Monsieur!" Ducroy cried in horror. "What are you doing?"

Lanyard favoured him with a look of surprise.

"I am about to destroy these films and prints."

"You must never do that!"

"Why not? They are mine, to do with as I like. If I cannot dispose of them at my price, I shall destroy them!"

"But—my God!—what you demand is impossible! Stay, monsieur! Think what your action means to France!"

"I have already thought of that. Now I must think of myself."

"But—one moment!"

Ducroy sat up in bed and dangled hairy fat legs over the side.

"But one moment only, monsieur. Don't make me waste your matches!"

"Monsieur, it shall be as you desire, if it lies in my power to accomplish it."

With this the Minister of War stood up and made for the telephone, in his agitation forgetful of dressing-gown and slippers.

"You must accomplish it, Monsieur Ducroy," Lanyard advised him gravely, puffing out the flame; "for if you fail, you make yourself the instrument of my death. Here are the plans."

"You trust them to me?" Ducroy asked in astonishment.

"But naturally: that makes it an affair of your honour," Lanyard explained suavely.

With a gesture of graceful capitulation the Frenchman accepted the little roll of film.

"Permit me," he said, "to acknowledge the honour of monsieur's confidence!"

Lanyard bowed low: "One knows with whom one deals, monsieur!... And now, if you will be good enough to excuse me..."

He turned to the door.

"But—eh—where are you going?" Ducroy demanded.

"Mademoiselle," Lanyard said, pausing on the threshold—"that is, the young lady who is to accompany me—is waiting anxiously in the garden, out yonder. I go to find and reassure her and—with your permission—to bring her in to the library, where we will await monsieur when he has finished telephoning and—ah—repaired the deficiencies in his attire; which one trusts he will forgive one's mentioning!"

He bowed again, impudently, gaily, and—when the Minister of War looked up again sheepishly from contemplation of his naked shanks—had vanished.

In high feather Lanyard made his way to a door at the rear of the house which gave upon the garden—in his new social status of Governmental protégé disdaining any such a commonplace avenue as that conservatory window whose fastenings he had forced on entering. And boldly unbolting the door, he ran out into the night, to rejoin his beloved, like a man waking to new life.

But she was no more there: the bench was vacant, the garden deserted, the gateway yawning on the street.

With a low, stifled cry, Lanyard turned from the bench and stumbled out to the junction of the cross-street. But nowhere in their several perspectives could he see anything that moved.

After some time he returned to the garden and quartered it with the thoroughness of a pointer beating a covert. But he did this hopelessly, bitterly aware that the outcome would be precisely what it eventually was, that is to say, nothing...

He was kneeling beside the bench—scrutinizing the turf with microscopic attention by aid of his flash-lamp, seeking some sign of struggle to prove she had not left him willingly, and finding none—when a voice brought him momentarily out of his distraction.

He looked up wildly, to discover Ducroy standing over him, his stout person chastely swathed in a quilted dressing-gown and trousers, his expression one of stupefaction.

"Well, monsieur—well?" the Minister of War demanded irritably. "What—I repeat—what are you doing there?"

Lanyard essayed response, choked up, and gulped. He rose and stood swaying, showing a stricken face.

"Eh?" Ducroy insisted with an accent of exasperation. "Why do you stand glaring at me like that—eh? Come, monsieur: what ails you? I have arranged everything, I say. Where is mademoiselle?"

Lanyard made a broken gesture.

"Gone!" he muttered forlornly.

Instantly the countenance of the stout Frenchman was lightened with a gleam of eager interest—inveterate romantic that he was!—and he stepped nearer, peering closely into the face of the adventurer.

"Gone?" he echoed. "Mademoiselle? Your sweetheart, eh?"

Lanyard assented with a disconsolate nod and sigh. Impatiently Ducroy caught him by the sleeve.

"Come!" he insisted, tugging—"but come at once into the house. Now, monsieur—now at length you enlist all one's sympathies! Come, I say! Is it your desire that I catch my death of cold?"

Indifferently Lanyard suffered himself to be led away.

He was, indeed, barely conscious of what was happening. All his being was possessed by the thought that she had forsaken him. And he could well guess why: impossible for such an one as she to contemplate without a shudder association with the man who had been what he had been! Infatuate!—to have dreamed that she would tolerate the devotion of a criminal, that she could ever forget his identity with the Lone Wolf. Inevitably—soon or late—she must have fled that ignominious thought in dread and horror, daring whatever consequences to escape and forget both it and him. And better now, perhaps, than later...

XVIII

ENIGMA

He found no reason to believe she had left him other than voluntarily, or that their adventures since the escape from the impasse Stanislas had been attended upon by spies of the Pack. He could have sworn they hadn't been followed either to or from the rue des Acacias; their way had been too long and purposely too roundabout, his vigilance too lively, for any sort of surveillance to have been practised without his remarking some indication thereof, at one time or another.

On the other hand (he told himself) there was every reason to believe she hadn't left him to go back to Bannon; concerning whom she had expressed herself too forcibly to excuse a surmise that she had preferred his protection to the Lone Wolf's.

Reasoning thus, he admitted, one couldn't blame her. He could readily see how, illuded at first by a certain romantic glamour, she had not, until left to herself in the garden, come to clear perception of the fact that she was casting her lot with a common criminal's. Then, horror overmastering her of a sudden she had fled—wildly, blindly, he didn't doubt. But whither? He looked in vain for her at their agreed rendezvous, the Sacré Coeur. She had neither money nor friends in Paris.

True: she had mentioned some personal jewellery she planned to hypothecate. Her first move, then, would be to seek the mont-de-piété—not to force himself again upon her, but to follow at a distance and ward off interference on Bannon's part.

The Government pawn-shop had its invitation for Lanyard himself: he was there before the doors were open for the day; and fortified by loans negotiated on his watch, cigarette-case, and a ring or two, retired to a café commanding a view of the entrance on the rue des Blancs-Manteaux, and settled himself against a day-long vigil.

It wasn't easy; drowsiness buzzed in his brain and weighted his eyelids; now and again, involuntarily, he nodded over his glass of black coffee. And when evening came and the mont-de-piété closed for the night, he rose and stumbled off, wondering if possibly he had napped a little without his knowledge and so missed her visit.

Engaging obscure lodgings close by the rue des Acacias, he slept till nearly noon of the following day, then rose to put into execution a design which had sprung full-winged from his brain at the instant of wakening.

He had not only his car but a chauffeur's license of long standing in the name of Pierre Lamier—was free, in short, to range at will the streets of Paris. And when he had levied on the stock of a second-hand clothing shop and a chemist's, he felt tolerably satisfied it would need sharp eyes—whether the Pack's or the Préfecture's—to identify "Pierre Lamier" with either Michael Lanyard or the Lone Wolf.

His face, ears and neck he stained a weather-beaten brown, a discreet application of rouge along his cheekbones enhancing the effect of daily exposure to the winter winds and rains of Paris; and he gave his hands an even darker shade, with the added verisimilitude of fingernails inked into permanent mourning. Also, he refrained from shaving: a stubble of two days' neglect bristled upon his chin and jowls. A rusty brown ulster with cap to match, shoddy trousers boasting conspicuous stripes of leaden colour, and patched boots completed the disguise.

Monsieur and madame of the conciergerie he deceived with a yarn of selling his all to purchase the motor-car and embark in business for himself; and with their blessing, sallied forth to scout Paris diligently for sight or sign of the woman to whom his every heartbeat was dedicated.

By the close of the third day he was ready to concede that she had managed to escape without his aid.

And he began to suspect that Bannon had fled the town as well; for the most diligent enquiries failed to educe the least clue to the movements of the American following the fire at Troyon's.

As for Troyon's, it was now nothing more than a gaping excavation choked with ashes and charred timbers; and though still rumours of police interest in the origin of the fire persisted, nothing in the papers linked the name of Michael Lanyard with their activities. His disappearance and Lucy Shannon's seemed to be accepted as due to death in the holocaust; the fact that their bodies hadn't been recovered was no longer a matter for comment.

In short, Paris had already lost interest in the affair.

Even so, it seemed, had the Pack lost interest in the Lone Wolf; or else his disguise was impenetrable. Twice he saw De Morbihan "flânning" elegantly on the Boulevards, and once he passed close by Popinot; but neither noticed him.

Toward midnight of the third day, Lanyard, driving slowly westward on the boulevard de la Madeleine, noticed a limousine of familiar aspect round a corner half a block ahead and, drawing up in front of Viel's, discharge four passengers.

The first was Wertheimer; and at sight of his rather striking figure, decked out in evening apparel from Conduit street and Bond, Lanyard slackened speed.

Turning as he alighted, the Englishman offered his hand to a young woman. She jumped down to the sidewalk in radiant attire and a laughing temper.

Involuntarily Lanyard stopped his car; and one immediately to the rear, swerving out to escape collision, shot past, its driver cursing him freely; while a sergent de ville scowled darkly and uttered an imperative word.

He pulled himself together, somehow, and drove on.

The girl was entering the restaurant by way of the revolving door, Wertheimer in attendance; while De Morbihan, having alighted, was lending a solicitous arm to Bannon.

Quite automatically the adventurer drove on, rounded the Madeleine, and turned up the boulevard Malesherbes. Paris and all its brisk midnight traffic swung by without claiming a tithe of his interest: he was mainly conscious of lights that reeled dizzily round him like a multitude of malicious, mocking eyes...

At the junction with the boulevard Haussmann a second sergent de ville roused him with a warning about careless driving. He went more sanely thereafter, but bore a heart of utter misery; his eyes still wore a dazed expression, and now and again he shook his head impatiently as though to rid it of a swarm of tormenting thoughts.

So, it seemed, he had all along been her dupe; all the while that he had been ostentatiously shielding her from harm and diffidently discovering every evidence of devotion, she had been laughing in her sleeve and planning to return to the service she pretended to despise, with her report of a fool self-duped.

A great anger welled in his bosom.

Turning round, he made back to the boulevard de la Madeleine, and on one pretext and another contrived to haunt the neighbourhood of Viel's until the party reappeared, something after one o'clock.

It was plain that they had supped merrily; the girl seemed in the gayest humour, Wertheimer a bit exhilarated, De Morbihan much amused; even Bannon—bearing heavily on the Frenchman's arm—was chuckling contentedly. The party piled back into De Morbihan's limousine and was driven up the avenue des Champs Élysées, pausing at the Élysée Palace Hotel to drop Bannon and the girl—his daughter?—whoever she was!

Whither it went thereafter, Lanyard didn't trouble to ascertain. He drove morosely home and went to bed, though not to sleep for many hours: bitterness of disillusion ate like an acid in his heart.

But for all his anguish, he continued in an uncertain temper. He had turned his back on the craft of which he was acknowledged master—for a woman's sake; for nothing else (he argued) had he dedicated himself to poverty and honest effort; and what little privation he had already endured was hopelessly distasteful to him. The art of the Lone Wolf, his consummate cunning and subtlety, was still at his command; with only himself to think of, he was profoundly contemptuous of the antagonism of the Pack; while none knew better than he with what ease the riches of careless Paris might be diverted to his own pockets. A single step aside from the path he had chosen—and tomorrow night he might dine at the Ritz instead of in some sordid cochers' cabaret!

And since no one cared—since *she* had betrayed his faith—what mattered?

Why not…?

Yet he could not come to a decision; the next day saw him obstinately, even a little stupidly, pursuing the course he had planned before his disheartening disillusionment.

Because his money was fast ebbing and motives of prudence alone—if none more worthy—forbade an attempt to replenish his pocketbook by revisiting the little rez-de-chaussée in the rue Roget and realizing on its treasures, he had determined to have a taximeter fitted to his car and ply for hire until time or chance should settle the question of his future.

Already, indeed, he had complied with the police regulations, and received permission to convert his voiture de remise into a taxicab; and leaving it before noon at the designated dépôt, he was told it would be ready for him at four with the "clock" installed. Returning at that hour, he learned that it couldn't be ready before six; and too bored and restless to while away two idle hours in a café, he wandered listlessly through the streets and boulevards—indifferent, in the black melancholy oppressing him, whether or not he were recognized—and eventually found himself turning from the rue St. Honoré through the place Vendôme to the rue de la Paix.

This was not wise, a perilous business, a course he had no right to pursue. And Lanyard knew it. Nonetheless, he persisted.

It was past five o'clock—deep twilight beneath a cloudless sky—the life of that street of streets fluent at its swiftest. All that Paris knew of wealth and beauty, fashion and high estate, moved between the curbs. One needed the temper of a Stoic to maintain indifference to the allure of its pageant.

Trudging steadily, he of the rusty brown ulster all but touched shoulders with men who were all that he had been but a few days since—hale, hearty, well-fed, well-dressed symbols of prosperity—and with exquisite women, exquisitely gowned, extravagantly be-furred and be-jewelled, of glowing faces and eyes dark with mystery and promise: spirited creatures whose laughter was soft music, whose gesture was pride and arrogance.

One and all looked past, over, and through him, unaffectedly unaware that he existed.

The roadway, its paving worn as smooth as glass, and tonight by grace of frost no less hard, rang with a clatter of hoofs high and clear above the resonance of motors. A myriad lights filled the wide channel with diffused radiance. Two endless ranks of shop-windows, facing one another—across the tide, flaunted treasures that kings might pardonably have coveted—and would.

Before one corner window, Lanyard paused instinctively.

The shop was that of a famous jeweller. Separated from him by only the thickness of plate-glass was the wealth of princes. Looking beyond that display, his attention focussed on the interior of an immense safe, to which a dapper French salesman was restoring velvet-lined trays of valuables. Lanyard studied the intricate, ponderous mechanism of the safe-door with a thoughtful gaze not altogether innocent of sardonic bias. It wore all the grim appearance of a strongbox that, once locked, would prove impregnable to everything save acquaintance with the combination and the consent of the time-lock. But give the Lone Wolf twenty minutes alone with it, twenty minutes free from interruption—he, the one man living who could seduce a time-lock and leave it apparently inviolate!...

To one side of that window stood a mirror, set at an angle, and suddenly Lanyard caught its presentment of himself—a gaunt and hungry apparition, with a wolfish air he had never worn when rejoicing in his sobriquet, staring with eyes of predaceous lustre.

Alarmed and fearing lest some passer-by be struck by this betrayal, he turned and moved on hastily.

But his mind was poisoned by this brutal revelation of the wide, deep gulf that yawned between the Lone Wolf of yesterday and Pierre Lamier of today; between Michael Lanyard the debonnaire, the amateur of fine arts and fine clothing, the beau sabreur of gentlemen-cracksmen and that lean, worn, shabby and dispirited animal who had glared back at him from the jeweller's mirror.

He quickened his pace, with something of that same instinct of self-preservation that bids the dipsomaniac avert his eyes and hurry past the corner gin-mill, and turned blindly off into the rue Danou, toward the avenue de l'Opéra.

But this only made it worse for him, for he could not avoid recognition of the softly glowing windows of the Café de Paris that knew him so well, or forget the memory of its shining rich linen, its silver and crystal, its perfumed atmosphere and luxury of warmth and music and shaded lights, its cuisine that even Paris cannot duplicate.

And the truth came home to him, that he was hungry not with that brute appetite he had money enough in his pocket to satisfy, but with the lust of flesh-pots, for rare viands and old vintage wines, to know once more the snug embrace of a dress-coat and to breathe again the atmosphere of ease and station.

In sudden panic he darted across the avenue and hurried north, determined to tantalize himself no longer with sights and sounds so provocative and so disturbing.

Half-way across the boulevard des Capucines, to the east of the Opéra, he leapt for his life from a man-killing taxi, found himself temporarily marooned upon one of those isles of safety which Paris has christened "thank-Gods," and stood waiting for an opening in the congestion of traffic to permit passage to the farther sidewalk.

And presently the policeman in the middle of the boulevard signalled with his little white wand; the stream of east-bound vehicles checked and began to close up to the right of the crossing, upon which they encroached jealously; and a taxi on the outside, next the island, overshot the mark, pulled up sharply, and began to back into place. Before Lanyard could stir, its window was opposite him, and he was looking in, transfixed.

There was sufficient light to enable him to see clearly the face of the passenger—its pale oval and the darkness of eyes whose gaze clung to his with an effect of confused fascination...

She sat quite motionless until one white-gloved hand moved uncertainly toward her bosom.

That brought him to; unconsciously lifting his cap, he stepped back a pace and started to move on.

At this, she bent quickly forward and unlatched the door. It swung wide to him.

Hardly knowing what he was doing, he accepted the dumb invitation, stepped in, took the empty seat, and closed the door.

Almost at once the car moved on with a jerk, the girl sinking back into her corner with a suggestion of breathlessness, as though her effort to seem composed had been almost too much for her strength.

Her face, turned toward Lanyard, seemed wan in the half light, but immobile, expressionless; only her eyes were darkly quick with anticipation.

On his part, Lanyard felt himself hopelessly confounded, in the grasp of emotions that would scarce suffer him to speak. A great wonder obsessed him that she should have opened that door to him no less than that he should have entered through it. Dimly he understood that each had acted without premeditation; and asked himself, was she already regretting that momentary weakness.

"Why did you do that?" he heard himself demand abruptly, his voice harsh, strained, and unnatural.

She stiffened slightly, with a nervous movement of her shoulders.

"Because I saw you… I was surprised; I had hoped—believed—you had left Paris."

"Without you? Hardly!"

"But you must," she insisted—"you *must* go, as quickly as possible. It isn't safe—"

"I'm all right," he insisted—"able-bodied—in full possession of my senses!"

"But any moment you may be recognized—"

"In this rig? It isn't likely... Not that I care."

She surveyed his costume curiously, perplexed.

"Why are you dressed that way? Is it a disguise?"

"A pretty good one. But in point of fact, it's the national livery of my present station in life."

"What do you mean by that?"

"Simply that, out of my old job, I've turned to the first resort of the incompetent: I'm driving a taxi."

"Isn't it awfully—risky?"

"You'd think so; but it isn't. Few people ever bother to look at a chauffeur. When they hail a taxi they're in a hurry, as a rule—preoccupied with business or pleasure. And then our uniforms are a disguise in themselves: to the public eye we look like so many Chinamen!"

"But you're mistaken: I knew you instantly, didn't I? And those others—they're as keen-witted as I—certainly. Oh, you should not have stopped on in Paris!"

"I couldn't go without knowing what had become of you."

"I was afraid of that," she confessed.

"Then why—?"

"Oh, I know what you're going to say! Why did I run away from you?" And then, since he said nothing, she continued unhappily: "I can't tell you... I mean, I don't know how to tell you!"

She kept her face averted, sat gazing blankly out of the window; but when he sat on, mute and unresponsive—in point of fact not knowing what to say—she turned to look at him, and the glare of a passing lamp showed her countenance profoundly distressed, mouth tense, brows knotted, eyes clouded with perplexity and appeal.

And of a sudden, seeing her so tormented and so piteous, his indignation ebbed, and with it all his doubts of her were dissipated; dimly he divined that something behind this dark fabric of mystery and inconsistency, no matter how inexplicable to him, excused all her apparent faithlessness and instability of character and purpose. He could not look upon this girl and hear her voice and believe that she was not at heart as sound and sweet, tender and loyal, as any that ever breathed.

A wave of tenderness and compassion brimmed his heart; he realized that he didn't matter, that his amour propre was of no account—that nothing mattered so long as she were spared one little pang of self-reproach.

He said, gently: "I wouldn't have you distress yourself on my account, Miss Shannon... I quite understand there must be things I *can't* understand—that you must have had your reasons for acting as you did."

"Yes," she said unevenly, but again with eyes averted—"I had; but they're not easy, they're impossible to explain—to you."

"Yet—when all's said and done—I've no right to exact any explanation."

"Ah, but how can you say that, remembering what we've been through together?"

"You owe me nothing," he insisted; "whereas I owe you everything, even unquestioning faith. Even though I fail, I have this to thank you for—this one not-ignoble impulse my life has known."

"You mustn't say that, you mustn't think it. I don't deserve it. You wouldn't say it—if you knew—"

"Perhaps I can guess enough to satisfy myself."

She gave him a swift, sidelong look of challenge, instinctively on the defensive.

"Why," she almost gasped—"what do you think—?"

"Does it matter what I think?"

"It does, to me: I wish to know!"

"Well," he conceded reluctantly, "I think that, when you had a chance to consider things calmly, waiting back there in the garden, you made up your mind it would be better to—to use your best judgment and—extricate yourself from an embarrassing position—"

"You think that!" she interrupted bitterly. "You think that, after you had confided in me; after you'd confessed—when I made you, led you on to it—that you cared for me; after you'd told me how much my faith meant to you—you think that, after all that, I deliberately abandoned you because I suddenly realized you had been the Lone Wolf—!"

"I'm sorry if I hurt you. But what can I think?"

"But you are wrong!" she protested vehemently—"quite, quite wrong! I ran away from myself—not from you—and with another motive, too, that I can't explain."

"You ran away from yourself—not from me?" he repeated, puzzled.

"Don't you understand? Why make it so hard for me? Why make me say outright what pains me so?"

"Oh, I beg of you—"

"But if you won't understand otherwise—I must tell you, I suppose." She checked, breathless, flushed, trembling. "You recall our talk after dinner, that night—how I asked what if you found out you'd been mistaken in me, that I had deceived you; and how I told you it would be impossible for me ever to marry you?"

"I remember."

"It was because of that," she said—"I ran away; because I hadn't been talking idly; because you *were* mistaken in me, because I *was* deceiving you, because I could never marry you, and because—suddenly—I came to know that, if I didn't go then and there, I might never find the strength to leave you, and only suffering and unhappiness could come of it all. I had to go, as much for your sake as for my own."

"You mean me to understand, you found you were beginning to—to care a little for me?"

She made an effort to speak, but in the end answered only with a dumb inclination of her head.

"And ran away because love wasn't possible between us?"

Again she nodded silently.

"Because I had been a criminal, I presume!"

"You've no right to say that—"

"What else can I think? You tell me you were afraid I might persuade you to become my wife—something which, for some inexplicable reason, you claim is impossible. What other explanation can I infer? What other explanation is needed? It's ample, it covers everything, and I've no warrant to complain—God knows!"

She tried to protest, but he cut her short.

"There's one thing I don't understand at all! If that is so, if your repugnance for criminal associations made you run away from me—why did you go back to Bannon?"

She started and gave him a furtive, frightened glance.

"You knew that?"

"I saw you—last night—followed you from Viel's to your hotel."

"And you thought," she flashed in a vibrant voice—"you thought I was in his company of my own choice!"

"You didn't seem altogether downcast," he countered, "Do you wish me to understand you were with him against your will?"

"No," she said slowly... "No: I returned to him voluntarily, knowing perfectly what I was about."

"Through fear of him—?"

"No. I can't claim that."

"Rather than me—?"

"You'll never understand," she told him a little wearily—"never. It was a matter of duty. I had to go back—I had to!"

Her voice trailed off into a broken little sob. But as, moved beyond his strength to resist, Lanyard put forth a hand to take the white-gloved one resting on the cushion beside her, she withdrew it with a swift gesture of denial.

"No!" she cried. "Please! You mustn't do that... You only make it harder..."

"But you love me!"

"I can't. It's impossible. I would—but I may not!"

"Why?"

"I can't tell you."

"If you love me, you must tell me."

She was silent, the white hands working nervously with her handkerchief.

"Lucy!" he insisted—"you must say what stands between you and my love. It's true, I've no right to ask, as I had no right to speak to you of love. But when we've said as much as we have said—we can't stop there. You will tell me, dear?"

She shook her head: "It—it's impossible."

"But you can't ask me to be content with that answer!"

"Oh!" she cried—"*how* can I make you understand?... When you said what you did, that night—it seemed as if a new day were dawning in my life. You made me believe it was because of me. You put me above you—where I'd no right to be; but the fact that you thought me worthy to be there, made me proud and happy: and for a little, in my blindness, I believed I could be worthy of your love and your respect. I thought that, if I could be as strong as you during that year you asked in which to prove your strength, I might listen to you, tell you everything, and be forgiven... But I was wrong, how wrong I soon learned... So I had to leave you at whatever cost!"

She ceased to speak, and for several minutes there was silence. But for her quick, convulsive breathing, the girl sat like a woman of stone, staring dry-eyed out of the window. And Lanyard sat as moveless, the heart in his bosom as heavy and cold as a stone.

At length, lifting his head, "You leave me no alternative," he said in a voice dull and hollow even in his own hearing: "I can only think one thing..."

"Think what you must," she said lifelessly: "it doesn't matter, so long as you renounce me, put me out of your heart and—leave me."

Without other response, he leaned forward and tapped the glass; and as the cab swung in toward the curb, he laid hold of the door-latch.

"Lucy," he pleaded, "don't let me go believing—"

She seemed suddenly infused with implacable hostility. "I tell you," she said cruelly—"I don't care what you think, so long as you go!"

The face she now showed him was ashen; its mouth was hard; her eyes shone feverishly.

And then, as still he hesitated, the cab pulled up and the driver, leaning back, unlatched the door and threw it open. With a curt, resigned nod, Lanyard rose and got out.

Immediately the girl bent forward and grasped the speaking-tube; the door slammed; the cab drew away and left him standing with the pose, with the gesture of one who has just heard his sentence of death pronounced.

When he roused to know his surroundings, he found himself standing on a corner of the avenue du Bois.

It was bitter cold in the wind sweeping down from the west, and it had grown very dark. Only in the sky above the Bois a long reef of crimson light hung motionless, against which leafless trees lifted gnarled, weird silhouettes.

While he watched, the pushing crimson ebbed swiftly and gave way to mauve, to violet, to black.

XIX

UNMASKED

When there was no more light in the sky, a profound sigh escaped Lanyard's lips; and with the gesture of one signifying submission to an omen, he turned and tramped heavily back across town.

More automaton than sentient being, he plodded on along the second enceinte of flaring, noisy boulevards, now and again narrowly escaping annihilation beneath the wheels of some coursing motor-cab or ponderous, grinding omnibus.

Barely conscious of such escapes, he was altogether indifferent to them: it would have required a mortal hurt to match the dumb, sick anguish of his soul; more than merely a sunset sky had turned black for him within that hour.

The cold was now intense, and he none too warmly clothed; yet there was sweat upon his brows.

Dully there recurred to him a figure he had employed in one of his talks with Lucy Shannon: that, lacking his faith in her, there would be only emptiness beneath his feet.

And now that faith was wanting in him, had been taken from him for all his struggles to retain it; and now indeed he danced on emptiness, the rope of temptation tightening round his neck, the weight of criminal instincts pulling it taut—strangling every right aspiration in him, robbing him of the very breath of that new life to which he had thought to give himself.

If she were not worthy, of what worth the fight...?

At one stage of his journey, he turned aside and, more through habit than desire or design, entered a cheap eating-place and consumed his customary evening meal without the slightest comprehension of what he ate or whether the food were good or poor.

When he had finished, he hurried away like a haunted man. There was little room in his mood for sustained thought: his wits were fathoming a bottomless pit of black despair. He felt like a man born blind, through skilful surgery given the boon of sight for a day or two, and suddenly and without any warning thrust back again into darkness.

He knew only that his brief struggle had been all wasted, that behind the flimsy barrier of his honourable ambition, the Lone Wolf was ravening. And he felt that, once he permitted that barrier to be broken down, it could never be repaired.

He had set it up by main strength of will, for love of a woman. He must maintain it now for no incentive other than to retain his own good will—or resign himself utterly to that darkness out of which he had fought his way, to its powers that now beset his soul.

And... he didn't care.

Quite without purpose he sought the machine-shop where he had left his car.

He had no plans; but it was in his mind, a murderous thought, that before another dawn he might encounter Bannon.

Interim, he would go to work. He could think out his problem while driving as readily as in seclusion; whatever he might ultimately elect to do, he could accomplish little before midnight.

Toward seven o'clock, with his machine in perfect running order, he took the seat and to the streets in a reckless humour, in the temper of a beast of prey.

The barrier was down: once more the Lone Wolf was on the prowl.

But for the present he controlled himself and acted perfectly his temporary rôle of taxi-bandit, fellow to those thousands who infest Paris. Half a dozen times in the course of the next three hours people hailed him from sidewalks and restaurants; he took them up, carried them to their several destinations, received payment, and acknowledged their gratuities with perfunctory thanks—thoroughly in character—but all with little conscious thought.

He saw but one thing, the face of Lucy Shannon, white, tense, glimmering wanly in shadow—the countenance with which she had dismissed him.

He had but one thought, the wish to read the riddle of her bondage. To accomplish this he was prepared to go to any extreme; if Bannon and his crew came between him and his purpose, so much the worse for them—and, incidentally, so much the better for society. What might befall himself was of no moment.

He entertained but one design, to become again what he had been, the supreme adventurer, the prince of plunderers, to lose himself once more in the delirium of adventurous days and peril-haunted nights, to reincarnate the Lone Wolf and in his guise loot the world anew, to court forgetfulness even at the prison's gates...

It was after ten when, cruising purposelessly, without a fare, he swung through the rue Auber into the place de l'Opéra and, approaching the Café de la Paix, was hailed by a door-boy of that restaurant.

Drawing in to the curb with the careless address that had distinguished his every action of that evening, he waited, with a throbbing motor, and with mind detached and gaze remote from the streams of foot and wheeled traffic that brawled past on either hand.

After a moment two men issued from the revolving door of the café, and approached the cab. Lanyard paid them no attention. His thoughts were now engaged with a certain hôtel particulier in the neighbourhood of La Muette and, in his preoccupation, he would need only the name of a destination and the sound of the cab-door slammed, to send him off like a shot.

Then he heard one of the men cough heavily, and in a twinkling stiffened to rigidity in his seat. If he had heard that cough but once before, that once had been too often. Without a glance aside, hardening his features to perfect immobility, he knew that the cough was shaking the slighter of those two figures.

And of a sudden he was acutely conscious of the clearness of the frosty atmosphere, of the merciless glare of electricity beating upon him from every side from the numberless street lamps and café lights. And poignantly he regretted neglecting to mask himself with his goggles.

He wasn't left long in suspense. The coughing died away by spasms; followed the unmistakable, sonorous accents of Bannon.

"Well, my dear boy! I have to thank you for an excellent dinner and a most interesting evening. Pity to break it up so early. Still, les affaires—you know! Sorry you're not going my way—but that's a handsome taxi you've drawn. What's its number—eh?"

"Haven't the faintest notion," a British voice drawled in response. "Never fret about a taxi's number until it has run over me."

"Great mistake," Bannon rejoined cheerfully. "Always take the number before entering. Then, if anything happens... However, that's a good-looking chap at the wheel—doesn't look as if he'd run you into any trouble."

"Oh, I fancy not," said the Englishman, bored.

"Well, you never can tell. The number's on the lamp. Make a note of it and be on the safe side. Or trust me—I never forget numbers."

With this speech Bannon ranged alongside Lanyard and looked him over, keenly malicious enjoyment gleaming in his evil old eyes.

"You are an honest-looking chap," he observed with a mocking smile but in a tone of the most inoffensive admiration—"honest and—ah—what shall I say?—what's the word we're all using nowadays?—efficient! Honest and efficient-looking, capable of better things, or I'm no judge! Forgive an old man's candour, my friend—and take good care of our British cousin here. He doesn't know his way around Paris very well. Still, I feel confident he'll come to no harm in *your* company. Here's a franc for you." With matchless effrontery, he produced a coin from the pocket of his fur-lined coat.

Unhesitatingly, permitting no expression to colour his features, Lanyard extended his palm, received the money, dropped it into his own pocket, and carried two fingers to the visor of his cap.

"Merci, monsieur," he said evenly.

"Ah, that's the right spirit!" the deep voice jeered. "Never be above your station, my man—never hesitate to take a tip! Here, I'll give you another, gratis: get out of this business: you're too good for it. Don't ask me how I know; I can tell by your face—Hello! Why do you turn down the flag? You haven't started yet!"

"Conversation goes up on the clock," Lanyard replied stolidly in French. He turned and faced Bannon squarely, loosing a glance of venomous hatred into the other's eyes. "The longer I have to stop here listening to your senile monologue, the more you'll have to pay. What address, please?" he added, turning back to get a glimpse of his passenger.

"Hotel Astoria," the porter supplied.

"Very good."

The porter closed the door.

"But remember my advice," Bannon counselled coolly, stepping back and waving his hand to the man in the cab. "Goodnight."

Lanyard took his car smartly away from the curb, wheeled round the corner into the boulevard des Capucines, and toward the rue Royale.

He had gone but a block when the window at his back was lowered and his fare observed pleasantly:

"That you, Lanyard?"

The adventurer hesitated an instant; then, without looking round, responded:

"Wertheimer, eh?"

"Right-O! The old man had me puzzled for a minute with his silly chaffing. Stupid of me, too, because we'd just been talking about you."

"Had you, though!"

"Rather. Hadn't you better take me where we can have a quiet little talk?"

"I'm not conscious of the necessity—"

"Oh, I say!" Wertheimer protested amiably—"don't be shirty, old top. Give a chap a chance. Besides, I have a bit of news from Antwerp that I guarantee will interest you."

"Antwerp?" Lanyard iterated, mystified.

"Antwerp, where the ships sail from," Wertheimer laughed: "not Amsterdam, where the diamonds flock together, as you may know."

"I don't follow you, I'm afraid."

"I shan't elucidate until we're under cover."

"All right. Where shall I take you?"

"Any quiet café will do. You must know one—"

"Thanks—no," said Lanyard dryly. "If I must confabulate with gentlemen of your kidney, I prefer to keep it dark. Even dressed as I am, I might be recognized, you know."

But it was evident that Wertheimer didn't mean to permit himself to be ruffled.

"Then will my modest diggings do?" he suggested pleasantly. "I've taken a suite in the rue Vernet, just back of the Hôtel Astoria, where we can be as private as you please, if you've no objection."

"None whatever."

Wertheimer gave him the number and replaced the window...

His rooms in the rue Vernet proved to be a small ground-floor apartment with private entrance to the street.

"Took the tip from you," he told Lanyard as he unlocked the door. "I daresay you'd be glad to get back to that rez-de-chaussée of yours. Ripping place, that... By the way—judging from your apparently robust state of health, you haven't been trying to live at home of late."

"Indeed?"

"Indeed yes, monsieur! If I may presume to advise—I'd pull wide of the rue Roget for a while—for as long, at least, as you remain in your present intractable temper."

"Daresay you're right," Lanyard assented carelessly, following, as Wertheimer turned up the lights, into a modest salon cosily furnished. "You live here alone, I understand?"

"Quite: make yourself perfectly at ease; nobody can hear us. And," the Englishman added with a laugh, "do forget your pistol, Mr Lanyard. I'm not Popinot, nor is this Troyon's."

"Still," Lanyard countered, "you've just been dining with Bannon."

Wertheimer laughed easily. "Had me there!" he admitted, unabashed. "I take it you know a bit more about the Old Man than you did a week ago?"

"Perhaps."

"But sit down: take that chair there, which commands both doors, if you don't trust me."

"Do you think I ought to?"

"Hardly. Otherwise I'd ask you to take my word that you're safe for the time being. As it is, I shan't be offended if you keep your gun handy and your sense of self-preservation running under forced draught. But you won't refuse to join me in a whiskey and soda?"

"No," said Lanyard slowly—"not if you drink from the same bottle."

Again the Englishman laughed unaffectedly as he fetched a decanter, glasses, bottled soda, and a box of cigarettes, and placed them within Lanyard's reach.

The adventurer eyed him narrowly, puzzled. He knew nothing of this man, beyond his reputation—something unsavoury enough, in all conscience!—had seen him only once, and then from a distance, before that conference in the rue Chaptal. And now he was becoming sensitive to a personality uncommonly insinuating: Wertheimer was displaying all the poise of an Englishman of the better caste. More than anybody in the underworld that Lanyard had ever known this blackmailer had an air of one acquainted with his own respect. And his nonchalance, the good nature with which he accepted Lanyard's pardonable distrust, his genial assumption of fellowship and a common footing, attracted even as it intrigued.

With the easy courtesy of a practised host, he measured whiskey into Lanyard's glass till checked by a "Thank you," then helped himself generously, and opened the soda.

"I'll not ask you to drink with me," he said with a twinkle, "but—chin-chin!"—and tilting his glass, half-emptied it at a draught.

Muttering formally, at a disadvantage and resenting it, Lanyard drank with less enthusiasm if without misgivings.

Wertheimer selected a cigarette and lighted it at leisure.

"Well," he laughed through a cloud of smoke—"I think we're fairly on our way to an understanding, considering you told me to go to hell when last we met!"

His spirit was irresistible: in spite of himself Lanyard returned the smile. "I never knew a man to take it with better grace," he admitted, lighting his own cigarette.

"Why not! I *liked* it: you gave us precisely what we asked for."

"Then," Lanyard demanded gravely, "if that's your viewpoint, if you're decent enough to see it that way—what the devil are you doing in that galley?"

"Mischief makes strange bedfellows, you'll admit. And if you think that a fair question—what are you doing here, with me?"

"Same excuse as before—trying to find out what your game is."

Wertheimer eyed the ceiling with an intimate grin. "My dear fellow!" he protested—"all *you* want to know is everything!"

"More or less," Lanyard admitted gracelessly. "One gathers that you mean to stop this side the Channel for some time."

"How so?"

"There's a settled, personal atmosphere about this establishment. It doesn't look as if half your things were still in trunks."

"Oh, these digs! Yes, they are comfy."

"You don't miss London?"

"Rather! But I shall appreciate it all the more when I go back."

"Then you can go back, if you like?"

"Meaning your impression is, I made it too hot for me?"

Wertheimer interposed with a quizzical glance. "I shan't tell you about that. But I'm hoping to be able to run home for an occasional weekend without vexing Scotland Yard. Why not come with me some time?"

Lanyard shook his head.

"Come!" the Englishman rallied him. "Don't put on so much side. I'm not bad company. Why not be sociable, since we're bound to be thrown together more or less in the way of business."

"Oh, I think not."

"But, my dear chap, you can't keep this up. Playing taxi-way man is hardly your shop. And of course you understand you won't be permitted to engage in any more profitable pursuit until you make terms with the powers that be—or leave Paris."

"Terms with Bannon, De Morbihan, Popinot and yourself—eh?"

"With the same."

"Mr Wertheimer," Lanyard told him quietly, "none of you will stop me if ever I make up my mind to take the field again."

"You haven't been thinking of quitting it—what?" Wertheimer demanded innocently, opening his eyes wide.

"Perhaps..."

"Ah, now I begin to see a light! So that's the reason you've come down to tooling a taxi. I wondered! But somehow, Mr Lanyard"—Wertheimer's eyes narrowed thoughtfully—"I can hardly see you content with that line... even if this reform notion isn't simple swank!"

"Well, what do you think?"

"I think," the Englishman laughed—"*I* think this conference doesn't get anywhere in particular. Our simple, trusting natures don't seem to fraternize as spontaneously as they might. We may as well cut the sparring and go, down to business—don't you think? But before we do, I'd like your leave to offer one word of friendly advice."

"And that is—?"

"'Ware Bannon!"

Lanyard nodded. "Thanks," he said simply.

"I say that in all sincerity," Wertheimer declared. "God knows you're nothing to me, but at least you've played the game like a man; and I won't see you butchered to make an Apache holiday for want of warning."

"Bannon's as vindictive as that, you think?"

"Holds you in the most poisonous regard, if you ask me. Perhaps you know why: I don't. Anyway, it was rotten luck that brought your car to the door tonight. He named you during dinner, and while apparently he doesn't know where to look for you, it is plain he's got no use for you—not, at least, until your attitude towards the organization changes."

"It hasn't. But I'm obliged."

"Sure you can't see your way to work with us?"

"Absolutely."

"Mind you, I'll have to report to the Old Man. I've got to tell him your answer."

"I don't think I need tell you what to tell him," said Lanyard with a grin.

"Still, it's worth thinking over. I know the Old Man's mind well enough to feel safe in offering you any inducement you can name, in reason, if you'll come to us. Ten thousand francs in your pocket before morning, if you like, and freedom to chuck this filthy job of yours—"

"Please stop there!" Lanyard interrupted hotly. "I was beginning to like you, too… Why persist in reminding me you're intimate with the brute who had Roddy butchered in his sleep?"

"Poor devil!" Wertheimer said gently. "That was a sickening business, I admit. But who told you—?"

"Never mind. It's true, isn't it?"

"Yes," the Englishman admitted gravely—"it's true. It lies at Bannon's door, when all's said... Perhaps you won't believe me, but it's a fact I didn't know positively who was responsible till tonight."

"You don't really expect me to swallow that? You were hand-in-glove—"

"Ah, but on probation only! When they voted Roddy out, I wasn't consulted. They kept me in the dark—mostly, I flatter myself, because I draw the line at murder. If I had known—this you won't believe, of course—Roddy would be alive today."

"I'd like to believe you," Lanyard admitted. "But when you ask me to sign articles with that damned assassin—!"

"You can't play our game with clean hands," Wertheimer retorted.

Lanyard found no answer to that.

"If you've said all you wished to," he suggested, rising, "I can assure you my answer is final—and go about my business."

"What's your hurry? Sit down. There's more to say—much more."

"As for instance—?"

"I had a fancy you might like to put a question or two."

Lanyard shook his head; it was plain that Wertheimer designed to draw him out through his interest in Lucy Shannon.

"I haven't the slightest curiosity concerning your affairs," he observed.

"But you should have; I could tell you a great many interesting things that intimately affect your affairs, if I liked. You must understand that I shall hold the balance of power here, from now on."

"Congratulations!" Lanyard laughed derisively.

"No joke, my dear chap: I've been promoted over the heads of your friends, De Morbihan and Popinot, and shall henceforth be—as they say in America—the whole works."

"By what warrant?"

"The illustrious Bannon's. I've been appointed his lieutenant—vice Greggs, deposed for bungling."

"Do you mean to tell me Bannon controls De Morbihan and Popinot?"

The Englishman smiled indulgently. "If you didn't know it, he's commander-in-chief of our allied forces, presiding genius of the International Underworld Unlimited."

"Bosh!" cried Lanyard contemptuously. "Why talk to me as if I were a child, to be frightened by a bogey-tale like that?"

"Take it or leave it: the fact remains... I know, if you don't. I confess I didn't till tonight; but I've learned some things that have opened my eyes... You see, we had a table in a quiet corner of the Café de la Paix, and since the Old Man's sailing for home before long it was time for him to unbosom rather thoroughly to the man he leaves to represent him in London and Paris. I never suspected our power before he began to talk..."

Lanyard, watching the man closely, would have sworn he had never seen one more sober. He was indescribably perplexed by this ostensible candour—mystified and mistrustful.

"And then there's this to be considered, from your side," Wertheimer resumed with the most business-like manner: "you can work with us without being obliged to deal in any way with the Old Man or De Morbihan, or Popinot. Bannon will never cross the Atlantic again, and you can do pretty much as you like, within reason—subject to my approval, that is."

"One of us is mad," Lanyard commented profoundly.

"One of us is blind to his best interests," Wertheimer amended with entire good-humour.

"Perhaps... Let it go at that. I'm not interested—never did care for fairy tales."

"Don't go yet. There is still much to be said on both sides of the argument."

"Has there been one?"

"Besides, I promised you news from Antwerp."

"To be sure," Lanyard said, and paused, his curiosity at length engaged.

Wertheimer delved into the breast-pocket of his dress-coat and produced a blue telegraph-form, handing it to the adventurer.

Of even date, from Antwerp, it read:

"*Underworld—Paris—Greggs arrested today boarding steamer for America after desperate struggle killed himself immediately afterward poison no confession—Q-2.*"

"*Underworld?*" Lanyard queried blankly.

"Our telegraphic address, of course. 'Q-2' is our chief factor in Antwerp."

"So they got Greggs!"

"Stupid oaf," Wertheimer observed; "I've no sympathy for him. The whole affair was a blunder, from first to last."

"But you got Greggs out and burned Troyon's—!"

"Still our friends at the Préfecture weren't satisfied. Something must have roused their suspicions."

"You don't know what?"

"There must have been a leak somewhere—"

"If so, it would certainly have led the police to me, after all the pains you were at to saddle me with the crime. There's something more than simple treachery in this, Mr Wertheimer."

"Perhaps you're right," said the other thoughtfully.

"And it doesn't speak well for the discipline of your precious organization—granting, for the sake of the argument, the possibility of such nonsense."

"Well, well, have your own way about that. I don't insist, so long as you agree to join forces with me."

"Oh, it's with you alone, now—is it? Not with that insane fiction, the International Underworld Unlimited?"

"With me alone. I offer you a clear field. Go where you like, do what you will—I wouldn't have the cheek to attempt to guide or influence you."

Lanyard kept himself in hand with considerable difficulty.

"But you?" he asked. "Where do you come in?"

Wertheimer lounged back in his chair and laughed quietly. "Need you ask? Must I recall to you the foundations of my prosperity? You had the name of it glib enough on your tongue the other night in the rue Chaptal... When you've done your work, you'll come to me and split the proceeds fairly—and as long as you do that, never a word will pass my lips!"

"Blackmail...!"

"Oh, if you insist! Odd, how I dislike that word!"

Abruptly the adventurer got to his feet. "By God!" he cried, "I'd better get out of this before I do you an injury!"

The door slammed behind him on a room ringing with Wertheimer's unaffected laughter.

XX

WAR

But why?—he asked himself as he swung his cab aimlessly away—why that blind rage with which he had welcomed Wertheimer's overtures?

Unquestionably the business of blackmailing was despicable enough; and as a master cracksman, of the highest caste of the criminal world, the Lone Wolf had warrantably treated with scorn and contempt the advances of a pariah like Wertheimer. But in no such spirit had he comprehended the Englishman's meaning, when finally that one came to the point; no cool disdain had coloured his attitude, but in the beginning hot indignation, in the end insensate rage...

He puzzled himself. That fit of passion had all the aspect of a psychical inconsistency impossible to reconcile with reason.

He recalled in perplexity how, toward the last, the face of the Englishman had swum in haze before his eyes; with what disfavour, approaching hatred, he had regarded its fixed, false smirk; with what loathing he had suffered the intimacy of Wertheimer's tone; how he had been tempted to fly at the man's throat and shake him senseless in reward of his effrontery: emotions that had suited better a man of unblemished honour and integrity subjected to the insolent addresses of a contemptible blackguard, emotions that might well have been expected of the man Lanyard had once dreamed to become.

But now, since he had resigned that infatuate ambition and turned apostate to all his vows, his part in character had been to laugh in Wertheimer's face and bid him go to the devil ere a worse thing befall him. Instead of which, he had flown into fury. And as he sat brooding over the wheel, he knew that, were the circumstances to be duplicated, his demeanour would be the same.

Was it possible he had changed so absolutely in the course of that short-lived spasm of reform?

He cried no to that: knowing well what he contemplated, that all his plans were laid and serious mischance alone could prevent him from putting them into effect, feeling himself once more quick with the wanton, ruthless spirit of the Lone Wolf, invincibly self-sufficient, strong and cunning.

When at length he roused from his reverie, it was to discover that his haphazard course had taken him back toward the heart of Paris; and presently, weary with futile cruising and being in the neighbourhood of the Madeleine, he sought the cab-rank there, silenced his motor, and relapsed into morose reflections so profound that nothing objective had any place in his consciousness.

Thus it was that without his knowledge a brace of furtive thugs were able to slouch down the rank, scrutinizing it covertly but in detail, pause opposite Lanyard's car under pretext of lighting cigarettes, identify him to their satisfaction, and hastily take themselves off.

Not until they were quite disappeared did the driver of the cab ahead dare warn him.

Lounging back, this last looked the adventurer over inquisitively.

"Is it, then," he enquired civilly, when Lanyard at length looked round, "that you are in the bad books of the good General Popinot, my friend?"

"Eh—what's that you say?" Lanyard asked, with a stare of blank misapprehension.

The man nodded wisely. "He who is at odds with Popinot," he observed, sententious, "does well not to sleep in public. You did not see those two who passed just now and took your number—rats of Montmartre, if I know my Paris! You were dreaming, my friend, and it is my impression that only the presence of those two flies over the way prevented your immediate assassination. If I were you, I should go away very quickly, and never stop till I had put stout walls between myself and Popinot."

A chill of apprehension sent a shiver stealing down Lanyard's spine.

"You're sure?"

"But of a certainty, my old one!"

"A thousand thanks!"

Jumping down, the adventurer cranked the motor, sprang back to his seat, and was off like a hunted hare...

And when, more than an hour later, he brought his panting car to a pause in a quiet and empty back-street of the Auteuil quarter, after a course that had involved the better part of Paris, it was with the conviction that he had beyond question shaken off pursuit—had there in fact been any attempt to follow him.

He took advantage of that secluded spot to substitute false numbers for those he was licensed to display; then at a more sedate pace followed the line of the fortifications northward as far as La Muette, where, branching off, he sought and made a circuit of two sides of the private park enclosing the hôtel of Madame Omber.

But the mansion showed no lights, and there was nothing in the aspect of the property to lead him to believe that the chatelaine had as yet returned to Paris.

Now the night was still young, but Lanyard had his cab to dispose of and not a few other essential details to arrange before he could take definite steps toward the reincarnation of the Lone Wolf.

Picking a most circumspect route across the river—via the Pont Mirabeau—to the all-night telegraph bureau in the rue de Grenelle he despatched a cryptic message to the Minister of War, then with the same pains to avoid notice made back toward the rue des Acacias. But it wasn't possible to recross the Seine secretly—in effect, at least—without returning the way he had come—a long detour that irked his impatient spirit to contemplate.

Unwisely he elected to cross by way of the Pont des Invalides—how unwisely was borne in upon him almost as soon as he turned from the brilliant Quai de la Conférence into the darkling rue François Premier. He had won scarcely twenty yards from the corner when, with a rush, its motor purring like some great tiger-cat, a powerful touring-car swept up from behind, drew abreast, but instead of passing checked speed until its pace was even with his own.

Struck by the strangeness of this manoeuvre, he looked quickly round, to recognize the moon-like mask of De Morbihan grinning sardonically at him over the steering-wheel of the black car.

A second hasty glance discovered four men in the tonneau. Lacking time to identify them, Lanyard questioned their character as little as their malign intent: Belleville bullies, beyond doubt, drafted from Popinot's batallions, with orders to bring in the Lone Wolf, dead or alive.

He had instant proof that his apprehensions were not exaggerated. Of a sudden De Morbihan cut out the muffler and turned loose, full strength, the electric horn. Between the harsh detonations of the exhaust and the mad, blatant shrieks of the warning, a hideous clamour echoed and re-echoed in that quiet street—a din in which the report of a revolver-shot was drowned out and went unnoticed. Lanyard himself might have been unaware of it, had he not caught out of the corner of his eye a flash that spat out at him like a fiery serpent's tongue, and heard the crash of the window behind him as it fell inward, shattered.

That the shot had no immediate successor was due almost wholly to Lanyard's instant and instinctive action.

Even before the clash of broken glass registered on his consciousness, he threw in the high speed and shot away like a frightened greyhound.

So sudden was this move that it caught De Morbihan himself unprepared. In an instant Lanyard had ten yards' lead. In another he was spinning on two wheels round an acute corner, into the rue Jean Goujon; and in a third, as he shot through that short block to the avenue d'Antin, had increased his lead to fifteen yards. But he could never hope to better that: rather, the contrary. The pursuit had the more powerful car, and it was captained by one said to be the most daring and skilful motorist in France.

The considerations that dictated Lanyard's simple strategy were sound if unformulated: barring interference on the part of the police—something he dared not count upon—his sole hope lay in open flight and in keeping persistently to the better-lighted, main-travelled thoroughfares, where a repetition of the attempt would be inadvisable—at least, less probable. There was always a bare chance of an accident—that De Morbihan's car would burst a tire or be pocketed by the traffic, enabling Lanyard to strike off into some maze of dark side-streets, abandon the cab, and take to cover in good earnest.

But that was a forlorn hope at best, and he knew it. Moreover, an accident was as apt to happen to him as to De Morbihan: given an unsound tire or a puncture, or let him be delayed two seconds by some traffic hindrance, and nothing short of a miracle could save him...

As he swung from the avenue d'Antin into Rond Point des Champs Élysées, the nose of the pursuing car inched up on his right, effectually blocking any attempt to strike off toward the east, to the Boulevards and the centre of the city's life by night. He had no choice but to fly westwards.

He cut an arc round the sexpartite circle of the Rond Point that lost no inch of advantage, and straightened out, ventre-à-terre, up the avenue for the place de l'Étoile, shooting madly in and out of the tide of more leisurely traffic—and ever the motor of the touring-car purred contentedly just at his elbow.

If there were police about, Lanyard saw nothing of them: not that he would have dreamed of stopping or even of checking speed for anything less than an immovable obstacle...

But as minutes sped it became apparent that there was to be no renewed attempt upon his life for the time being. The pursuers could afford to wait. They could afford to ape the patience of Death itself.

And it came then to Lanyard that he drove no more alone: Death was his passenger.

Absorbed though he was with the control of his machine and the ever-shifting problems of the road, he still found time to think quite clearly of himself, to recognize the fact that he was very likely looking his last on Paris... on life...

But a little longer, and the name of Michael Lanyard would be not even a memory to those whose lives composed the untiring life of this broad avenue.

Before him the Arc de Triomphe loomed ever larger and more darkly beautiful against the field of midnight stars He wondered, would he reach it alive...

He did: still the pursuit bided its time. But the hood of the touring-car nosed him inexorably round the arch, away from the avenue de la Grande Armée and into the avenue du Bois.

Only when in full course for Porte Dauphine did he appreciate De Morbihan's design. He was to be rushed out into the midnight solitudes of the Bois de Boulogne and there run down and slain.

But now he began to nurse a feeble thrill of hope.

Once inside the park enclosure, he reckoned vaguely on some opportunity to make sudden halt, abandon the car and, taking refuge in the friendly obscurity of trees and shrubbery, either make good his escape afoot or stand off the Apaches until police came to his aid. With night to cloak his movements and with a clump of trees to shelter in, he dared believe he would have a chance for his life—whereas in naked streets any such attempt would prove simply suicidal.

Infrequent glances over shoulder showed no change in the gap between his own and the car of the assassins. But his motor ran sweet and true: humouring it, coaxing it, he contrived a little longer to hold his own.

Approaching the Porte Dauphine he became aware of two sergents de ville standing in the middle of the way and wildly brandishing their arms. He held on toward them relentlessly—it was their lives or his—and they leaped aside barely in time to save themselves.

And as he slipped into the park like a hunted shadow, he fancied that he heard a pistol-shot—whether directed at himself by the Apaches, or fired by the police to emphasize their indignation, he couldn't say. But he was grateful enough it was a taxicab he drove, not a touring-car: lacking the body of his vehicle to shield him, he little doubted that a bullet would long since have found him.

In that dead hour the drives of the Bois were almost deserted. Between the porte and the first carrefour he passed only one motor-car, a limousine whose driver shouted something inarticulate as Lanyard hummed past. The freedom from traffic dangers was a relief: but the pursuit was creeping up, inch by inch, as he swung down the roadway along the eastern border of the lake; and still he had found no opening, had recognized no invitation in the lay of the land to attempt his one plan; as matters stood, the Apaches would be upon him before he could jump from his seat.

Bending low over the wheel, searching with anxious eyes the shadowed reaches of that winding drive, he steered for a time with one hand, while the other tore open his ulster and brought his pistol into readiness.

Then, as he topped the brow of the incline, above the whine of his motor, the crackle of road-metal beneath the tires, and the boom of the rushing air in his ears, he heard the sharp clatter of hoofs, and surmised that the gendarmerie had given chase.

And then, on a slight downgrade, though he took it at perilous speed and seemed veritably to ride the wind, the following machine, aided by its greater weight, began to close in still more rapidly. Momentarily the hoarse snoring of its motor sounded more loud and menacing. It was now a mere question of seconds...

Inspiration of despair came to him, as wild as any ever conceived by mind of man.

They approached a point where, on the left, a dense plantation walled the road. To the right a wide foot walk separated the drive from a gentle declivity sown with saplings, running down to the water.

Rising in his place, Lanyard slipped from under him the heavy waterproof cushion.

Then edging over to the left of the middle of the road, abruptly he shut off power and applied the brakes with all his might.

From its terrific speed the cab came to a stop within twice its length.

Lanyard was thrown forward against the wheel, but having braced in anticipation, escaped injury and effected instant recovery.

The car of the Apaches was upon him in a pulse beat. With no least warning of his intention, De Morbihan had no time to employ brakes. Lanyard saw its dark shape flash past the windows of his cab and heard a shout of triumph. Then with all his might he flung the heavy cushion across that scant space, directly into the face of De Morbihan.

His aim was straight and true.

In alarm, unable to comprehend the nature of that large, dark, whirling mass, De Morbihan attempted to lift a warding elbow. He was too slow: the cushion caught him in the face, full-force, and before he could recover or guess what he was doing, he had twisted the wheel sharply to the right.

The car, running a little less than locomotive speed, shot across the strip of sidewalk, caught its right forewheel against a sapling, swung heavily broadside to the drive, and turned completely over as it shot down the slope to the lake.

A terrific crash was followed by a hideous chorus of oaths, shrieks, cries and groans. Promptly Lanyard started his motor anew and, trembling in every limb, ran on for several hundred yards. But time pressed, and the usefulness of his car was at an end, as far as he was concerned; there was no saying how many times its identity might not have been established by the police in the course of that wild chase through Paris, or how soon these last might contrive to overhaul and apprehend him; and as soon as a bend in the road shut off the scene of wreck, he stopped finally, jumped down, and plunged headlong into the dark midnight heart of the Bois, seeking its silences where trees stood thickest and lights were few.

Later, like some worried creature of the night, panting, dishevelled, his rough clothing stained and muddied, he slunk across an open space, a mile or so from his point of disappearance, dropped cautiously down into the dry bed of the moat, climbed as stealthily a slippery glacis of the fortifications, darted across the inner boulevard, and began to describe a wide arc toward his destination, the hôtel Omber.

XXI

APOSTATE

He was singularly free from any sort of exultation over the manner in which he had at once compassed his own escape and brought down catastrophe upon his self-appointed murderers; his mood was quick with wonder and foreboding and bewilderment. The more closely he examined the affair, the more strange and inexplicable it bulked in his understanding. He had not thought to defy the Pack and get off lightly; but he had looked for no such overt effort at disciplining him so long as he kept out of the way and suspended his criminal activities. An unwilling recruit is a potential traitor in the camp; and retired competition isn't to be feared. So it seemed that Wertheimer hadn't believed his protestations, or else Bannon had rejected the report which must have been made him by the girl. In either case, the Pack had not waited for the Lone Wolf to prove his insincerity; it hadn't bothered to declare war; it had simply struck; with less warning than a rattlesnake gives, it had struck—out of the dark—at his back.

And so—Lanyard swore grimly—even so would he strike, now that it was his turn, now that his hour dawned.

But he would have given much for a clue to the riddle. Why must he be saddled with this necessity of striking in self-defence? Why had this feud been forced upon him, who asked nothing better than to be let alone? He told himself it wasn't altogether the professional jealousy of De Morbihan, Popinot and Wertheimer; it was the strange, rancorous spite that animated Bannon.

But, again, why? Could it be that Bannon so resented the aid and encouragement Lanyard had afforded the girl in her abortive attempt to escape? Or was it, perhaps, that Bannon held Lanyard responsible for the arrest and death of Greggs?

Could it be possible that there was really anything substantial at the bottom of Wertheimer's wild yarn about the pretentiously named "International Underworld Unlimited"? Was this really a demonstration of purpose to crush out competition—"and hang the expense"?

Or was there some less superficially tangible motive to be sought? Did Bannon entertain some secret, personal animus against Michael Lanyard himself as distinguished from the Lone Wolf?

Debating these questions from every angle but to no end, he worked himself into a fine fury of exasperation, vowing he would consummate this one final coup, sequestrate himself in England until the affair had blown over, and in his own good time return to Paris to expose De Morbihan (presuming he survived the wreck in the Bois) exterminate Popinot utterly, drive Wertheimer into permanent retirement at Dartmoor, and force an accounting from Bannon though it were surrendered together with that invalid's last wheezing breaths...

In this temper he arrived, past one in the morning, under the walls of the hôtel Omber, and prudently selected a new point of attack. In the course of his preliminary examinations of the walls, it hadn't escaped him that their brick-and-plaster construction was in bad repair; he had marked down several spots where the weather had eaten the outer coat of plaster completely away. At one of these, midway between the avenue and the junction of the side-streets, he hesitated.

As he had foreseen, the mortar that bound the bricks together was all dry and crumbling; it was no great task to work one of them loose, making a foothold from which he might grasp with a gloved hand the glass-toothed curbing, cast his ulster across this for further protection, and swing himself bodily atop the wall.

But there, momentarily, he paused in doubt and trembling. In that exposed and comfortless perch, the lifeless street on one hand, the black mystery of the neglected park on the other, he was seized and shaken by a sudden revulsion of feeling like a sickness of his very soul. Physical fear had nothing to do with this, for he was quite alone and unobserved; had it been otherwise faculties trained through a lifetime to such work as this and now keyed to concert pitch would not have failed to give warning of whatever danger his grosser senses might have overlooked.

Notwithstanding, he was afraid as though Fear's very self had laid hold of his soul by the heels and would not let it go until its vision of itself was absolute. He was afraid with a great fear such as he had never dreamed to know; who knew well the wincing of the flesh from risk of pain, the shuddering of the spirit in the shadow of death, and horror such as had gripped him that morning in poor Roddy's bedchamber.

But none of these had in any way taught him the measure of such fear as now possessed him, so absolute that he quaked like a naked soul in the inexorable presence of the Eternal.

He was afraid of himself, in panic terror of that ego which tenanted the shell of functioning, sensitive stuff called Michael Lanyard: he was afraid of the strange, silent, incomprehensible Self lurking occult in him, that masked mysterious Self which in its inscrutable whim could make him fine or make him base, that Self impalpable and elusive as any shadow yet invincibly strong, his master and his fate, in one the grave of Yesterday, the cup of Today, the womb of Tomorrow...

He looked up at the tired, dull faces of those old dwellings that loomed across the way with blind and lightless windows, sleeping without suspicion that he had stolen in among them—the grim and deadly thing that walked by night, the Lone Wolf, creature of pillage and rapine, scourged slave of that Self which knew no law...

Then slowly that obsession lifted like the passing of a nightmare; and with a start, a little shiver and a sigh, Lanyard roused and went on to do the bidding of his Self for its unfathomable ends...

Dropping silently to the soft, damp turf, he made himself one with the shadows of the park, as mute, intangible and fugitive as they, until presently coming out beneath the stars, on an open lawn running up to the library wing of the hôtel, he approached a shallow stone balcony which jutted forth eight feet above the lawn—an elevation so inconsiderable that, with one bound grasping its stone balustrade, the adventurer was upon it in a brace of seconds.

Nor did the long French windows that opened on the balcony offer him any real hindrance: a penknife quickly removed the dried putty round one small, lozenge-shaped pane, then pried out the pane itself; a hand through this space readily found and turned the latch; a cautious pressure opened the two wings far enough to admit his body; and—he stood inside the library.

He had made no sound; and thanks to thorough familiarity with the ground, he needed no light. The screen of cinnabar afforded all the protection he required; and because he meant to accomplish his purpose and be out of the house with the utmost expedition, he didn't trouble to explore beyond a swift, casual review of the adjoining salons.

The clock was chiming the three-quarters as he knelt behind the screen and grasped the combination-knob.

But he did not turn it. That mellow music died out slowly, and left him transfixed, there in the silence and gloom, his eyes staring wide into blackness at nothing, his jaw set and rigid, his forehead knotted and damp with sweat, his hands so clenched that the nails bit deep into his palms; while he looked back over the abyss yawning between the Lone Wolf of tonight and the man who had, within the week, knelt in that spot in company with the woman he loved, bent on making restitution that his soul might be saved through her faith in him.

He was visited by clear vision of himself: the thief caught in his crime by his conscience—or whatever it was, what for want of a better name he must call his conscience: this thing within him that revolted from his purpose, mutinied against the dictates of his Self, and stopped his hand from reaping the harvest of his cunning and daring; this sense of honour and of honesty that in a few brief days had grown more dear to him than all else in life, knitting itself inextricably into the fibre of his being, so that to deny it were against Nature...

He closed his eyes to shut out the accusing vision, and knelt on, unstirring, though torn this way and that in the conflict of man's dual nature.

Minutes passed without his knowledge.

But in time he grew more calm; his hands relaxed, the muscles of his brow smoothed out, he breathed more slowly and deeply; his set lips parted and a profound sigh whispered in the stillness. A great weariness upon him, he rose slowly and heavily from the floor, and stood erect, free at last and forever from that ancient evil which so long had held his soul in bondage.

And in that moment of victory, through the deep hush reigning in the house, he detected an incautious footfall on the parquetry of the reception-hall.

XXII

TRAPPED

It was a sound so slight, so very small and still, that only a super-subtle sense of hearing could have discriminated it from the confused multiplicity of almost inaudible, interwoven, interdependent sounds that make up the slumberous quiet of every human habitation, by night.

Lanyard, whose training had taught him how to listen, had learned that the nocturnal hush of each and every house has its singular cadence, its own gentle movement of muted but harmonious sound in which the introduction of an alien sound produces immediate discord, and to which, while at his work, he need attend only subconsciously since the least variation from the norm would give him warning.

Now, in the silence of this old mansion, he detected a faint flutter of discordance that sounded a note of stealth; such a note as no move of his since entering had evoked.

He was no longer alone, but shared the empty magnificence of those vast salons with one whose purpose was as furtive, as secret, as wary as his own; no servant or watchman roused by an intuition of evil, but one who had no more than he any lawful business there.

And while he stood at alert attention the sound was repeated from a point less distant, indicating that the second intruder was moving toward the library.

In two swift strides Lanyard left the shelter of the screen and took to cover in the recess of one of the tall windows, behind its heavy velvet hangings: an action that could have been timed no more precisely had it been rehearsed; he was barely in hiding when a shape of shadow slipped into the library, paused beside the massive desk, and raked the room with the light of a powerful flash-lamp.

Its initial glare struck squarely into Lanyard's eyes, dazzling them, as he peered through a narrow opening in the portières; and though the light was instantly shifted, for several moments a blur of peacock colour, blending, ebbing, hung like a curtain in the darkness, and he could see nothing distinctly—only the trail traced by that dancing spotlight over walls and furnishings.

When at length his vision cleared, the newcomer was kneeling in turn before the safe; but more light was needed, and this one, lacking Lanyard's patience and studious caution, turned back to the desk, and, taking the reading-lamp, transferred it to the floor behind the screen.

But even before the flood of light followed the dull click of the switch, Lanyard had recognized the woman.

For an instant he felt dazed, half-stunned, suffocating, much as he had felt with Greggs' fingers tightening on his windpipe, that week-old night at Troyon's; he experienced real difficulty about breathing, and was conscious of a sickish throbbing in his temples and a pounding in his bosom like the tolling of a great bell. He stared, swaying...

The light, gushing from the opaque hood, made the safe door a glare, and was thrown back into her intent, masked face, throwing out in sharp silhouette her lithe, sweet body, indisputably identified by the individual poise of her head and shoulders and the gracious contours of her tailored coat.

She was all in black, even to her hands, no trace of white or any colour showing but the fair curve of the cheek below her mask and the red of her lips. And if more evidence were needed, the intelligence with which she attacked the combination, the confident, business-like precision distinguishing her every action, proved her an apt pupil in that business.

His thoughts were all in a welter of miserable confusion. He knew that this explained many things he would have held questionable had not his infatuation forbidden him to consider them at all, lest he be disloyal to this woman whom he adored; but in the anguish of that moment he could entertain but one thought, and that possessed him altogether—that she must somehow be saved from the evil she contemplated...

But while he hesitated, she became sensitive to his presence; though he had made no sound since her entrance, though he had not even stirred, somehow she divined that he—someone—was there in the recess of the window, watching her.

In the act of opening the safe—using the memorandum of its combination which he had jotted down in her presence—he saw her pause, freeze to a pose of attention, then turn to stare directly at the portière that hid him. And for an eternal second she remained kneeling there, so still that she seemed not even to breathe, her gaze fixed and level, waiting for some sound, some sign, some tremor of the curtain's folds, to confirm her suspicion.

When at length she rose it was in one swift, alert movement. And as she paused with her slight shoulders squared and her head thrown back defiantly, challengingly, as one without will of his own but drawn irresistibly by her gaze, he stepped out into the room.

And since he was no more the Lone Wolf, but now a simple man in agony, with no thought for their circumstances—for the fact that they were both housebreakers and that the slightest sound might raise a hue-and-cry upon them—he took one faltering step toward her, stopped, lifted a hand in a gesture of appeal, and stammered:

"Lucy—you—"

His voice broke and failed.

She didn't answer, more than by recoiling as though he had offered to strike her, until the table stopped her, and she leaned back as if glad of its support.

"Oh!" she cried, trembling—"why—why did you do it?"

He might have answered her in kind, but self-justification passed his power. He couldn't say, "Because this evening you made me lose faith in everything, and I thought to forget you by going to the devil the quickest way I knew—this way!"—though that was true. He couldn't say: "Because, a thief from boyhood, habit proved too strong for me, and I couldn't withstand temptation!"—for that was untrue. He could only hang his head and mumble the wretched confession: "I don't know."

As if he hadn't spoken, she cried again: "Why—*why* did you do it? I was so proud of you, so sure of you, the man who had turned straight because of me!... It compensated... But now...!"

Her voice broke in a short, dry sob.

"Compensated?" he repeated stupidly.

"Yes, compensated!" She lifted her head with a gesture of impatience: "For this—don't you understand?—for this that I'm doing! You don't imagine I'm here of my own will?—that I went back to Bannon for any reason but to try to save you from him? I knew something of his power, and you didn't; I knew if I went away with you he'd never rest until he had you murdered. And I thought if I could mislead him by lies for a little time—long enough to give you a chance to escape—I thought—perhaps—I might be able to communicate with the police, denounce him—"

She hesitated, breathless and appealing.

At her first words he had drawn close to her; and all their talk was murmurings. But this was quite instinctive; for both were beyond considerations of prudence, the one coherent thought of each being that now, once and forever, all misunderstanding must be done away with.

Now, as naturally as though they had been lovers always, Lanyard took her hand, and clasped it between his own.

"You cared as much as that!"

"I love you," she told him—"I love you so much I am ready to sacrifice everything for you—life, liberty, honour—"

"Hush, dearest, hush!" he begged, half distracted.

"I mean it: if honour could hold me back, do you think I would have broken in here tonight to steal for Bannon?"

"He sent you, eh?" Lanyard commented in a dangerous voice.

"He was too cunning for me... I was afraid to tell you... I meant to tell—to warn you, this evening in the cab. But then I thought perhaps if I said nothing and sent you away believing the worst of me—perhaps you would save yourself and forget me—"

"But never!"

"I tried my best to deceive him, but couldn't. They got the truth from me by threats—"

"They wouldn't dare—"

"They dare anything, I tell you! They knew enough of what had happened, through their spies, to go on, and they tormented and bullied me until I broke down and told them everything... And when they learned you had brought the jewels back here, Bannon told me I must bring them to him—that, if I refused, he'd have you killed. I held out until tonight; then just as I was about to go to bed he received a telephone message, and told me you were driving a taxi and followed by Apaches and wouldn't live till daylight if I persisted in refusing."

"You came alone?"

"No. Three men brought me to the gate. They're waiting outside, in the park."

"Apaches?"

"Two of them. The other is Captain Ekstrom."

"Ekstrom!" Lanyard cried in despair. "Is he—"

The dull, heavy, crashing slam of the great front doors silenced him.

XXIII

MADAME OMBER

Before the echo of that crash ceased to reverberate from room to room, Lanyard slipped to one side of the doorway, from which point he could command the perspective of the salons together with a partial view of the front doors. And he was no more than there, in the shadow of the portières, when light from an electrolier flooded the reception-hall.

It showed him a single figure, that of a handsome woman, considerably beyond middle age but still a well-poised, vigorous, and commanding presence, in full evening dress of such magnificence as to suggest recent attendance at some State function.

Standing beneath the light, she was restoring a key to a brocaded handbag. This done, she turned her head and spoke indistinguishably over her shoulder. Promptly there came into view a second woman of about the same age, but even more strong and able of appearance—a serving-woman, in plain, dark garments, undoubtedly madame's maid.

Handing over the brocaded bag, madame unlatched the throat of her ermine cloak and surrendered it to the servant's care.

Her next words were audible, and reassuring in as far as they indicated ignorance of anything amiss.

"Thank you, Sidonie. You may go to bed now."

"Madame will not need me to undress her?"

"I'm not ready yet. When I am—I'm old enough to take care of myself. Besides, I prefer you to go to bed, Sidonie. It doesn't improve your temper to lose your beauty sleep."

"Many thanks, madame. Goodnight."

"Goodnight."

The maid moved off toward the main staircase, while her mistress turned deliberately through the salons toward the library.

At this, swinging back to the girl in a stride, and grasping her wrist to compel attention, Lanyard spoke in a rapid whisper, mouth close to her ear, but his solicitude so unselfish and so intense that for the moment he was altogether unconscious of either her allure or his passion.

"This way," he said, imperatively drawing her toward the window by which he had entered: "there's a balcony outside—a short drop to the ground." And unlatching the window, he urged her through it. "Try to leave by the back gateway—the one I showed you before—avoiding Ekstrom—"

"But surely you are coming too?" she insisted, hanging back.

"Impossible: there's no time for us both to escape undetected. I shall keep madame interested only long enough for you to get away. But take this"—and he pressed his automatic into her hand. "No—take it; I've another," he lied, "and you may need it. Don't fear for me, but go—O my heart!—go!"

The footfalls of Madame Omber were sounding dangerously near, and without giving the girl more opportunity to protest, Lanyard closed the windows, shot the latch and stole like a cat round the farther side of the desk, pausing within a few feet of the screen and safe.

The desk-lamp was still burning, where the girl had left it behind the cinnabar screen; and Lanyard knew that the diffusion of its rays was enough to render his figure distinctly and immediately visible to one entering the doorway.

Now everything hung upon the temper of the householder, whether she would take that apparition quietly, deceived by Lanyard's mumming into believing she had only a poor thievish fool to deal with, or with a storm of bourgeois hysteria. In the latter event, Lanyard's hand was ready planted, palm down, on the top of the desk: should the woman attempt to give the alarm, a single bound would carry the adventurer across it in full flight for the front doors.

In the doorway the mistress of the house appeared and halted, her quick bright eyes shifting from the light on the floor to the dark figure of the thief. Then, in a stride, she found a switch and turned on the chandelier, a blaze of light.

As this happened, Lanyard cowered, lifting an elbow as though to guard his face—as though expecting to find himself under the muzzle of a revolver.

The gesture had the calculated effect of focussing the attention of the woman exclusively to him, after one swift glance round had shown her a room tenanted only by herself and a cringing thief. And immediately it was made manifest that, whether or not deceived, she meant to take the situation quietly, if in a strong hand.

Her eyes narrowed and the muscles of her square, almost masculine jaw hardened ominously as she looked the intruder up and down. Then a flicker of contempt modified the grimness of her countenance. She took three steps forward, pausing on the other side of the desk, her back to the doorway.

Lanyard trembled visibly...

"Well!"—the word boomed like the opening gun of an engagement—"Well, my man!"—the shrewd eyes swerved to the closed door of the safe and quickly back again—"you don't seem to have accomplished much!"

"For God's sake, madame!" Lanyard blurted in a husky, shaken voice, nothing like his own—"don't have me arrested! Give me a chance! I haven't taken anything. Don't call the flics!"

He checked, moving an uncertain hand towards his throat as if his tongue had gone dry.

"Come, come!" the woman answered, with a look almost of pity. "I haven't called anyone—as yet."

The fingers of one strong white hand were drumming gently on the top of the desk; then, with a movement so quick and sure that Lanyard himself could hardly have bettered it, they slipped down to a handle of a drawer, jerked it open, closed round the butt of a revolver, and presented it at the adventurer's head.

Automatically he raised both hands.

"Don't shoot!" he cried. "I'm not armed—"

"Is that the truth?"

"You've only to search me, madame!"

"Thanks!" Madame's accents now discovered a trace of dry humour. "I'll leave that to you. Turn out your pockets on the desk there—and, remember, I'll stand no nonsense!"

The weapon covered Lanyard steadily, leaving him no choice but to obey. As it happened, he was glad of the excuse to listen for sounds to tell how the girl was faring in her flight, and made a pretence of trembling fingers cover the slowness with which he complied.

But he heard nothing.

When he had visibly turned every pocket inside out, and their contents lay upon the desk, the woman looked the exhibits over incuriously.

"Put them back," she said curtly. "And then fetch that chair over there—the one in the corner. I've a notion I'd like to talk to you. That's the usual thing, isn't it?"

"How?" Lanyard demanded with a vacant stare.

"In all the criminal novels I've ever read, the law-abiding householder always sits down and has a sociable chat with the housebreaker—before calling in the police. I'm afraid that's part of the price you've got to pay for my hospitality."

She paused, eyeing Lanyard inquisitively while he restored his belongings to his pockets. "Now, get that chair!" she ordered; and waited, standing, until she had been obeyed. "That's it—there! Sit down."

Leaning against the desk, her revolver held negligently, the speaker favoured Lanyard with a more leisurely inspection; the harshness of her stare was softened, and the anger which at first had darkened her countenance was gone by the time she chose to pursue her catechism.

"What's your name? No—don't answer! I saw your eyes waver, and I'm not interested in a makeshift alias. But it's the stock question, you know... Do you care for a cigar?"

She opened a mahogany humidor on the desk.

"No, thanks."

"Right—according to Hoyle: the criminal always refuses to smoke in these scenes. But let's forget the book and write our own lines. I'll ask you an original question: Why were you acting just now?"

"Acting?" Lanyard repeated, intrigued by the acuteness of this masterful woman's mentality.

"Precisely—pretending you were a common thief. For a moment you actually made me think you afraid of me. But you're neither the one nor the other. How do I know? Because you're unarmed, your voice has changed in the last two minutes to that of a cultivated man, you've stopped cringing and started thinking, and the way you walked across the floor and handled that chair showed how powerfully you're made. If I didn't have this revolver, you could overpower me in an instant—and I'm no weakling, as women go. So—why the acting?"

Studying his captor with narrow interest, Lanyard smiled faintly and shrugged, but made no answer. He could do no more than this—no more than spare for time: the longer he indulged madame in her whim, the better Lucy's chances of scot-free escape. By this time, he reckoned, she would have found her way through the service gate to the street. But he was on edge with unending apprehension of mischance.

"Come, come!" Madame Omber insisted. "You're hardly civil, my man. Answer my question!"

"You don't expect me to—do you?"

"Why not? You owe me at least satisfaction of my curiosity, in return for breaking into my house."

"But if, as you suggest, I am—or was—acting with a purpose, why expect me to give the show away?"

"That's logic. I knew you could think. More's the pity!"

"Pity I can think?"

"Pity you can get your own consent to waste yourself like this. I'm an old woman, and I know men better than most; I can see ability in you. So I say, it's a pity you won't use yourself to better advantage. Don't misunderstand me: this isn't the conventional act; I don't hold with encouraging a fool in his folly. You're a fool, for all your intelligence, and the only cure I can see for you is drastic punishment."

"Meaning the Santé, madame?"

"Quite so. I tell you frankly, when I'm finished lecturing you, off you go to prison."

"If that's the case I don't see I stand to gain much by retailing the history of my life. This seems to be your cue to ring for servants to call the police."

A trace of anger shone in the woman's eyes. "You're right," she said shortly; "I dare say Sidonie isn't asleep yet. I'll get her to telephone while I keep an eye on you."

Bending over the desk, without removing her gaze from the adventurer, his captor groped for, found, and pressed a call-button.

From some remote quarter of the house sounded the grumble of an electric bell.

"Pity you're so brazen," she observed. "Just a little less side, and you'd be a rather engaging person!"

Lanyard made no reply. In fact he wasn't listening.

Under the strain of that suspense, the iron control which had always been his was breaking down—since now it was for another he was concerned. And he wasted no strength trying to enforce it. The stress of his anxiety was both undisguised and undisguisable. Nor did Madame Omber overlook it.

"What's the trouble, eh? Is it that already you hear the cell door clang in your ears?"

As she spoke, Lanyard left his chair with a movement in the execution of which all his wits co-operated, with a spring as lithe and sure and swift as an animal's, that carried him like a shot across the two yards or so between them.

The slightest error in his reckoning would have finished him: for the other had been watching for just such a move, and the revolver was nearly level with Lanyard's head when he grasped it by the barrel, turned that to the ceiling, imprisoned the woman's wrist with his other hand, and in two movements had captured the weapon without injuring its owner.

"Don't be alarmed," he said quietly. "I'm not going to do anything more violent than to put this weapon out of commission."

Breaking it smartly, he shot a shower of cartridges to the door, and tossed the now-useless weapon into a wastebasket beneath the desk.

"Hope I didn't hurt you," he added abstractedly—"but your pistol was in my way!"

He took a stride toward the door, pulled up, and hung in hesitation, frowning absently at the woman; who, without moving, laughed quietly and watched him with a twinkle of malicious diversion.

He repaid this with a stare of thoughtful appraisal; from the first he had recognized in her a character of uncommon tolerance and amiability.

"Pardon, madame, but—" he began abruptly—and checked in constrained appreciation of his impudence.

"If that's permission to interrupt your reverie," Madame Omber remarked, "I don't mind telling you, you're the most extraordinary burglar I ever heard of!"

Footfalls became audible on the staircase—the hasty scuffling of slippered feet.

"Is that you, Sidonie?" madame called.

The voice of the maid replied: "Yes, madame—coming!"

"Well—don't, just yet—not till I call you."

"Very good, madame."

The woman returned complete attention to Lanyard.

"Now, monsieur-of-two-minds, what is it you wish to say to me?"

"Why did you do that?" the adventurer asked, with a jerk of his head toward the hall.

"Tell Sidonie to wait instead of calling for help? Because—well, because you interest me strangely. I've got a theory you're in a desperate quandary and are about to throw yourself on my mercy."

"You are right," Lanyard admitted tersely.

"Ah! Now you do begin to grow interesting! Would you mind explaining why you think I'll be merciful?"

"Because, madame, I've done you a great service, and feel I can count upon your gratitude."

The Frenchwoman's eyebrows lifted at this. "Doubtless, monsieur knows what he's talking about—"

"Listen, madame: I am in love with a young woman, an American, a stranger and friendless in Paris. If anything happens to me tonight, if I am arrested or assassinated—"

"Is that likely?"

"Quite likely, madame: I have enemies among the Apaches, and in my own profession as well; and I have reason to believe that several of them are in this neighbourhood tonight. I may possibly not escape their attentions. In that event, this young lady of whom I speak will need a protector."

"And why must I interest myself in her fate, pray?"

"Because, madame, of this service I have done you... Recently, in London, you were robbed—"

The woman started and coloured with excitement: "You know something of my jewels?"

"Everything, madame: it was I who stole them."

"You? You are, then, that Lone Wolf?"

"I was, madame."

"Why the past tense?" the woman demanded, eyeing him with a portentous frown.

"Because I am done with thieving."

She threw back her head and laughed, but without mirth: "A likely story, monsieur! Have you reformed since I caught you here—?"

"Does it matter when? I take it that proof, visible, tangible proof of my sincerity, more than a meaningless date, would be needed to convince you."

"No doubt of that, Monsieur the Lone Wolf!"

"Could you ask better proof than the restoration of your stolen property?"

"Are you trying to bribe me to let you off with an offer to return my jewels?"

"I'm afraid emergency reformation wouldn't persuade you—"

"You may well be afraid, monsieur!"

"But if I can prove I've already restored your jewels—?"

"But you have not."

"If madame will do me the favour to open her safe, she will find them there—conspicuously placed."

"What nonsense—!"

"Am I wrong in assuming that madame didn't return from England until quite recently?"

"But today, in fact—"

"And you haven't troubled to investigate your safe since returning?"

"It had not occurred to me—"

"Then why not test my statement before denying it?"

With an incredulous shrug Madame Omber terminated a puzzled scrutiny of Lanyard's countenance, and turned to the safe.

"But to have done what you declare you have," she argued, "you must have known the combination—since it appears you haven't broken this open."

The combination ran glibly off Lanyard's tongue. And at this, with every evidence of excitement, at length beginning to hope if not to believe, the woman set herself to open the safe. Within a minute she had succeeded, the morocco-bound jewel-case was in her hand, and a hasty examination had assured her its treasure was intact.

"But why—?" she stammered, pale with emotion—"why, monsieur, *why*?"

"Because I decided to leave off stealing for a livelihood."

"When did you bring these jewels here?"

"Within the week—four or five nights since—"

"And then—repented, eh?"

"I own it."

"But came here again tonight, to steal a second time what you had stolen once?"

"That's true, too."

"And I interrupted you—"

"Pardon, madame: not you, but my better self. I came to steal—I could not."

"Monsieur—you do not convince. I fail to fathom your motives, but—"

A sudden shock of heavy trampling feet in the reception-hall, accompanied by a clash of excited voices, silenced her and brought Lanyard instantly to the face-about.

Above that loud wrangle—of which neither had received the least warning, so completely had their argument absorbed them—Sidonie's accents were audible:

"Madame—madame!"—a cry of protest.

"What is it?" madame demanded of Lanyard.

He threw her the word "Police!" as he turned and flung himself into the recess of the window.

But when he wrenched it open the voice of a picket on the lawn saluted him in sharp warning; and when, involuntarily, he stepped out upon the balcony, a flash of flame split the gloom below, a loud report rang in the quiet of the park, and a bullet slapped viciously the stone facing of the window.

XXIV

RENDEZVOUS

With as little ceremony as though the bullet had lodged in himself, Lanyard tumbled back into the room, tripped, and fell sprawling; while to a tune of clattering boots two sergents de ville lumbered valiantly into the library and pulled up to discover Madame Omber standing calmly, safe and sound, beside her desk, and Lanyard picking himself up from the floor by the open window.

Behind them Sidonie trotted, wringing her hands.

"Madame!" she bleated—"they wouldn't listen to me, madame—I couldn't stop them!"

"All right, Sidonie. Go back to the hall. I'll call you when needed... Messieurs, goodmorning!"

One of the sergents advanced with an uncertain salute and a superfluous question: "Madame Omber—?" The other waited on the threshold, barring the way.

Lanyard measured the two speculatively: the spokesman seemed a bit old and fat, ripe for his pension, little apt to prove seriously effective in a rough-and-tumble; but the other was young, sturdy, and broad-chested, with the poise of an athlete, and carried in addition to his sword a pistol naked in his hand, while his clear blue eyes, meeting the adventurer's, lighted up with a glint of invitation.

For the present, however, Lanyard wasn't taking any. He met that challenge with a look of utter stupidity, folded his arms, lounged against the desk, and watched Madame Omber acknowledge, none too cordially, the other sergent's query.

"I am Madame Omber—yes. What can I do for you?"

The sergent gaped. "Pardon!" he stammered, then laughed as one who tardily appreciates a joke. "It is well we are arrived in time, madame," he added—"though it would seem you have not had great trouble with this miscreant. Where is the woman?"

He moved a pace toward Lanyard: hand-cuffs jingled in his grasp.

"But a moment!" madame interposed. "Woman? What woman?"

Pausing, the older sergent explained in a tone of surprise:

"But his accomplice, naturally! Such were our instructions—to proceed at once to madame's hôtel, come in quietly by the servants' entrance—which would be open—and arrest a burglar with his female accomplice."

Again the stout sergent moved toward Lanyard; again Madame Omber stopped him.

"But one moment more, if you please!"

Her eyes, dense with suspicion, questioned Lanyard; who, with a significant nod toward the jewel-case still in her hands, gave her a glance of dumb entreaty.

After brief hesitation, "It is a mistake," madame declared; "there is no woman in this house, to my certain knowledge, who has no right to be here... But you say you received a message? I sent none!"

The fat sergent shrugged. "That is not for me to dispute, madame. I have only my orders to go by."

He glared sullenly at Lanyard; who returned a placid smile that (despite such hope as he might derive from madame's irresolute manner) masked a vast amount of trepidation. He felt tolerably sure Madame Omber had not sent for police on prior knowledge of his presence in the library. All this, then, would seem to indicate a new form of attack on the part of the Pack. He had probably been followed and seen to enter; or else the girl had been caught attempting to steal away and the information wrung from her by *force majeure*... Moreover, he could hear two more pair of feet tramping through the salons.

Pending the arrival of these last, Madame Omber said nothing more.

And, unceremoniously enough, the newcomers shouldered into the library—one pompous uniformed body, of otherwise undistinguished appearance, promptly identified by the sergents de ville as monsieur le commissaire of that quarter; the other, a puffy mediocrity, known to Lanyard at least (if apparently to no one else) as Popinot.

At this confirmation of his darkest fears, the adventurer abandoned hope of aid from Madame Omber and began quietly to reckon his chances of escape through his own efforts.

But he was quite unarmed, and the odds were heavy: four against one, all four no doubt under arms, and two at least—the sergents—men of sound military training.

"Madame Omber?" enquired the commissaire, saluting that lady with immense dignity. "One trusts that this intrusion may be pardoned, the circumstances remembered. In an affair of this nature, involving this repository of so historic treasures—"

"That is quite well understood, monsieur le commissaire," madame replied distantly. "And this monsieur is, no doubt, your aide?"

"Pardon!" the official hastened to identify his companion: "Monsieur Popinot, agent de la Sûreté, who lays these informations!"

With a profound obeisance to Madame Omber, Popinot strode dramatically over to confront Lanyard and explore his features with his small, keen, shifty eyes of a pig; a scrutiny which the adventurer suffered with superficial calm.

"It is he!" Popinot announced with a gesture. "Messieurs, I call upon you to arrest this man, Michael Lanyard, alias 'The Lone Wolf'."

He stepped back a pace, expanding his chest in vain effort to eclipse his abdomen, and glanced triumphantly at his respectful audience.

"Accused," he added with intense relish, "of the murder of Inspector Roddy of Scotland Yard at Troyon's, as well as of setting fire to that establishment—"

"For this, Popinot," Lanyard interrupted in an undertone, "I shall some day cut off your ears!" He turned to Madame Omber: "Accept, if you please, madame, my sincere regrets... but this charge happens to be one of which I am altogether innocent."

Instantly, from lounging against the desk, Lanyard straightened up: and the heavy humidor of brass and mahogany, on which his right hand had been resting, seemed fairly to leap from its place as, with a sweep of his arm, he sent it spinning point-blank at the younger sergent.

Before that one, wholly unprepared, could more than gasp, the humidor caught him a blow like a kick just below the breastbone. He reeled, the breath left him in one great gust, he sat down abruptly—blue eyes wide with a look of aggrieved surprise—clapped both hands to his middle, blinked, turned pale, and keeled over on his side.

But Lanyard hadn't waited to note results. He was busy. The fat sergent had leaped snarling upon his arm, and was struggling to hold it still long enough to snap a handcuff round the wrist; while the commissaire had started forward with a bellow of rage and two hands extended and itching for the adventurer's throat.

The first received a half-arm jab on the point of his chin that jarred his entire system, and without in the least understanding how it happened, found himself whirled around and laid prostrate in the commissaire's path. The latter tripped, fell, and planted two hard knees, with the bulk of his weight atop them, on the apex of the sergent's paunch.

At the same time Lanyard, leaping toward the doorway, noticed Popinot tugging at something in his hip-pocket.

Followed a vivid flash, then complete darkness: with a well-aimed kick—an elementary movement of la savate—Lanyard had dislocated the switch of the electric lights, knocking its porcelain box from the wall, breaking the connection, and creating a short-circuit which extinguished every light in that part of the house.

With his way thus apparently cleared, the police in confusion, darkness aiding him, Lanyard plunged on; but in mid-stride, as he crossed the threshold, his ankle was caught by the still prostrate younger sergent and jerked from under him.

His momentum threw him with a crash—and may have spared him a worse mishap; for in the same breath he heard the report of a pistol and knew that Popinot had fired at his fugitive shadow.

As he brought one heel down with crushing force on the sergent's wrist, freeing his foot, he was dimly conscious of the voice of the commissaire shouting frantic prayers to cease firing. Then the pain-maddened sergent crawled to his knees, lunged blindly forward, knocked the adventurer back in the act of rising, and fell on top of him.

Hampered by two hundred pounds of fighting Frenchman, Lanyard felt his cause was lost, yet battled on—and would while breath was in him.

With a heave, a twist and a squirm, he slipped from under, and swinging a fist at random barked his knuckles against the mouth of the sergent. Momentarily that one relaxed his hold, and Lanyard struggled to his knees, only to go down as the indomitable Frenchman grappled yet a second time.

Now, however, as they fell, Lanyard was on top: and shifting both hands to his antagonist's left forearm, he wrenched it up and around. There was a cry of pain, and he jumped clear of one no longer to be reckoned with.

Nevertheless, as he had feared, the delay had proved ruinous. He had only found his feet when an unidentified person hurled himself bodily through the gloom and wrapped his arms round Lanyard's thighs. And as both went down, two others piled up on top...

For the next minute or two, Lanyard fought blindly, madly, viciously, striking and kicking at random. For all that—even with one sergent hors de combat—they were three to one; and though with the ferocity of sheer desperation he shook them all off, at one time, and gained a few yards more, it was only again to be overcome and borne down, crushed beneath the weight of three.

His wind was going, his strength was leaving him. He mustered up every ounce of energy, all his wit and courage, for one last effort: fought like a cat, tooth and nail; toiled once more to his knees, with two clinging to him like wolves to the flanks of a stag; shook one off, regained his feet, swayed; and in one final gust of ferocity dashed both fists repeatedly into the face of him who still clung to him.

That one was Popinot; he knew instinctively that this was so; and a grim joy filled him as he felt the man's clutches relax and fall away, and guessed how brutal was the damage he had done that fat, evil face.

At length free, he made off, running, stumbling, reeling: gained the hall; flung open the door; and heedless of the picket who had fired on him from below the window, dashed down the steps and away...

Three shots sped him through that intricate tangle of night-bound park. But all went wide; the pursuit—what little there was—blundered off at haphazard and lost itself, as well.

He came to the wall, crept along in shelter of its shadow until he found a tree with a low-swung branch that jutted out over the street, climbed this, edged out over the wall, and dropped to the sidewalk.

A shout from the quarter of the carriage gates greeted his appearance. He turned and ran again. Flying footsteps for a time pursued him; and once, with a sinking heart, he heard the rumble of a motor. But he recovered quickly, regained his wind, and ran well, with long, steady, ground-consuming strides; and he doubled, turned and twisted in a manner to wake the envy of the most subtle fox.

In time he felt warranted in slowing down to a rapid walk.

Weariness was now a heavy burden upon him, and his spirit numb with desperate need of rest; but his pace did not flag, nor his purpose falter from its goal.

It was a long walk if a direct one to which he set himself as soon as confident the pursuit had failed once more. He plodded on, without faltering, to the one place where he might feel sure of finding his beloved, if she lived and were free. He knew that she had not forgotten, and in his heart he knew that she would never again of her own will fail him...

Nor had she: when—weary and spent from that heartbreaking climb up the merciless acclivity of the Butte Montmartre—he staggered rather than walked past the sleepy verger and found his way through the crowding shadows to the softly luminous heart of the basilica of the Sacré-Cour, he found her there, kneeling, her head bowed upon hands resting on the back of the chair before her: a slight and timid figure, lost and lonely in the long ranks of empty chairs that filled the nave.

Slowly, almost fearfully, he went to her, and silently he slipped into the chair by her side.

She knew, without looking up, that it was he...

After a little her hand stole out, closed round his fingers, and drew him forward with a gentle, insistent pressure. He knelt then with her, hand in hand—filled with the wonder of it, that he to whom religion had been nothing should have been brought to this by a woman's hand.

He knelt for a long time, for many minutes, profoundly intrigued, his sombre gaze questioning the golden shadows and ancient mystery of the distant choir and shining altar: and there was no question in his heart but that, whatever should ensue of this, the unquiet spirit of the Lone Wolf was forevermore at rest.

XXV

WINGS OF THE MORNING

About half-past six Lanyard left the dressing-room assigned him in the barracks at Port Aviation and, waddling quaintly in the heavy wind-resisting garments supplied him at the instance of Ducroy, made his way between two hangars toward the practice field.

Now the eastern skies were pulsing with fitful promise of the dawn; but within the vast enclosure of the aerodrome the gloom of night lingered so stubbornly that two huge searchlights had been pressed into the service of those engaged in tuning up the motor of the Parrott biplane.

In the intense, white, concentrated glare—that rippled oddly upon the wrinkled, oily garments of the dozen or so mechanics busy about the machine—the undersides of those wide, motionless planes hung against the dark with an effect of impermanence: as though they were already afloat and needed but a breath to send them winging skyward...

To one side a number of young and keen-faced Frenchmen, officers of the corps, were lounging and watching the preparations with alert and intelligent interest.

To the other, all the majesty of Mars was incarnate in the person of Monsieur Ducroy, posing valiantly in fur-lined coat and shining top hat while he chatted with an officer whose trim, athletic figure was well set off by his aviating uniform.

As Lanyard drew near, this last brought his heels together smartly, saluted the Minister of War, and strode off toward the flying-machine.

"Captain Vauquelin informs me he will be ready to start in five minutes, monsieur," Ducroy announced. "You are in good time."

"And mademoiselle?" the adventurer asked, peering anxiously round.

Almost immediately the girl came forward from the shadows, with a smile apologetic for the strangeness of her attire.

She had donned, over her street dress, an ample leather garment which enveloped her completely, buttoning tight at throat and wrists and ankles. Her small hat had been replaced by a leather helmet which left only her eyes, nose, mouth and chin exposed, and even these were soon to be hidden by a heavy veil for protection against spattering oil.

"Mademoiselle is not nervous?" Ducroy enquired politely.

Lucy smiled brightly.

"I? Why should I be, monsieur?"

"I trust mademoiselle will permit me to commend her courage. But pardon! I have one last word for the ear of Captain Vauquelin."

Lifting his hat, the Frenchman joined the group near the machine.

Lanyard stared unaffectedly at the girl, unable to disguise his wonder at the high spirits advertised by her rekindled colour and brilliant eyes.

"Well?" she demanded gaily. "Don't tell me I don't look like a fright! I know I do!"

"I daren't tell you how you look to me," Lanyard replied soberly. "But I will say this, that for sheer, down right pluck, you—"

"Thank you, monsieur! And you?"

He glanced with a deprecatory smile at the flimsy-looking contrivance to which they were presently to entrust their lives.

"Somehow," said he doubtfully, "I don't feel in the least upset or exhilarated. It seems little out of the average run of life—all in the day's work!"

"I think," she said, judgmatical, "that you're very like the other lone wolf, the fictitious one—Lupin, you know—a bit of a blagueur. If you're not nervous, why keep glancing over there?—as if you were rather expecting somebody—as if you wouldn't be surprised to see Popinot or De Morbihan pop out of the ground—or Ekstrom!"

"Hum!" he said gravely. "I don't mind telling you now, that's precisely what I am afraid of."

"Nonsense!" the girl cried in open contempt. "What could they do?"

"Please don't ask me," Lanyard begged seriously. "I might try to tell you."

"But don't worry, my dear!" Fugitively her hand touched his. "We're ready."

It was true enough: Ducroy was moving impressively back toward them.

"All is prepared," he announced in sonorous accents.

A bit sobered, in silence they approached the machine.

Vauquelin kept himself aloof while Lanyard and a young officer helped the girl to the seat to the right of the pilot, and strapped her in. When Lanyard had been similarly secured in the place on the left, the two sat, imprisoned, some six feet above the ground.

Lanyard found his perch comfortable enough. A broad band of webbing furnished support for his back; another crossed his chest by way of provision against forward pitching; there were rests for his feet, and for his hands cloth-wound grips fixed to struts on either side.

He smiled at Lucy across the empty seat, and was surprised at the clearness with which her answering smile was visible. But he wasn't to see it again for a long and weary time; almost immediately she began to adjust her veil.

The morning had grown much lighter within the last few minutes.

A long wait ensued, during which the swarm of mechanics, assistants and military aviators buzzed round their feet like bees.

The sky was now pale to the western horizon. A fleet of heavy clouds was drifting off into the south, leaving in their wake thin veils of mist that promised soon to disappear before the rays of the sun. The air seemed tolerably clear and not unseasonably cold.

The light grew stronger still: features of distant objects defined themselves; traces of colour warmed the winter landscape.

At length their pilot, wearing his wind-mask, appeared and began to climb to his perch. With a cool nod for Lanyard and a civil bow to his woman passenger, he settled himself, adjusted several levers, and flirted a gay hand to his brother-officers.

There was a warning cry. The crowd dropped back rapidly to either side. Ducroy lifted his hat in parting salute, cried "Bon voyage!" and scuttled clear like a startled rooster before a motor-car. And the motor and propeller broke loose with a mighty roar comparable only, in Lanyard's fancy, to the chant of ten thousand rivetting locusts.

He felt momentarily as if his eardrums must burst with the incessant and tremendous concussions registered upon them; but presently this sensation passed, leaving him with that of permanent deafness.

Before he could recover and regain control of his startled wits the aviator had thrown down a lever, and the great fabric was in motion.

It swept down the field like a frightened swan; and the wheels of its chassis, registering every infinitesimal irregularity in the surface of the ground, magnified them all a hundred-fold. It was like riding in a tumbril driven at top-speed over the Giant's Causeway. Lanyard was shaken violently to the very marrow of his bones; he believed that even his eyes must be rattling in their sockets...

Then the Parrott began to ascend. Singularly enough, this change was marked, at first, by no more than slight lessening of the vibration: still the machine seemed to be dashing over a cobbled thoroughfare at breakneck speed; and Lanyard found it difficult to appreciate that they were afloat, even when he looked down and discovered a hundred feet of space between himself and the practice-field.

In another breath they were soaring over housetops.

Momentarily, now, the shocks became less frequent. And presently they ceased almost altogether, to be repeated only at rare intervals, when the drift of air opposing the planes developed irregularities in its velocity. There succeeded, in contrast, the sublimest peace; even the roaring of the propeller dwindled to a sustained drone; the biplane seemed to float without an effort upon a vast, still sea, flawed only occasionally by inconsiderable ripples.

Still rising, they surprised the earliest rays of the sun; and in their virgin light the aeroplane was transformed into a thing of gossamer gold.

Continually the air buffeted their faces like a flood of icy water.

Below, the scroll of the world unrolled like some vast and intricately illuminated missal, or like some strange mosaic, marvellously minute...

Lanyard could see the dial of the compass, fixed to a strut on the pilot's left. By that telltale their course lay nearly due northeast. Already the weltering roofs of Paris were in sight, to the right, the Eiffel Tower spearing up like a fairy pillar of gold lace-work, the Seine looping the cluttered acres like a sleek brown serpent, the Sacré-Coeur a dream-palace of opalescent walls.

Versailles broke the horizon to port and slipped astern. Paris closed up, telescoped its panorama, became a mere blur, a smoky smudge. But it was long before the distance eclipsed that admonitory finger of the Eiffel.

Vauquelin manipulating the levers, the plane tilted its nose and swam higher and yet higher. The song of the motor dropped an octave to a richer tone. The speed was sensibly increased.

Lanyard contemplated with untempered wonder the fact of his equanimity: there seemed nothing at all strange in this extraordinary experience; he was by no means excited, remained merely if deeply interested. And he could detect in his physical sensations no trace of that qualmish dread he always experienced in high places: the sense he had of security, of solidity, was and ever remained wholly unaccountable in his understanding.

Of a sudden, surprised by a touch on his arm, he turned to see through the mica windows of the wind-mask the eyes of the aviator informed with importunate doubt. Infinitely mystified and so an easy prey to sickening fear lest something were going wrong with the machine, Lanyard shook his head to indicate lack of comprehension. With an impatient gesture the aviator pointed downward. Appreciating the fact that speech was impossible, Lanyard clutched the struts and bent forward. But the pace was now so fast and their elevation so great that the landscape swimming beneath his vision was no more than a brownish plain fugitively maculated with blots of contrasting colour.

He looked up blankly, but only to be treated to the same gesture.

Piqued, he concentrated attention more closely upon the flat, streaming landscape. And suddenly he recognized something oddly familiar in an approaching bend of the Seine.

"St. Germain-en-Laye!" he exclaimed with a start of alarm.

This was the danger point...

"And over there," he reminded himself—"to the left—that wide field with a queer white thing in the middle that looks like a winged grub—that must be De Morbihan's aerodrome and his Valkyr monoplane! Are they bringing it out? Is that what Vauquelin means? And if so—what of it? I don't see..."

Suddenly doubt and wonder chilled the adventurer.

Temporarily Vauquelin returned entire attention to the management of the biplane. The wind was now blowing more fitfully, creating pockets—those holes in the air so dreaded by cloud pilots—and in quest of more constant resistance the aviator was swinging his craft in a wide northerly curve, climbing ever higher and more high.

The earth soon lost all semblance of design; even the twisted silver wire of the Seine vanished, far over to the left; remained only the effect of firm suspension in that high blue vault, of a continuous low of iced water in the face, together with the tuneless chanting of the motor.

After some forty minutes of this—it may have been an hour, for time was then an incalculable thing—Lanyard, in a mood of abnormal sensitiveness, began to divine additional disquiet in the mind of the aviator, and stared until he caught his eye.

"What is it?" he screamed in futile effort to lift his voice above the din.

But the Frenchman understood, and responded with a sweep of his arm toward the horizon ahead. And seeing nothing but cloud in the quarter indicated, Lanyard grasped the nature of a phenomenon which, from the first, had been vaguely troubling him. The reason why he had been able to perceive no real rim to the world was that the earth was all a-steam from the recent heavy rains; all the more remote distances were veiled with rising vapour. And now they were approaching the coast, to which, it seemed, the mists clung closest; for all the world before them slept beneath a blanket of dull grey.

Nor was it difficult now to understand why the aviator was ill at ease facing the prospect of navigating a Channel fog.

Several minutes later, he startled Lanyard with another peremptory touch on his arm followed by a significant glance over his shoulder.

Lanyard turned quickly.

Behind them, at a distance which he calculated roughly as two miles, the silhouette of a monoplane hung against the brilliant firmament, resembling, with its single spread of wings, more a solitary, soaring gull than any man-directed mechanism.

Only an infrequent and almost imperceptible shifting of the wings proved that it was moving.

He watched it for several seconds, in deepening perplexity and anxiety, finding it impossible to guess whether it were gaining or losing in that long chase, or who might be its pilot.

Yet he had little doubt but that the pursuing machine had risen from the aerodrome of Count Remy de Morbihan at St.-Germain-en-Laye; that it was nothing less, in fact, than De Morbihan's Valkyr, reputed the fastest monoplane in Europe and winner of a dozen International events; and that it was guided, if not by De Morbihan himself, by one of the creatures of the Pack—quite possibly, even more probably, by Ekstrom!

But—assuming all this—what evil could such pursuit portend? In what conceivable manner could the Pack reckon to further its ends by commissioning the monoplane to overtake or distance the Parrott? They could not hinder the escape of Lanyard and Lucy Shannon to England in any way, by any means reasonably to be imagined.

Was this simply one more move to keep the pair under espionage? But that might more readily have been accomplished by telegraphing or telephoning the Pack's confreres, Wertheimer's associates in England!

Lanyard gave it up, admitting his inability to trump up any sane excuse for such conduct; but the riddle continued to fret his mind without respite.

From the first, from that moment when Lucy's disappearance had required postponement of this flight, he had feared trouble; it hadn't seemed reasonable to hope that the Parrott could be held in waiting on his convenience for many days without the secret leaking out; but it was trouble to develop before the start from Port Aviation that he had anticipated. The possibility that the Pack would be able to work any mischief to him, after that, had never entered his calculations. Even now he found it difficult to give it serious consideration.

Again he glanced back. Now, in his judgment, the monoplane loomed larger than before against the glowing sky, indicating that it was overtaking them.

Beneath his breath Lanyard swore from a brimming heart.

The Parrott was capable of a speed of eighty miles an hour; and unquestionably Vauquelin was wheedling every ounce of power out of its willing motor. Since drawing Lanyard's attention to the pursuer he had brought about appreciable acceleration.

But would even that pace serve to hold the Valkyr if not to distance it?

His next backward look reckoned the monoplane no nearer.

And another thirty minutes or go elapsed without the relative positions of the two flying machines undergoing any perceptible change.

In the course of this period the Parrott rose to an altitude, indicated by the barograph at Lanyard's elbow, of more than half a mile. Below, the Channel fog spread itself out like a sea of milk, slowly churning.

Staring down in fascination, Lanyard told himself gravely: "Blue water below that, my friend!"

It seemed difficult to credit the fact that they had made the flight from Paris in so short a time.

By his reckoning—a very rough one—the Parrott was then somewhere off Dieppe: it ought to pick up England, in such case, not far from Brighton. If only one could see...!

By bending forward a little and staring past the aviator Lanyard could catch a glimpse of Lucy Shannon.

Though all her beauty and grace of person were lost in the clumsy swaddling of her makeshift costume, she seemed to be comfortable enough; and the rushing air, keen with the chill of that great altitude, moulded her wind-veil precisely to the exquisite contours of her face and stung her firm cheeks until they glowed with a rare fire that even that thick dark mesh could not wholly quench.

The sun crept above the floor of mist, played upon it with iridescent rays, shot it through and through with a warm, pulsating glow like that of a fire opal, and suddenly turned it to a tumbled sea of gold which, apparently boundless, baffled every effort to surmise their position, whether they were above land or sea.

Nonetheless Lanyard's rough and rapid calculations persuaded him that they were then about Mid-Channel.

He had no more than arrived at this conclusion when a sharp, startled movement, that rocked the planes, drew his attention to the man at his side.

Glancing in alarm at the aviator's face, he saw it as white as marble—what little of it was visible beyond and beneath the wind-mask.

Vauquelin was holding out an arm, and staring at it incredulously; Lanyard's gaze was drawn to the same spot—a ragged perforation in the sleeve of the pilot's leather surtout, just above the elbow.

"What is it?" he enquired stupidly, again forgetting that he could not be heard.

The eyes of the aviator, lifting from the perforation to meet Lanyard's stare, were clouded with consternation.

Then Vauquelin turned quickly and looked back. Simultaneously he ducked his head and something slipped whining past Lanyard's cheek, touching his flesh with a touch more chill than that of the icy air itself.

"Damnation!" he shrieked, almost hysterically. "That madman in the Valkyr is firing at us!"

XXVI

THE FLYING DEATH

Steadying himself with a splendid display of self-control and sheer courage, Captain Vauquelin concentrated upon the management of the biplane.

The drone of its motor thickened again, its speed became greater, and the machine began to rise still higher, tracing a long, graceful curve.

Lanyard glanced apprehensively toward the girl, but apparently she remained unconscious of anything out of the ordinary. Her face was still turned forward, and still the wind-veil trembled against her glowing cheeks.

Thanks to the racket of the motor, no audible reports had accompanied the sharp-shooting of the man in the monoplane; while Lanyard's cry of horror and dismay had been audible to himself exclusively. Hearing nothing, Lucy suspected nothing.

Again Lanyard looked back.

Now the Valkyr seemed to have crept up to within the quarter of a mile of the biplane, and was boring on at a tremendous pace, its single spread of wings on an approximate level with that of the lower plane of the Parrott.

But this last was rising steadily...

The driver's seat of the Valkyr held a muffled, burly figure that might be anybody—De Morbihan, Ekstrom, or any other homicidal maniac. At the distance its actions were as illegible as their results were unquestionable: Lanyard saw a little tongue of flame lick out from a point close beside the head of the figure—he couldn't distinguish the firearm itself—and, like Vauquelin, quite without premeditation, he ducked.

At the same time there sounded a harsh, ripping noise immediately above his head; and he found himself staring up at a long ragged tear in the canvas, caused by the bullet striking it aslant.

"What's to be done?" he screamed passionately at Vauquelin.

The aviator shook his head impatiently; and they continued to ascend; already the web of gold that cloaked earth and sea seemed thrice as far beneath their feet as it had when Vauquelin made the appalling discovery of his bullet-punctured sleeve.

But the monoplane was doggedly following suit; as the Parrott rose, so did the Valkyr, if a trace more slowly and less flexibly.

Lanyard had read somewhere, or heard it said, that monoplanes were poor machines for climbing. He told himself that, if this were true, Vauquelin knew his business; and from this reflection drew what comfort he might.

And he was glad, very glad of the dark wind-veil that shrouded his face, which he believed to be nothing less than a mask of panic terror.

He was, in fact, quite rigid with fright and horror. It were idle to argue that only unlikely chance would wing one of the bullets from the Valkyr to a vital point: there was the torn canvas overhead, there was that hole through Vauquelin's sleeve...

And then the barograph on the strut beside Lanyard disappeared as if by magic. He was aware of a slight jar; the framework of the biplane quivered as from a heavy blow; something that resembled a handful of black crumbs sprayed out into the air ahead and vanished: and where the instrument had been, nothing remained but an iron clamp gripping the strut.

And even as any one of these bullets might have proved fatal, their first successor might disable the aviator if it did not slay him outright; in either case, the inevitable result would be death following a fall from a height, as recorded on the barograph dial an instant before its destruction, of more than four thousand feet.

They were still climbing...

Now the pursuer was losing some of the advantage of his superior speed; the Parrott was perceptibly higher; the Valkyr must needs mount in a more sweeping curve.

Nonetheless, Lanyard, peering down, saw still another tongue of flame spit out at him; and two bullet-holes appeared in the port-side wings of the biplane, one in the lower, one in the upper spread of canvas.

White-lipped and trembling, the adventurer began to work at the fastenings of his surtout. After a moment he plucked off one of his gloves and cast it impatiently from him. A-sprawl, it sailed down the wind like a wounded sparrow. He caught Vauquelin's eye upon him, quick with a curiosity which changed to a sudden gleam of comprehension as Lanyard, thrusting his hand under the leather coat, groped for his pocket and produced an automatic pistol which Ducroy had pressed upon his acceptance.

They were now perhaps a hundred feet higher than the Valkyr, which was soaring a quarter of a mile off to starboard. Under the guidance of the Frenchman, the Parrott swooped round in a narrow circle until it hung almost immediately above the other—a manoeuvre requiring, first and last, something more than five minutes to effect.

Meanwhile, Lanyard rebuttoned his surtout and clutched the pistol, trying hard not to think. But already his imagination was sick with the thought of what would ensue when the time came for him to carry out his purpose.

Vauquelin touched his arm with urgent pressure; but Lanyard only shook his head, gulped, and without looking surrendered the weapon to the aviator...

Bearing heavily against the chest-band, he commanded the broad white spread of the Valkyr's back and wings. Invisible beneath these hung the motor and driver's seat.

An instant more, and he was aware that Vauquelin was leaning forward and looking down.

Aiming with what deliberation was possible, the aviator emptied the clip of its eight cartridges in less than a minute.

The vicious reports rang out against the drum of the motor like the cracking of a blacksnake-whip.

Momentarily, Lanyard doubted if any one bullet had taken effect. He could not, with his swimming vision, detect sign of damage in the canvas of the Valkyr.

He saw the empty automatic slip from Vauquelin'p numb and nerveless fingers. It vanished...

A frightful fascination kept his gaze constant to the soaring Valkyr.

Beyond it, down, deep down a mile of emptiness, was that golden floor of tumbled cloud, waiting...

He saw the monoplane check abruptly in its strong onward surge—as if it had run, full-tilt, head-on, against an invisible obstacle—and for what seemed a round minute it hung so, veering and wobbling, nuzzling the wind. Then like a sounding whale it turned and dived headlong, propeller spinning like a top.

Down through the eighth of a mile of space it plunged plummet-like; then, perhaps caught in a flaw of wind, it turned sideways and began to revolve, at first slowly, but with increasing rapidity in its fatally swift descent.

Toward the beginning of its revolutions, something was thrown off, something small, dark and sprawling... like that glove which Lanyard had discarded. But this object dropped with a speed even greater than that of the Valkyr, in a brace of seconds had diminished to the proportions of a gnat, in another was engulfed in that vast sea of golden vapour.

Even so the monoplane itself, scarcely less precipitate, spun down through the abyss and plunged to oblivion in the fog-rack...

And Lanyard was still hanging against the chest-band, limp and spent and trying not to vomit, when, of a sudden and without any warning whatever, the stentorian chant of the motor ceased and was blotted up by that immense silence, by the terrible silence of those vast solitudes of the upper air, where never a sound is heard save the voices of the elements at war among themselves: a silence that rang with an accent as dreadful as the crack of Doom in the ears of those three suspended there, in the heart of that unimaginably pellucid and immaculate radiance, in the vast hollow of the heavens, midway between the deep blue of the eternal dome and the rose and golden welter of the fog—that fog which, cloaking earth and sea, hid as well every vestige of the tragedy they had wrought, every sign of the murder that they had done that they themselves might not be murdered and cast down to destruction.

And, its propeller no longer gripping the air, the aeroplane drifted on at ever-lessening speed, until it had no way whatever and rested without motion of any sort; as it might have been in the cup of some mighty and invisible hand, held up to that stark and merciless light, under the passionless eye of the Infinite, to await a Judgment...

Then, with a little shudder of hesitation, the planes dipped, inclined slightly earthwards, and began slowly and as if reluctantly to slip down the long and empty channels of the air.

At this, rousing, Lanyard became aware of his own voice yammering wildly at Vauquelin:

"Good God, man! Why did you do that?"

Vauquelin answered only with a pale grimace and a barely perceptible shrug.

Momentarily gathering momentum, the biplane sped downward with a resistless rush, with the speed of a great wind—a speed so great that when Lanyard again attempted speech, the breath was whipped from his lips and he could utter no sound.

Thus from that awful height, from the still heart of that immeasurable void, they swept down and ever down, in a long series of sickening swoops, broken only by negligible pauses. And though they approached it on a long slant, the floor of vapour rose to meet them like a mighty rushing wave: in a trice the biplane was hovering instantaneously before plunging on down into that cold, grey world of fog.

In that moment of hesitation, while still the adventurer gasped for breath and pawed at his streaming eyes with an aching hand, pierced through and through with cold, the fog showed itself as something less substantial than it had seemed; blurs of colour glowed through its folds of gauze, and with these the rounded summit of a brownish, knoll.

Then they plunged on, down out of the bleak, bright sunshine into cool twilight depths of clinging vapours; and the good green earth lifted its warm bosom to receive them.

Tilting its nose a trifle, fluttering as though undecided, the Parrott settled gracefully, with scarcely a Jar, upon a wide sweep of untilled land covered with short coarse grass.

For some time the three remained in their perches like petrified things, quite moveless and—with the possible exception of the aviator—hardly conscious.

But presently Lanyard became aware that he was regularly filling his lungs with air sweet, damp, wholesome, and by comparison warm, and that the blood was tingling painfully in his half-frozen hands and feet.

He sighed as one waking from a strange dream.

At the same time the aviator bestirred himself, and began a bit stiffly to climb down.

Feeling the earth beneath his feet, he took a step or two away from the machine, reeling and stumbling like a drunken man, then turned back.

"Come, my friend!" he urged Lanyard in a voice of strangely normal intonation—"look alive—if you're able—and lend me a hand with mademoiselle. I'm afraid she has fainted."

The girl was reclining inertly in the bands of webbing, her eyes closed, her lips ajar, her limbs slackened.

"Small blame to her!" Lanyard commented, fumbling clumsily with the chest-band. "That dive was enough to drive a body mad!"

"But I had to do it!" the aviator protested earnestly. "I dared not remain longer up there. I have never before been afraid in the air, but after *that* I was terribly afraid. I could feel myself going—taking leave of my senses—and I knew I must act if we were not to follow that other... God! what a death!"

He paused, shuddered, and drew the back of his hand across his eyes before continuing: "So I cut off the ignition and volplaned. Here—my hand. So-o! All right, eh?"

"Oh, I'm all right," Lanyard insisted confidently.

But his confidence was belied by a look of daze; for the earth was billowing and reeling round him as though bewitched; and before he knew what had happened he sat down hard and stared foolishly up at the aviator.

"Here!" said the latter courteously, his wind-mask hiding a smile—"my hand again, monsieur. You've endured more than you know. And now for mademoiselle."

But when they approached the girl, she surprised both by shivering, sitting up, and obviously pulling herself together.

"You feel better now, mademoiselle?" Vauquelin enquired, hastening to loosen her fastenings.

"I'm better—yes, thank you," she admitted in a small, broken voice—"but not yet quite myself."

She gave a hand to the aviator, the other to Lanyard, and as they helped her to the ground, Lanyard, warned by his experience, stood by with a ready arm.

She needed that support, and for a few minutes didn't seem even conscious of it. Then gently disengaging, she moved a foot or two away.

"Where are we—do you know?"

"On the South Downs, somewhere?" Lanyard suggested, consulting Vauquelin.

"That is probable," this last affirmed—"at all events, judging from the course I steered. Somewhere well in from the coast, at a venture; I don't hear the sea."

"Near Lewes, perhaps?"

"I have no reason to doubt that."

A constrained pause ensued. The girl looked from the aviator to Lanyard, then turned away from both and, trembling with fatigue and enforcing self-control by clenching her hands, stared aimlessly off into the mist.

Painfully, Lanyard set himself to consider their position.

The Parrott had come to rest in what seemed to be a wide, shallow, saucer-like depression, whose irregular bounds were cloaked in fog. In this space no living thing stirred save themselves; and the waste was crossed by not so much as a sheep track. In brief, they were lost. There might be a road running past the saucer ten yards from its brim in any quarter. There might not. Possibly there was a town or village immediately adjacent. Quite as possibly the Downs billowed away for desolate miles on either hand.

"Well—what do we do now?" the girl demanded suddenly, in a nervous voice, sharp and jarring.

"Oh, we'll find a way out of this somehow," Vauquelin asserted confidently. "England isn't big enough for anybody to remain lost in it—not for long, at all events. I'm sorry only on Miss Shannon's account."

"We'll manage, somehow," Lanyard affirmed stoutly.

The aviator smiled curiously. "To begin with," he advanced, "I daresay we might as well get rid of these awkward costumes. They'll hamper walking—rather."

In spite of his fatigue Lanyard was so struck by the circumstances that he couldn't help remarking it as he tore off his wind-veil.

"Your English is remarkably good, Captain Vauquelin," he observed.

The other laughed shortly.

"Why not?" said he, removing his mask.

Lanyard looked up into his face, stared, and fell back a pace.

"Wertheimer!" he gasped.

XXVII

DAYBREAK

The Englishman smiled cheerfully in response to Lanyard's cry of astonishment.

"In effect," he observed, stripping off his gauntlets, "you're right, Mr Lanyard. 'Wertheimer' isn't my name, but it is so closely identified with my—ah—insinuative personality as to warrant the misapprehension. I shan't demand an apology so long as you permit me to preserve an incognito which may yet prove somewhat useful."

"Incognito!" Lanyard stammered, utterly discountenanced. "Useful!"

"You have my meaning exactly; although my work in Paris is now ended, there's no saying when it may not be convenient to be able to go back without establishing a new identity."

Before Lanyard replied to this the look of wonder in his eyes had yielded to one of understanding.

"Scotland Yard, eh?" he queried curtly.

Wertheimer bowed. "Special agent," he added.

"I might have guessed, if I'd had the wit of a goose!" Lanyard affirmed bitterly. "But I must admit..."

"Yes," the Englishman assented pleasantly; "I did pull your leg—didn't I? But not more than our other friends. Of course, it's taken some time: I had to establish myself firmly as a shining light of the swell mob over here before De Morbihan would take me to his hospitable bosom."

"I presume I'm to consider myself under arrest?"

With a laugh, the Englishman shook his head vigorously.

"No, thank you!" he declared. "I've had too convincing proof of your distaste for interference in your affairs. You fight too sincerely, Mr Lanyard—and I'm a tired sleuth this very morning as ever was! I would need a week's rest to fit me for the job of taking you into custody—a week and some able-bodied assistance!... But," he amended with graver countenance, "I will say this: if you're in England a week hence, I'll be tempted to undertake the job on general principles. I don't in the least question the sincerity of your intention to behave yourself hereafter; but as a servant of the King, it's my duty to advise you that England would prefer you to start life anew—as they say—in another country. Several steamers sail for the States before the end of the week: further details I leave entirely to your discretion. But go you must," he concluded firmly.

"I understand..." said Lanyard; and would have said more, but couldn't. There was something suspiciously like a mist before his eyes.

Avoiding the faces of his sweetheart and the Englishman, he turned aside, put forth a hand blindly to a wing of the biplane to steady himself, and stood with head bowed and limbs trembling.

Moving quietly to his side, the girl took his other hand and held it tight...

Presently Lanyard shook himself impatiently and lifted his head again.

"Sorry," he said, apologetic—"but your generosity—when I looked for nothing better than arrest—was a bit too much for my nerves!"

"Nonsense!" the Englishman commented with brusque good-humour. "We're all upset. A drop of brandy will do us no end of good."

Unbuttoning his leather surtout, he produced a flask from an inner pocket, filled its metal cup, and offered it to the girl.

"You first, if you please, Miss Shannon. No—I insist. You positively need it."

She allowed herself to be persuaded, drank, coughed, gasped, and returned the cup, which Wertheimer promptly refilled and passed to Lanyard.

The raw spirits stung like fire, but proved an instant aid to the badly jangled nerves of the adventurer. In another moment he was much more himself.

Drinking in turn, Wertheimer put away the flask. "That's better!" he commented. "Now I'll be able to cut along with this blessed machine without fretting over the fate of Ekstrom. But till now I haven't been able to forget—"

He paused and drew a hand across his eyes.

"It was, then, Ekstrom—you think?" Lanyard demanded.

"Unquestionably! De Morbihan had learned—I know—of your bargain with Ducroy; and I know, too, that he and Ekstrom spent each morning in the hangars at St. Germain, after your sensational evasion. It never entered my head, of course, that they had any such insane scheme brewing as that—else I would never have so giddily arranged with Ducroy—through the Sûreté, you understand—to take Vauquelin's place... Besides, who else could it have been? Not De Morbihan, for he's crippled for life, thanks to that affair in the Bois; not Popinot, who was on his way to the Santé, last I saw of him; and never Bannon—he was dead before I left Paris for Port Aviation."

"Dead!"

"Oh, quite!" the Englishman affirmed nonchalantly, "When we arrested him at three this morning—charged with complicity in the murder of Roddy—he flew into a passion that brought on a fatal haemorrhage. He died within ten minutes."

There was a little silence...

"I may tell you, Mr Lanyard," the Englishman resumed, looking up from the motor, to which he was paying attentions with monkey-wrench and oil-can, "that you were quite off your bat when you ridiculed the idea of the 'International Underworld Unlimited.' Of course, if you *hadn't* laughed, I shouldn't feel quite as much respect for you as I do; in fact, the chances are you'd be in handcuffs or in a cell of the Santé, this very minute... But, absurd as it sounded—and was—the 'Underworld' project was a pet hobby of Bannon's—who'd been the brains of a gang of criminals in New York for many years. He was a bit touched on the subject: a monomaniac, if you ask me. And his enthusiasm won De Morbihan and Popinot over... and me! He took a wonderful fancy to me, Bannon did; I really was appointed first-lieutenant in Greggs' stead... So you first won my sympathy by laughing at my offer," said Wertheimer, restoring the oil-can to its place in the tool-kit; "wherein you were very wise... In fact, my personal feeling for you is one of growing esteem, if you'll permit me to say so. You've most of the makings of a man. Will you shake hands—with a copper's nark?"

He gave Lanyard's hand a firm and friendly grasp, and turned to the girl.

"Goodbye, Miss Shannon. I'm truly grateful for the assistance you gave us. Without you, we'd have been sadly handicapped. I understand you have sent in your resignation? It's too bad: the Service will feel the loss of you. But I think you were right to leave us, the circumstances considered... And now it's goodbye and good luck! I hope you may be happy... I'm sure you can't go far without coming across a highroad or a village; but—for reasons not unconnected with my profession—I prefer to remain in ignorance of the way you go."

Releasing her hand, he stepped back, saluted the lovers with a smile and gay gesture, and clambered briskly to the pilot's seat of the biplane.

When firmly established, he turned the switch of the starting mechanism.

The heavy, distinctive hum of the great motor filled that isolated hollow in the Downs like the purring of a dynamo.

With a final wave of his hand, Wertheimer grasped the starting-lever.

Its *brool* deepening, the Parrott stirred, shot forward abruptly. In two seconds it was fifty yards distant, its silhouette already blurred, its wheels lifting from the rim of the hollow.

Then lightly it leaped, soared, parted the mists, vanished...

For some time Lanyard and Lucy Shannon remained motionless, clinging together, hand-in-hand, listening to the drone that presently dwindled to a mere thread of sound and died out altogether in the obscurity above them.

Then, turning, they faced each other, smiling a trace uncertainly, a smile that said: "So all that is finished...! Or, perhaps, we dreamed it...!"

Suddenly, with a low cry, the girl gave herself to Lanyard's arms; and as this happened the mists parted and bright sunlight flooded the hollow in the Downs.

THE END

Edgar
Wallace
THE COMPLETE J. G. REEDER STORIES

E.W.
HORNUNG
THE COMPLETE RAFFLES

Edgar
Wallace
THE COMPLETE JUST MEN
VOLUME 2

Arthur
Morrison
THE COMPLETE MARTIN HEWITT COLLECTION
VOLUME 1

E. Phillips
Oppenheim
THE GREAT IMPERSONATION

Allan
Pinkerton
THE EXPRESSMAN AND THE DETECTIVE

H. Rider Haggard
MR. MEESON'S WILL

Melville Davisson Post
MASTER OF MYSTERIES
THE COMPLETE UNCLE ABNER COLLECTION

Jack London
THE ASSASSINATION BUREAU LTD.

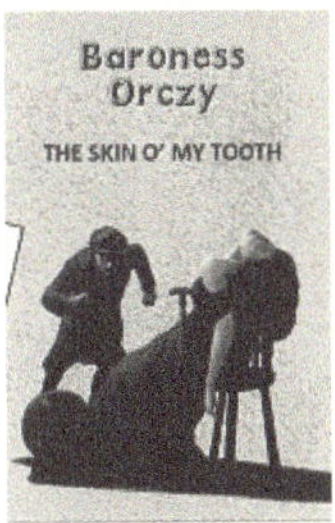
Baroness Orczy
THE SKIN O' MY TOOTH

Earl Derr Biggers
SEVEN KEYS TO BALDPATE

Horace Walpole
THE CASTLE OF OTRANTO

Sexton Blake
THE SEXTON BLAKE COLLECTION
VOLUME 1

Francis Beeding
THE HOUSE OF DR. EDWARDES

A. E. W. Mason
AT THE VILLA ROSE

Fergus Hume
THE MILLIONAIRE MYSTERY

Donald Henderson
A VOICE LIKE VELVET

Richard Hallas
YOU PLAY THE BLACK AND THE RED COMES UP